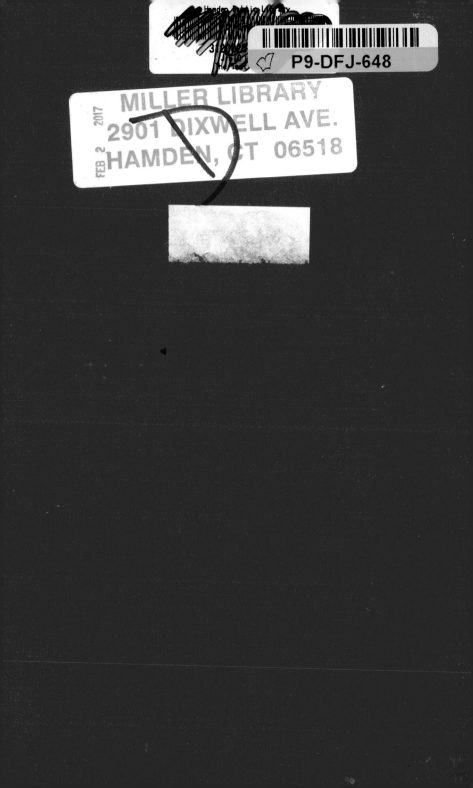

THE
LAST
HARVEST

THE
LAST
HARVEST

KIM LIGGETT

TOR TEEN

A TOM DOHERTY ASSOCIATES BOOK · NEW YORK

THE LAST HARVEST

Copyright © 2017 by Kim Liggett

All rights reserved.

A Tor Teen Book
Published by Tom Doherty Associates
175 Fifth Avenue
New York, NY 10010

www.tor-forge.com

Tor® is a registered trademark of Macmillan Publishing Group, LLC.

The Library of Congress Cataloging-in-Publication Data is available upon request.

ISBN 978-0-7653-8098-2 (hardcover)
ISBN 978-1-4668-7630-9 (e-book)

Our books may be purchased in bulk for promotional, educational, or business use. Please contact your local bookseller or the Macmillan Corporate and Premium Sales Department at 1-800-221-7945, extension 5442, or by e-mail at MacmillanSpecialMarkets@macmillan.com.

First Edition: January 2017

Printed in the United States of America

10 9 8 7 6 5 4 3 2 1

For Rahm
Seek and ye shall find

THE
LAST
HARVEST

1

PEOPLE CALL this God's country, but you can't have God without the Devil.

I see it in the cutworms threatening to take over the crops and the katydids with their bright-green wings fluttering as they drown in the troughs.

When I'm riding the combine like this, watching the sun rise over the fields, I can't help thinking about my ancestors who claimed this piece of shit parcel in the 1889 land rush. The majestic display of color and light must've felt like God himself was rising up to pass judgment on them every single day. I know it's just a bunch of particles making the light rays scatter, but it still gets to me. An Oklahoma sky will make a believer out of anybody.

I pull my sleeves down over my frozen knuckles and concentrate on annihilating the wheat in front of me. The last harvest of the season. Man, I hate wheat. It's so old school. Soybeans—that's the wave of the future. I kept telling Dad, but he was too stuck in his ways. Now he's really stuck. Six feet under.

I glance at the Neely Cattle Ranch on the western edge of our property, and a sick feeling twists my insides. I tell myself it's only an abandoned barn now, but I swear I can feel it pressing in on me, like it's trying to suffocate me. I'll never understand why they didn't burn it to the ground after what happened. After what Dad did.

"Just keep it together, Clay," I say to myself as I twist my cap around and crank up the music. We need the money and I'm already behind schedule. I had a hard time getting the combine going again this morning. Dad's the one who was good at all this. Sometimes I catch myself daydreaming about what my life would've been like if it never happened. I'd still be playing football, looking at colleges, going down to the quarry to drink beer with my friends.

As I make my last turn to head back home and get ready for school, I catch a glimpse of something moving low through the wheat. I rise up in my seat, peering through the dusty windshield, watching it move back toward the house, when I hit something solid. The cutting blades grind to a halt, making the combine rock forward and stall out.

"Come on," I groan as I pull out my earbuds.

The sound of screaming guitars fades as I slide out of the cab and trudge toward the front of the harvester.

Hope I didn't run over my little sister's bike. I've been looking everywhere for that hunk of junk. I thought about getting her a new one, roughing it up a little, telling her I found it out by Harmon Lake, but Noodle's sharp. Dad put it together for her sixth birthday last year—wasn't worth a dime, just a bunch of scraps from mine and Jess's old bikes. Guess it has sentimental value.

As I lean down to look under the cutting platform, a musky copper smell flares in my nostrils. There, stuck in the blade, is a gnarled hoof. My stomach lurches; my throat feels so thick I can barely swallow. Frantically, I dig around in the discarded wheat stems to uncover the rest of it—a newborn calf, throat slit wide open, bright-red blood splattered against golden fur. My eyes well up as I try and find a pulse, but it's no use. It's just a heap of warm blood, bone, and fur.

"Jesus!" I stagger back, tearing off my work gloves to try and get away from the sweet repulsive odor, but it's all around me . . . inside me.

Pacing around the combine, I scan the fields, searching for an explanation. We don't have any cattle around here, not since Mr. Neely shut down the ranch last year. Did I do this or did somebody kill it and ditch it here for me to find, like some kind of sick joke?

Bracing my hands against my knees, I stare down at the calf, its eyes black as tar, and all I see is Dad lying on the breeding floor, arms outstretched, his last breath rattling in his throat.

"I plead the blood," he whispered.

He looked terrified—not of death, but of me.

The wind rushes over the crops, pulling me back. It sounds like sandpaper scraping against skin.

I take off running back toward the house.

I know it's only the sun chasing my shadow, but I swear, it feels like the Devil himself is right on my heels.

2

"YOU'RE LATE," Noodle says, completely out of breath, her lopsided pigtails bouncing around like they have their own motors.

"I know, I know." I hand over my cap and field jacket.

"Gloves?" She hangs everything on its proper peg.

I grasp the banister, feeling the worn wood beneath my fingertips, the dead calf still fresh in my mind. Noodle can't find out about that. No one can. Not until I figure out where it came from. This town doesn't need more reason to think we're monsters.

"I must've left them behind." I peer down the hall toward the kitchen to make sure no one's listening. Mom's hunched over the stove, still half in a dream, using all her concentration to keep the bacon grease from escaping the cast-iron skillet, and Jess is too busy being miserable to give a flying crap. If that girl doesn't end up on the *Maury* show, it'll be a miracle.

Noodle tugs on the hem of my shirt. "How many acres did you finish today?"

"Two."

She purses her lips as she pulls two gold stars from her sticker bag, placing them in the little squares on the sheet of poster board she "borrowed" from Sunday school. Each square represents an acre for the harvest. We need every penny this year. One hundred and thirteen acres all squeezed into early mornings and after school. It's a hell of a lot of work to handle on my own, and if the first frost beats me to it, we'll be shit out of luck.

Noodle does the math, tapping out the remaining acres on the side of her leg. She counts everything. I read somewhere it's a form of OCD, but I think she's just too smart for her own good.

"Can you keep a secret?" I crouch down so I can look her in the eye.

She knots her hands on her scrawny waist. "You know I can."

"Hey, what happened to your finger?"

"Just a paper cut and no changing the subject."

I rub the back of my neck. "I had a little engine trouble this morning . . . nothing I can't fix." Her glance veers toward the window, and I know exactly what she's thinking. "Don't worry. I'll catch up. And don't be going out there." I reach out to muss up her wispy light-blond bangs; she ducks out of the way. She doesn't like anyone touching her hair anymore. "I'll take care of it after school. Deal?"

She zips her lips and locks them, pressing the imaginary key into my hand, before skipping off to the kitchen.

"And put a Band-Aid on that, okay?"

A fly buzzes past. I watch it as it lands on the bare wall above the mantel in the living room, where the crucifix used to hang.

It takes me right back to that night.

Dad came home from the Preservation Society meeting all wild-eyed. "Ian Neely knew . . . they all knew," he said.

Mom just thought he'd gotten into Charlie Miller's homemade rye again, but I knew he wasn't drunk. He was alert, too alert, like he was operating on pure adrenaline.

As he lifted the heavy metal crucifix down from over the mantel-piece, he kept saying, "The golden calf . . . it's the sixth generation . . . the seed." He stared right at me when he said it with a look of disgust. Mom tried to get him to calm down, but he shoved her against the wall and stormed out of the house. I followed him to the edge of the untilled wheat, grabbing on to his arm to stop him. He turned, clutching the crucifix tight to his chest. "I have to stop the evil before it's born," he said, his eyes drilling me in place. "God forgive us, son."

There was no moon that night. No stars, like they knew what my dad was about to do, like they couldn't bear to watch.

"Fifteen minutes, Clay," Mom calls from the kitchen.

Letting go of the memory, I rush upstairs, turn on the faucet, and strip off my clothes. I'm shivering my ass off waiting for the water to heat up, though it never makes it past lukewarm. One of the many perks of living with three girls. I step in the tub and tug the plastic curtain shut. The sound of the rusty metal loops scraping against the curtain rod reminds me of the hoof jammed in the cutting blades. It sets my teeth on edge.

I try not to think about it, but for the life of me I can't figure out how the calf got there. Since the Neely ranch closed, the closest cattle ranch is two towns over in Monroe. It had golden fur, the same color as the wheat. Just like my dad talked about before he died. I've never seen a calf that color before. It couldn't have been more than a day old. No way it could've wandered all the way over here on its own.

Unless someone put it there.

Wouldn't put it past Tyler, Ian Neely's son. It's more than bad blood. Ever since Dad died, Tyler's always staring at me in this strange expectant way. Maybe he's just waiting for me to lose my shit like my dad did. Maybe everyone is.

Grabbing a towel from the rack, I coax it around my waist; it's still pretty stiff from drying on the line. I shuffle down the hall to my room. Besides the thick black garbage bags taped up over the windows and the pill bottles cluttering my bedside table, it looks just like it did before. At first, the garbage bags were just a way to keep out the light, but then it became this weird thing, almost like I wanted to preserve everything inside. Sometimes I think about taking it all down—the mementos, the posters, the football trophies—but I can't bring myself to do it. Dad took me to every practice, stood on the sidelines for every game. Outside this room, people can say whatever they want about him, but in here, he's still just my dad.

Peeling back a corner of one of the garbage bags, I peer out over the crops. Hammy's out there pacing the perimeter of the wheat. For a second, I wonder if he somehow got to the calf and dragged it out into the field, but that mutt hasn't set foot in the wheat since Dad died, almost like he's scared of it.

We've run over plenty of animals in the fields. It's awful, but that's life on the farm. One time we even found a black bear. We figured he must've tried to make a den out there. But seeing the newborn calf rattled me. With good fucking reason.

I try not to read too much into it. Noodle says that's the trouble with me: I keep trying to make sense out of everything.

"Clay?" Mom hollers up the stairs. "Five minutes, okay, hon?" The sound of her voice makes me wince. She tries so hard to keep it light and sunny, but it just reeks of desperation, like she's one step away from being sent to Oakmoor.

I pull on some boxers and a T-shirt. For the millionth time, I think about selling the farm. Mr. Neely offered a while back, enough to get us out of town. But it feels like I'd be betraying Dad, betraying our entire family history. We weren't Sooners like some of the other families in neighboring counties. We didn't steal the land by camping out before the land rush and hiding in the brush like little assholes. My family started at the roundup and fought it out with the best of them. We got the best parcel, too. Dad always used to joke around that our family used up all their luck getting this land. Either that or they made some kind of deal with the Devil. Besides, Noodle'd be crushed if I sold. She has this crazy idea she wants to run the farm someday. It's not that she can't do it; when she puts her mind to it, Noodle can do anything. I just want something better for her.

"Clay?" Mom hollers.

"Coming." I pull on some fresh jeans and a flannel and grab my backpack. No time for breakfast so I snatch a handful of bacon, kiss Mom on the cheek, and give Noodle a high five as I head out to the truck.

I open the driver's-side door to find Jess scrunched down in the cab with her army surplus boots pressing up against the dash. I slap her feet down. "No way, Jess. Take the bus with Noodle."

"I'm sick of the bus." She sighs as she settles into the seat. "Please, Clay." She bats her thickly coated eyelashes. They're all clumped together like black sticky webs.

I want to tell her to get lost. The drive into town is the only peace I get, when I can turn up the radio and pretend nothing ever happened. But I hold my tongue. Maybe this one time, she'll talk . . . open up.

"Fine." I shoot her a sideways glance and rev Old Blue to life. "But you're not wearing that to school." I take off my flannel and toss it onto her lap.

She puts it on over her tank top and too-short skirt like it's the most exhausting thing she'll do all day.

"You need a haircut." She pops her gum. "Unless you're *trying* to look like a surfer girl."

I grab my cap from the dash, pulling it down low. I used to keep my hair buzzed for football season. Haven't cut it in over a year. It's not some dramatic protest or anything, just haven't gotten around to it. No need.

We reach the end of the long dirt drive, and a guy in a brand-new F-150 with tricked-out radials drives by, giving me the reverent head nod. Townie. Most people look at our farm and get all nostalgic. They don't see the termites eating up the barn or the endless crops I'll have to work. They see the American flag and apple pie and John fucking Mellencamp.

As we pull onto Route 17, Jess fiddles with the radio dial.

"We both know you're never going to find a song you like, so what's the point?"

"Because it bugs the crap out of you?" she snaps, and then turns off the radio. She knows I hate the silence.

Instead of kicking her out on the side of the road, I try to think of our time together like POW training. If I'm ever captured behind enemy lines, I'll be immune to certain forms of torture.

Just as I'm working up the nerve to ask her how she's doing with everything, she rolls down her window and closes her eyes. I wonder what she's thinking, but I don't ask.

I used to love this time of year—football, the scent of burning leaves hanging on the brittle morning air. Now it just reminds me of what happened. Of death. Tonight will be the one-year anniversary. I don't need a calendar to remind me. I can feel it, the memory buried deep within my bones. I wonder if Jess can feel it, too.

I turn right onto Main Street and that sick feeling swells in my stomach as we pass the Preservation Society. The gleaming white paint, the manicured lawn edged with orange, yellow, and rust-colored flowers. People think it's all ice cream socials, deb balls, and ribbon-cutting ceremonies, but there are secrets, too. I think my dad uncovered something . . . something big. He'd been acting strange for weeks, staying up all night poring over family Bibles and tattered documents, but it was that final meeting with Ian Neely and the Preservation Society that sent him over the edge.

The last time I set foot in the place was right after Dad's funeral. Mr. Neely said he wanted to talk to me man-to-man. He told me everything happens for a reason, that it's all part of God's plan. "Clay, we all have our roles to play," Mr. Neely had said. "And you're very important to the Preservation Society. It's time for you to take your place on the council. It's time to move forward, into the future."

Something about his words felt wrong. Like putting weight on a broken bone.

"I don't have all day, Grandpa." Jess drums her black nails on the edge of the window.

I press on the gas.

Some people say Jess's gone goth, because of the nail polish and everything. They say she's headed for a fall. I just hope it doesn't take a world of hurt to bring her back to us.

"Pull over," she says.

I stop the car in front of a boarded-up house with a foreclosure sign out front. "Why? We're four blocks away from your school."

"Exactly."

I decide to take a more direct approach. "Why. Am. I. Dropping. You. Off. Here?"

"Duh." She rolls her eyes as she gets out of the car and slams the door shut. "Because I don't want to be seen with you."

"Then ride the bus!" I yell back at her.

She doubles back to lean against the open window. "I don't get you. You have a car. You're going to be eighteen in a couple of days. Nothing's stopping you from leaving."

I take a deep breath, reminding myself she's just a kid, trying to get a rise out of me. "Except a family I have to take care of."

"We both know you could've sold the farm to Neely."

I look up at her in shock. I had no idea she knew about that.

A sly smile curls the corner of her mouth. "I thought so. We would've been fine. You just don't have the balls to leave. You're going to live with Mom forever like that perv from *Psycho*."

"Have a great day, Jess!" I lean over and roll up the window. She gives me the finger and kicks my truck as I pull away.

3

CRANKING UP the radio, I drive the half mile to Midland High. All I get is some lame soft rock station from Tulsa, but it feels good to numb out even if it's just for a few minutes.

I park in the back of the lot—last one in, first one out. That probably says a lot about my personality. Tyler Neely, on the other hand, parks front row, center.

He's the biggest dick at school, or at least he thinks he has the biggest dick. He's got this beautiful '66 Mustang, and he had to ruin it by painting bright-yellow racing stripes down the middle.

As soon as I cut the engine, Tyler looks back at me as if on cue. Normally, I'd turn away, pretend not to notice, but I'm sick of his shit. I hold his stare. If he had anything to do with that calf, I want him to know he didn't get to me.

Ben says something to him, probably some stupid joke, and when Tyler finally looks away, I let out a huge burst of pent-up air.

It's the strangest crew.

Ben Gillman's a good guy, decent tight end, but dumber than a bucket of gravel.

Tammy Perry's one of those girls you'd be hard-pressed to notice. Never in trouble, hardly makes a peep. Beige clothes . . . beige hair . . . beige freckles. The girl practically screams *oatmeal*.

Less oatmeal but still no prize is Jimmy Doogan. I swear he's scared of his own shadow. One time a bird flew into the window of our fifth-grade math class and he pissed his pants, like a *river* of pee.

And then there's Ali Miller.

It's complicated.

I watch her cross the parking lot to Tyler's car—legs for days. She has this way about her, I mean, she's so far above all these hicks, and she doesn't even know it.

I've known her since Sunday school, hell, probably since I was born. I don't remember anything without her. Catching crawdads in Harmon Lake, turtle races, riding our bikes all over the county. One time we found ten bucks on the side of Route 17 and bought a whole mess of penny candy from Merritt's gas station. Just a bunch of stale baby-teeth bait, but when we tossed it onto people's front steps, we felt like Santa in the middle of summer. We talked about saving the world, or at least saving ourselves.

I try not to go there, but I can't help thinking about the last time Ali came to see me. It was right after the funeral. She sat on the edge of my bed and cried.

"Promise you won't forget me," she whispered.

To this day, I have no idea what she was talking about, or why she was crying. Maybe she was just trying to say goodbye and I was too stupid to notice. All I wanted to do was wipe the tears off her cheeks and maybe hold her and tell her it was going to be okay, but the smell of her skin, the softness of her long dark-brown hair, the feel of her body pressing against me was more than I could bear. I leaned in and kissed her. Her lips were so warm and wet. She took in a tiny gasp of air, and when I went in for another kiss, she started crying even harder and ran out of the house. I wanted to tell her I was caught up in the grief, plead temporary insanity, but the truth was I really just loved her. I think I've always loved her. She hasn't spoken to me since.

Tyler snatches the red hoodie tied around Ali's waist and smacks her ass with it. She shoots him a lopsided grin as she grabs it back from him and pulls it on over her faded-tan shoulders. I wonder if he even notices her shoulders—that constellation of freckles on the right one. That's the arm she was always hanging out of her mom's Cadillac when they delivered Avon around town.

The only thing they have in common is they're the eldest sons and daughters of the founders of our glorious Preservation Society—the six families who rode in together and settled this county in the 1889 land rush. The Neelys, the Gillmans, the Perrys, the Millers, the Doogans, and yours truly, the Tates. I guess it's about as close to royalty as this town will ever get.

It wouldn't have been so weird if they'd all been friends before, but it seemed like as soon as my dad died, as soon as they stepped up to take their seats on the council, they suddenly became inseparable.

I'd never admit this to anyone, but sometimes I envy them—their freedom, their wide-open futures. It feels like my fate was sealed the moment my dad walked toward the cattle ranch holding that crucifix.

"Mooder in Midland." That's what the newspeople called it.

Real catchy.

At first, I kept waiting for the council to reach out to me, offer condolences or something . . . *anything*. But no one said a word to me. Not a single word. And Tyler was more than happy to step into my shoes in every way possible. I thought it was only a matter of time before Ali figured out what a tool he was, but I guess I was wrong.

She used to make fun of the Preservation Society just as much as I did. Sometimes when I look at her like this, surrounded by sycophants and assholes, it feels like I never knew her at all. Like I never knew any of them. Like I don't even exist.

As I open my door, my cousin Dale jumps in front of my truck. "If you liked it then you shoulda put a ring on it. If you liked it then you shoulda put a ring on it," he sings obnoxiously as he swivels his hips in front of me.

Three freshman girls walk by, giggling their heads off.

I slide out of my truck. "You shouldn't do that. Ever."

"Come on, loosen up, cuz. They love it, doncha ladies?" He shakes his hips again, and they all look back and laugh.

"I hate to break it to you, but it's never gonna happen."

"They don't call 'em freshies for nothing. For all they know I could be the coolest guy at school."

"They call them freshies because they're fourteen-year-old girls, not because they're stupid. And Jess is going to be one of them next year, so lay off."

"Don't be such an old man." He punches me in the shoulder. "Hang out with me tonight."

"Can't, last harvest," I say as I hoist my backpack up on my shoulder. "Besides, all you're going to do is park up at the Quick Trip and holler at girls all night from the back of your pickup."

"I've got it all figured out. You need to catch 'em when they're feeling all vulnerable—on a late-night ice cream run in sweats and no makeup. You tell them they look beautiful and they're yours."

"You're an idiot," I say as we make our way across the lot.

"Or I'm a genius. Fine line, my friend. It was a lot easier to get girls to talk to me when you were QB. All I had to do was drop your name, tell 'em we're cousins."

"Second cousins."

"Whatever."

Some pep girls run by, and Dale elbows me. "Big game tomorrow."

"Oh yeah?" I act like I don't know it's the biggest game of the season. Homecoming.

I should've never stepped on that field last year. My dad wasn't even in the ground yet. I'd like to say I did it for him, or coach, or the team, but the truth was I did it for me. And look where that got me.

"He's a shit quarterback," Dale mutters as we edge around Tyler's car. "Everybody knows the only reason he's starting is 'cause his old man paid for the new stadium."

"If you love football so much, maybe *you* should play."

"Please. They wouldn't even know what to do with this much power." Dale clenches his fist, trying to make a bicep appear, but it's no use. Dale was born with a tiny hole in his heart. Can't play sports. Doc's orders.

"Hey, has anyone started raising cattle around here?" I ask as casually as possible.

"Why? Are those jerks still mooing at you?" Dale bristles.

"What? No. I don't know . . . I was just curious. Wait, who was mooing at me?"

"No cattle, dude." He tries to play it off, but he looks concerned. "If something's going on, you'd tell me, right?"

"Sure. 'Course, man." I manage my best "I'm not going crazy" smile.

Dale wanders off after some girl in a low-cut top. I swear, he's got the attention span of a cicada in heat.

As I wait for him at the top of the steps, I look out over the lot, my gaze immediately drawn back to Ali. She's gathering her hair over her shoulder when I notice a mark on the nape of her neck.

It isn't anything pretty like angel wings or a butterfly. It looks like the same thing Tyler has on his inner wrist. An upside-down U with two dots above and below. The harder I look at it, the more disgusted I get.

It doesn't make any sense. Ali's too squeamish for that. I had to hold her hand when they pricked her finger in seventh grade for blood testing in science class. And this isn't any tattoo. It looks hard-core, like some kind of prison tattoo. Or a brand.

Tyler moves into my line of sight, staring right at me as he pulls Ali's hair away from her neck, like he wants to give me a better view.

A blistering rage pulses through my entire body.

In a panic, I rush into school. My chest feels tight, my eyes blurry as I barrel through a group of students. I don't know where I'm going; all I know is I need to get away. I slam into the emergency exit door at the end of the hall, triggering the alarm. I scream as loud as I can over the piercing wail.

Why would she let him do that to her?

Mark her like fucking cattle.

4

I MAKE it through most of my classes, but the idea of facing any
of them in the cafeteria makes my skin crawl, so I sneak out to the
booth above the football field and hide out until last period. I still
have the key from when I used to come out here at night and go
through plays.

Settling myself on the concrete floor beneath the control panel,
I pull out my lunch. Noodle always puts something on the outside
of the brown paper bag. Today, it's a smiley face sticker. She makes
me the same lunch every day. I don't even like grape jelly anymore,
but I don't have the heart to tell her.

I try to concentrate on finishing up my algebra, but I find myself drawing the symbol I saw on Ali's neck over and over again on
the front of my folder.

Yeah, I want to beat the shit out of Tyler, but I feel more bummed than anything else. I mean, it's her body, Ali can do whatever she wants with it, but something about that mark makes me feel like it's too late for me, like maybe I never even had a shot.

The booth has a musky damp smell, same smell as the locker room. I try not to think about it, but I miss it. It's not about the trophies, or even being part of a team. I miss it like you'd miss a limb. It's like I can feel the memory in my muscles, my fingers naturally curving around the ball. But when I think of my last game, them hauling off that poor kid in a back brace, I clench my hand in a tight fist. They said I just snapped, that it could happen to anyone. But that's what they said about my dad, too. All I know is that I didn't need to tackle him. I wanted to do it. I wanted to hurt someone, and that scares me more than anything. What I'm capable of . . . what's in my blood.

I always thought of Coach Pearson like a second father, but when I quit the team, he left Midland. Heard he took a job in Arkansas, and that's that.

Neely brought in some fancy coach from Texas. The team moved on. The town moved on. The council moved on. Ali moved on.

I'm the only one who kept hanging on to the past.

It's only when I dared to accuse the Preservation Society of pushing my dad over the edge that everyone got real "concerned." Dr. Perry, Tammy's dad, stepped in, said all I needed was sleep. He gave me a bottomless supply of sleeping pills and I've been uncomfortably numb since. They even started sending me to counseling at school. Every day, last period.

The bell rings and I head back in. Skipping math and health class is one thing, but if I miss counseling, there'll be hell to pay.

"MISS GRANGER?" I knock on the open door.

She looks up briefly from her computer and smiles. "Emma . . . please."

"Sure." I sit down in my usual chair. She thinks it's weird I call her Miss Granger because she's just a handful of years older than me, but that's how I was raised.

She unfolds the magnetic chessboard on her desk and pushes it toward me. "Your move," she says as she scoops some loose tea from a metal tin into a teapot. I don't know anybody else who makes tea like that. It smells good, like spicy oranges and lemons and something else I can't quite figure out, maybe some kind of herb.

One look at her and you can tell she's not from around here— tailored clothes, clear nail polish, long hair pulled back into a fancy bun thing. Pretty in that *Playboy* librarian kind of way, but I shouldn't be thinking about her like that.

Edging forward in my seat, I move my bishop. I act like it's a big drag coming here, but I've grown accustomed to it . . . to her. It's calming in a weird way. And she never asks me about football. Sometimes we don't talk at all, which is nice. Sometimes we just sit and stare out the window. There's always music on—it's classical, but it's good. She doesn't like the quiet, either.

"Here." She leans over her desk to hand me a cup of tea.

The only jewelry she wears is a small clear cross around her neck with a little mustard seed floating around inside. She doesn't go to church at Midland Baptist like everyone else. She's Catholic, which is pretty exotic around here. Nearest Catholic church is four towns over in Murpheyville. Folks are nice to her, but they keep her at arm's length. Hell, Garry Henderson's family moved here when he was two and he's still considered an outsider.

Miss Granger's been real helpful with Noodle's application to All Saints—the private school connected with the church over there. Sure, there's nuns and that's weird, but I can't let what happened to Jess happen to Noodle. This town has a way of ruining people.

"Any news about Noodle?" I ask as I take a sip of the tea. I don't really like it, but I'm trying.

She sits back, studying the board. "Not yet."

"I've been checking the mail twice a day. If she doesn't get in, I don't know what I'm going to do."

"I wouldn't worry." Miss Granger smiles. "She's gifted."

"It's going to be tight, money-wise, but it's worth it. She's worth it."

Miss Granger moves her queen. "How's the harvest coming along?"

Maybe it's the classical music, or the smell of the tea, or maybe it's just her, but I blurt, "I ran over an animal with the combine this morning."

She looks up at me from the board. Her gray eyes are soft, but curious. "And how do you feel about that?"

"Pissed." I force a chuckle. "It got caught up in the cutting blade. It's going to take me an hour to get that thing running again."

Instead of turning up her nose, she seems interested. "What kind of animal?"

I think about lying, just telling her it was a fox. But there's something about her that makes me want to open up like one of her Chinese puzzle boxes. I open my mouth to speak, but I can't seem to make myself do it.

She leans forward. "Clay, what is it?"

"Look." I let out a heavy sigh. "If I tell you, you have to promise you won't tell anyone . . . or freak out."

"I told you, you can trust me."

I run my sweaty palms down the front of my jeans. "A calf."

"A *calf*?" She nearly chokes on the word. She gets up and closes the door then sits in the chair next to me. "Have you told anyone else about this?"

"No, but I'm pretty sure I know who did it. Tonight's the one-year anniversary and he's been staring at me nonstop."

"Are we talking about Tyler Neely again?" Her razor-sharp brows knit together. "You think he placed a dead calf in your field? We've talked about this, Clay. How are you doing on the medication? Those sleeping pills can have some serious side—"

"It wasn't dead . . . at least not for long." I shake my head. "The blood . . . it was fresh. I saw someone moving low through the wheat to the east and then I hit it. The cut on its throat looked too clean for the combine. It had golden fur." Just thinking about it makes me feel sick to my stomach. "Have you ever seen a calf with golden fur?" I lean my elbows on the desk, accidentally knocking over my cup.

She springs up to grab a couple of tissues. As she's dabbing the tea from my folder, her movement slows and her eyes narrow on the drawing of the upside-down U with two dots above and below.

"Where did you see this?"

"It's nothing. Just something I've seen around," I say as I take the folders from her and cram them into my backpack.

"Around where?" she asks, scratching the side of her head with her pencil.

"Tyler Neely." I look up to gauge her response, but she's hard to read. "He has it on his wrist. And then I saw it on the back of Ali

Miller's neck this morning." Just saying it out loud ticks me off all over again.

I notice Miss Granger's slender fingers gripping the pencil, her knuckles straining white.

"Why?" I ask. "Does it mean something?"

She reaches her hand to her neck, twisting the cross between her fingers.

The bell rings, startling us both.

She opens her mouth like she's going to say something more, but then changes her mind. "You can go."

I gather up my bag.

"And, Clay?" She gives a tight smile. "You can call me anytime."

I nod and head for the exit, making a beeline for my truck.

As I sink into the driver's seat, I see Ali and the rest of the pack gathering around Tyler's dickmobile.

Tyler's on his phone, trying to look like some kind of hotshot. He grabs Ali by a belt loop, pulling her toward him. As his hand moves lower, dangerously close to her ass, a searing heat creeps up the sides of my neck. I want to rip his arm off his body.

For the life of me, I can't figure out what she sees in him, but it's like she's under some kind of spell.

He whispers something in her ear. Ali turns to look over her shoulder. I swear, she's staring right at me. But that's crazy. She hasn't so much as glanced at me since the night I kissed her and she went running out of my house. I look behind me, but there's no one there. Ali Miller is smiling at *me* . . . all seductive like.

In a panic, I try to put my key in the ignition, but my hands are shaking so bad I can't seem to find the keyhole. When I look up again, Ali's standing right next to my truck. My heart's pounding in my ears, and my throat's bone dry. Hesitantly, I roll down my window.

"Ali?" I hardly recognize my own voice. It's like I'm a kid all over again.

She drapes her arms inside the truck and leans in close. I feel her breath on my cheek, smell the faint hint of flowers in her hair. Her fingertips graze the top of my thigh, dangerously close to my zipper. Adrenaline rushes through every part of me.

"Meet me at midnight," she whispers, "at the breeding barn."

As she turns to walk back to Tyler's car, I force the key into the ignition and pull out of the lot, ignoring the angry car horns.

I almost crash into some poor girl in a powder-blue Buick, but I have to get out of here. I turn up the stereo as loud as it will go, but it still doesn't drown out the screaming in my head. The Ali I knew would never go to the Neely ranch after what happened there. She would never ask *me* to go there.

I'm glancing in the rearview mirror to make sure no one's following when I catch my reflection. My eyes—they look just like Dad's on the night he died. His last words cling to the back of my throat like thick bile.

"I plead the blood."

5

As I turn on to Route 17, I spot a bunch of punk kids ducking into the woods behind Merritt's gas station. There's an old campsite out there where nothing good ever happens. Through the pines, I catch a glimpse of what looks like chestnut hair. Pale skin. A black boot.

Jess.

Without even thinking, I whip the truck around and pull into the lot, kicking up a mess of red earth and gravel.

The kids take off running. By the time I break through the trees, they've scattered.

"Jess," I call as I chase them through the woods, but I don't see her anywhere.

I catch up to a scrawny kid with a dirty-blond mullet, tackling him to the ground.

"Where's Jess?" I flip him over to see his face and I feel like I'm going to throw up.

Lee Wiggins. He used to be in my class. It's like he's wearing a Halloween mask year round—face like a gnawed-up cheese pizza.

They say the chemicals melted off half the skin on his body. Left nothing behind of his dumbass brothers. A family full of meth heads, bootleggers before that. They blew themselves up in a trailer behind Ted Bannon's junkyard on the same night my dad died.

"Jess!" I scan the woods, her name echoing through the pines.

"He's coming." Lee smiles up at me, clutching my shirt. He reeks of cigarettes, burnt hair, and iodine.

"What the hell are you talking about?" I try to pry his hands free. "And what are you doing with my sister?"

The woods are dense; it'd be so easy to get lost back here. Disappear.

"He who slays the golden calf will be chosen," Lee whispers, spit bubbles specking his scarred lips.

My heart stutters. "Wait . . . what . . . what do you know about the calf?" I grab his shoulders and shake him. "Was it you? Did you put it there?"

"It could be me. The seed. The Devil told me so . . . from the flames." He grins, his grotesque skin stretching tight across his bones like thick rubber bands.

"Stop smiling at me!" I scream, rage boiling inside of me.

Before I even know what I'm doing, I haul back and punch him in the face. The sick feel of his waxy gnarled skin against my knuckles makes me cringe. Horrified by what I've done, I clutch my fist

34

tight to my chest and crawl off him. "I . . . I'm sorry. I didn't mean to do that."

"Sure you did." Lee just lies there on the pine straw, smiling, blood seeping from the corner of his mouth. "I know all about you. We're the same, you and me."

Molten heat radiates through my muscles. I clench my fists tighter.

I tower over him, the edge of my boot inches away from his head. "I don't know what your deal is, but if you don't stay away from my sister, I'll come back and put you out of your misery. You understand me?"

His grin stretches wider, exposing his crooked bottom teeth, swimming in blood. "I'm counting on it."

"You're crazy." I stagger back.

His laughter follows me out of the woods.

My truck door's still wide open, engine running, music full blast.

I tear out of the lot, back toward home.

I don't know what the hell got into me back there.

As hard as I try, I can't get Lee out of my head. His face. His words.

The Devil.

I PARK in back of the equipment shed so Noodle won't see the truck. I can't look at her. Not right now. Not after what I just did.

As soon as I enter the shed, my eyes settle on the spot where I discovered all those explosives last year. I buried them on a patch of barren land on the back acres. I don't know what Dad was doing with all that, but it didn't matter. He was gone.

Grabbing a hatchet, a shovel, and a couple of heavy-duty black compost bags, I head out to the combine.

I feel the weight of what I'm about to do in my limbs, like I'm moving underwater.

A turkey vulture passes overhead; I wonder if we're headed to the same place. Shading my eyes from the sun, I peer up at the sky—an endless gunmetal blue with long white clouds stretching out like continents I'll never see.

As I get closer to the combine, I tie a bandana around my nose and mouth and brace myself for the stench of the calf, the sound of the maggots worming their way through the innards, a glistening moist endless rattle that makes my stomach churn. I'll never forget that sound when I found Dad in the breeding barn.

God, I hate maggots. When I die I want to be cremated. I know it's not the Tate way, but this land's already taken so much from us. I want to leave this earth nothing more than a pile of ash.

I crouch so I can peer under the cutting platform, but there's nothing there. No maggots, no fur, no blood.

When I reach my hand in to see if it somehow settled under the discarded wheat stems, the engine roars to life, the cutting blade nicking my arm.

I scramble back from the combine, my adrenaline setting my nerves on fire.

"Tyler, is that you?" I peer in the cab, but there's no one there. I run around the tractor. "This isn't funny," I yell over the roar of the engine.

I search for my gloves, the ones I left behind this morning, the gloves that should be covered in blood, but they're nowhere to be found.

Holding my head in my hands, like I can press the madness from my brain, I scan the fields. I'm desperate for a logical explanation. Anything other than I'm just going crazy.

The wind stings as it hits my cut. I glance down at the bright-red blood trickling onto the golden wheat and I feel dizzy. Bleary-eyed, I stare out over the untilled crops waving in the wind like a churning sea.

I understand how the settlers got lost in the plains. It'd be so easy to lose your bearings out here, get separated from the herd. Once you're isolated, the predators can pick you off.

My breath is coming in short bursts now; it feels like the wheat, the sky, and the earth are squeezing me from all sides.

Backing up to the combine, I climb into the cab and cut the engine. There's no way it could've started on its own. I listen closely, but the only thing I hear is the occasional ting of the engine cooling down and the faint buzz of the train whistling through the crossing on Route 17. It's so quiet I swear I can hear my heartbeat thrumming in the slash across my arm. I pull the first-aid kit from under the seat to find Noodle's put heart stickers over everything. My chin quivers.

"Just keep it together, Clay," I whisper as I rip open a packet of gauze and wrap it around my wrist. The combine's been acting up lately. And it's just a surface cut.

I notice my bruised knuckles and a fresh wave of guilt washes over me. No one needs to know about this. About any of it. I think about heading home, barricading myself in my room for the rest of the day, but then I think of Noodle standing there with her sticker bag. That goofy Kool-Aid-stained grin, her front two teeth missing. I can't let her down. I can't let the family down.

All of this could be caused by lack of sleep. I mean, even when I'm asleep, it's a restless sleep. I keep having the weirdest dreams—Noodle whispering in my ear, telling me to work the wheat. It has to mean something. This last harvest will bring in the money we need to pay for that school over in Murpheyville. It might be too late for the rest of us, but Noodle deserves this. I'll do whatever it takes to help her get out of here . . . make something of her life.

I take in a deep shaky breath and let it all out. Okay . . . so there's no calf. Maybe there never was a calf. Maybe I fell asleep in the cab this morning and dreamt the entire thing. That could happen. Same with Ali. I mean, if she smiled at me like that, walked over to my truck, Dale would be calling me nonstop to get all the details. And Lee Wiggins . . . who the hell knows. I lost my temper, that was a mistake, but he's not going to say anything. Even if he did, everybody thinks the Wiggins are crazy trash.

As much as I explain it away, a part of me wonders if this is how it all started for Dad. Maybe it's schizophrenia.

Maybe it's in my blood.

I drag my hands through my hair as I look back toward the house. The house my ancestors built from nothing. I need to man up. The fields aren't going to work themselves.

I force myself to turn the ignition. The combine purrs to life so easily, it takes me aback.

Like it's been waiting for me.

6

By the time I notice the front porch light flickering, dusk has come and gone. I worked the fields with a kind of focus only the heaviest of death metal can bring. As I climb out of the cab, I feel completely spent, but my mind's still reeling.

Noodle doesn't ask me how many acres I did, but I can tell she's dying to know by the way she's gripping her sticker bag. I dig my hand in and count out six gold stars for her. She hums a little tune as she places them in the squares.

Standing back so she can admire her work, she slips her hand into mine. "More than halfway there."

That's Noodle for you—glass half-full.

"Clay?" Mom calls from the kitchen. "Supper's ready."

"Finally." Jess clomps down the stairs.

Noodle skips off to help with the plates.

"Were you out by Merritt's today?" I ask, trying to keep my voice down.

Jess lets out a heavy sigh. "What's it to you?"

"I saw that Wiggins kid out there."

"So?"

"So, I want you to stay away from him. Stay away from those woods."

She rolls her eyes at me.

"I'm serious, Jess."

"I'm starving." She barges past. "It's stupid we have to wait for you to eat. King of the castle . . . just like Dad."

I grab her arm, yanking her back. "I'm *nothing* like Dad."

She looks down at my hand in shock, and jerks away. "Leave me alone, psycho."

"I'm sorry, I didn't mean—" But she's already gone.

We sit in our usual spots, while Mom waits on us hand and foot. I'm always telling her she doesn't have to do it, but I think it's a way to keep the attention off her, keep busy.

Dad's chair sits empty at the head of the table, like a ghost. We never talk about it, but that's the Tate way—there's honor in the pain. Tragedy is a way of life, right? Why should we be immune? Right after the funeral, during one of her *spells,* Mom told me she thought it was God's punishment for having so much—being blessed with healthy children, a fruitful farm. But I don't believe that. Not even God can be that big of an asshole.

Noodle starts grace. A little whistle escapes through the gap in her teeth every time she makes the "th" sound. I never say grace anymore. Feels wrong.

"And God bless potpie night. Amen."

Thursday night, potpie night. Basically all the leftovers from the week thrown in a dish with gravy and a piecrust tucked over the top. It sounds gross, but it's pretty good.

Jess takes the best piece, the one on the far side where the oven's the hottest and the crust gets real crunchy. Mom always gets stuck with the soggy middle piece. She claims she likes it best, but we know she won't touch it anyway. She'll just move it around the plate over and over again in the same pattern, a sweeping arc with a couple of stabs for good measure.

Each of us had our own way of dealing with what happened, but sometimes I think Mom took on the worst of it—the shame.

"How are you coming on the wheat?" Mom asks as she finally sits down and picks up her fork. I look away. I can't stand watching her going through the motions anymore.

Noodle sits up all proud. "Right on schedule, forty-four acres left."

I feel her tapping the leg of the chair, no doubt, forty-four times.

"I need new clothes," Jess says, more as a demand than a request.

I'm saving for Noodle's tuition at All Saints, but I don't want anyone to know about that yet. Not until she gets in. "Well, I'm sure as hell not giving you hard-earned crop money to buy clothes you're just going to cut holes in anyway."

Jess opens her mouth as wide as she can to show me her half-chewed food.

Noodle giggles at her. "I don't need new clothes."

"Duh." Jess looks her up and down. "It's not like any boy is ever going to be interested in you anyway, unless it's COUNT Dracula."

Noodle kicks her hard under the table. Mom and I ignore it. If Noodle kicks you, you probably deserve it.

"Tomorrow's homecoming," Mom says with a gasp as she looks

up at the wall where the calendar used to hang, like she can still see the date circled. "You should have an extra piece tonight. You'll need your strength."

We all freeze in place, looking at each other anxiously. It's usually best to play along. She'll remember eventually, and when she does, she'll take to her bed. To be honest, I'm not sure which is worse.

"Do you need a corsage . . . for Ali?" she asks as she moves her food around.

I flinch at the memory. Last year, after the game, I was going to take Ali to the dance, finally tell her how I felt. Instead, I spent it in the wheat alone, mourning my dad, thinking I'd just killed that halfback, and cursing the day I'd ever been born.

I glance into the living room. Even though the lights are off, I swear I can still see the faint outline where the metal crucifix used to hang.

I force myself to swallow another bite and glance at the clock on the wall: 9:06 P.M. I don't know how much more of this I can take.

"Your dad sure is working late these days, but don't worry, we'll be there in time for kickoff. He wouldn't miss that."

"Why can't anyone say it?" Jess drops her silverware on the table with a loud clang. "You know what tonight is, right? It's the one-year anniversary. Can we at least take Dad's chair away now? It's not like he's ever coming back. He's dead, Mom. He went crazy and now we're paying the price."

Noodle's smile melts away. Mom looks down at her plate.

I'm partly relieved for the interruption, but I can't believe she said that.

I glare at her.

"What?" Jess wads up her napkin.

42

As I look down at the flesh-colored vegetables and meat oozing with gravy, I feel sick to my stomach. I poke at my plate with my fork a few times and then ask if I can be excused.

"Of course, honey," Mom says with a weary smile. "You'll need your rest for the big game tomorrow." She starts to get up to clear my plate, but I carry it to the sink on my own. I can't look at her right now. It hurts too much.

"I don't want you waiting on me for supper anymore." I walk away before getting a response.

I make it to the foot of the stairs when Noodle comes crashing into me from behind with a hug. "You're good, Clay. Don't forget that."

I pull her around and hold her tight. I have no idea what she's talking about, but somehow it's exactly what I need.

MY ROOM is stifling.

Who am I kidding? This house is stifling.

Peeling back the garbage bag, I open up my window and take in a deep breath of fresh air. My eyes automatically zero in on the Neely ranch. No lights—nothing but dead space.

All I can think about is Ali leaning into my truck, her fingertips almost grazing the top of my thighs, my zipper. I feel stupid for thinking it was real. No way she'd even look at me, let alone ask me to meet her at the breeding barn. Maybe Miss Granger's right. Maybe it's the sleeping pills.

I grab one of the bottles from my bedside table and read the side effects. *Warning: This medication may cause drowsiness.* Sure as hell hope so. *In some cases this may cause delusions,* check. *Tremors,* check. *Hallucinations,* check. *And severe mood disorders.* Awesome.

"Thanks for nothing, Dr. Perry." I gather up all the pill bottles and empty them into the toilet, flushing them before I have a chance to change my mind.

Stripping down to my boxers, I climb into bed. The sheets feel clammier than my skin.

I left my music on the combine, but I'm not about to go back out there and get it. So what if I have to lie here all night? It's not like it's going to kill me. I can still read.

I pull out the family Bibles and farm ledgers stashed under my bed.

At first, I was looking for clues, but now it's just habit. The last few weeks of his life, Dad couldn't stop poring over these books. And when he didn't have his nose buried in one of them, he was down at the Preservation Society looking through the archives.

I feel like the answer's here, staring me right in the face, but I just can't see it. The only thing remotely interesting is the family tree. That night, Dad kept talking about the sixth generation . . . the seed. It must have something to do with the family tree.

I trace my finger across the names.

Thomas Tate came here and settled this farm in 1889. So I guess he's the first. It passed on to his son Benjamin Tate in 1919. And then to his son Lyle Tate in 1950. Then Heath Tate in 1979. My dad, Neil Tate, in 2000.

Which leaves me. I'm the sixth. I just wish I knew what it meant. There's a line drawn next to my name, stretching out to the margins, with "L.A.W. 11:26" written in my dad's chicken scrawl. I've gone over every corresponding Bible passage, every possible acronym I can think of and I still can't make heads or tails of it. There were lots of entries for L.A.W. in the checkbook the last month of my dad's life. A hundred dollars here, fifty dollars there. When I asked Mom about it, she got so agitated, I had to stop.

Written around the perimeter of the page, in a circular pattern, is a passage from Exodus 32—The Golden Calf.

"I will make your descendants as numerous as the stars in the sky and I will give your descendants all this land I promised them, and it will be their inheritance forever."

As hard as I try to piece it all together, I can't help thinking maybe it's just the ramblings of a crazy person. Nothing more. Maybe I should be thankful I don't understand it, because understanding it would mean I'm crazy, too.

Rubbing the goose bumps from my arms, I set the books aside and turn off my light.

It's a little chilly, but the breeze feels good. The way the wind rustles against the garbage bag almost sounds like wind chimes.

For the longest time after Dad's death, I thought I could still hear the cattle bellowing and mewing. I know that's nuts.

People think cows are these dumb docile animals, but you should've seen what they did to him. Teeth, hooves, a thousand pounds of pressure crushing his bones.

But that's nothing compared to what he did to them.

7

A DULL creaking sound pulls me through the wheat. The sky is so blue, like it's been painted on. I reach a clearing in the wheat to find a girl with long, dark-brown hair swinging on a rusted-out swing set. The curves of her body are barely concealed under a sheer white slip.

She glances at me over her shoulder, a sly smile playing across her cherry lips.

Ali.

I walk around the clearing so I can face her. She stretches out her long tan legs in front of her like she's trying to reach heaven with her tiptoes. Her legs are slightly parted. Catching my gaze, her smile deepens. Her hazel eyes look darker than normal, like the algae clinging to the rocks at the bottom of Harmon Lake.

"I want to go higher," she says. "Don't you want to push me?"

"Sure." I cross behind her.

She comes back to me like an arrow, legs tucked beneath her.

I reach out to give her a push. The feel of her warm body against my hands sends a surge of raw electricity through me.

The sky begins to darken, ominous clouds rolling in all around us, but I don't care. All I want to do is touch her again.

I push her. She laughs as she swings higher and higher away from me.

When she returns, Ali tilts her head back; her eyes are black. Pure black, like pools of crude.

I stumble back into the wheat, and on the upswing Ali lets go, disappearing into the churning sky.

Calling her name, I careen around the clearing, the empty swing whipping all around me, but she never comes back down.

The swing sways and creaks, over and over. The sound grates on my nerves, like a dull knife sawing through bone, but there's another sound, a warm wet sucking sound coming from a hollow in the wheat. Something about that sound makes me want to crawl out of my skin, but I have to know what it is. With each step forward, a sickeningly sweet metallic odor fills my senses, making me want to gag.

I try to turn back, but it's too late. The wheat has closed in all around me, leading me to a nest made up of discarded wheat stems.

Inside, a little girl with light-blond pigtails lies next to a calf with golden fur.

The little girl is suckling from the dead calf.

"Noodle?" I gasp.

She sits up, blood dripping from her mouth. "He's coming."

———

I JOLT upright in bed, chest heaving, my skin covered in a thick sheen of cold sweat. My entire body's trembling. Dragging my hand through my damp hair, I think maybe it's withdrawal symptoms. I've been popping those sleeping pills like candy for the past year. But that dream . . . *Jesus*. I can't shake the image of Noodle with that calf.

I get up to shut the window, and that's when I notice a warm glow coming from the western edge of our property, from the Neely ranch. It looks like it's spilling from every crack of the breeding barn.

I clench my eyes shut. Whatever this is, I need to snap out of it. I press my hand against the glass, and a shock of cold sinks into my flesh, making the hair on my arms stand up.

This isn't a dream.

I glance back at the clock. 11:59 P.M. "No way." I exhale as I brace myself against the window frame. Could it be Ali? Could she seriously be waiting for me there?

"Come on, Clay. Don't do this to yourself." I shut the window and start to resecure the garbage bag, but I can't take it. I have to know. If Ali's there, waiting for me, and I don't go, I'll never forgive myself.

Pulling on my jeans and a T-shirt, I creep down the stairs. I know exactly where the creaks are in the pine floors, from when Dale used to stay over and we'd sneak out and run around like idiots, playing Marco Polo in the wheat.

My heart aches when I see Noodle's arranged my work boots next to the door, exactly one inch apart. There's a note tucked in the right one. I put the note in my pocket and slip on my boots, stepping outside into the brisk air.

As I head toward the Neely ranch, my breath hovers all around me. The only sound is the wheat being crushed beneath my boots, like tiny skeletons.

The sky looks the same as it did on the night Dad marched into the wheat clutching that crucifix. And I think to myself, what the hell am I even doing out here? This is just morbid . . . and pathetic. It's probably nothing. Just my imagination or some dumbass kids from the city. But if they're looking for ghosts, I can sure lend a hand. Serve them right.

As I reach the edge of our property, I duck under the broken-down fence and walk straight for the breeding barn. I try not to think about the last time I made this trip. The blood. The carnage. When they finally cleared the breeding-floor drains, they found the metal crucifix at the bottom of the pool of blood all twisted up with chunks of fur and intestines.

A soft whisper stops me in my tracks.

At first, it's so low I wonder if it's just the wheat swaying in the bitter wind, but it feels more sinister than that.

I force myself to step forward, slow and steady. The closer I get to the breeding barn, the more intense the sound grows. It's more than one voice. It sounds like people are whispering . . . in unison. And there's a beat, a low thud that feels like it's reverberating up from the soil.

The glow I saw from my bedroom window is candlelight. I can tell by the way it softly flickers through the gaps in the wood of the barn, but I've never smelled candles like these. There's a strange odor in the air . . . maybe some kind of flower, but with a strong scent of decay, like rotting meat.

I creep around the back of the barn and peek through one of the cracks in the wood. I don't see anyone, but I hear them, that soft chanting along with the steady boom, like they're stomping their feet.

A hulking form stretches along the breeding platform, covered by a dingy tarp the police must've left behind.

A figure approaches the breeding platform. He's wearing jeans and a hoodie. When he grabs the edge of the tarp, I notice the symbol on his wrist—the upside-down U with two dots above and below. Fucking Tyler. I should've known.

Three other people move into view and my heart picks up speed. I crane my neck to see Ben, Tammy, and Jimmy—all the Preservation Society kids. Everyone except Ali. Thank God she's not involved in whatever this is, but why would she ask me to meet her here? Did she want me to see this? Maybe she wanted me to stop it. Maybe this was the only way she could tell me they're messing with me, or Tyler put her up to it. Either way, I'm not having it.

Just as I open my mouth to holler at them, tell them the joke's over, Tyler pulls off the tarp to reveal a dead cow. Must be at least twelve hundred pounds, split right down the middle. My stomach lurches; bile rises in my throat. Is this where the calf came from? Did they cut it out of her stomach? But the cow's stomach looks full, bloated even.

I'm trying to get control of my breath when I see something roil inside the cow's stomach. I clamp my hand tight over my mouth, my eyes beginning to water.

Something's *alive* in there.

My knees buckle. I press my forehead against the splintery wood to steady myself.

A hand thrusts out from the cow's stomach.

A human hand, fingers outstretched.

Tyler steps into my line of sight, blocking my view, and I take off running down the length of the barn to get a better look.

The next gap in the dilapidated wood reveals the crown of a head emerging from the cow, dark hair slick with blood.

The chanting and stomping grow louder, more frenetic, but I can hardly hear a word over the siren-like ringing in my ears. Tyler and the others are circling the cow like a sick merry-go-round, creepy smiles plastered on their glowing faces. Dizziness washes over me. I only catch glimpses, slivers of movement inside the circle.

I sprint for the next gap in the wood to see arms and a torso rise from the cow's stomach. A girl. My heart's beating so hard I'm afraid it'll burst. I can't stop staring at her chest. I know I should feel repulsed, but the sharp curve from her waist to her hip bone fills me with something ancient and primal. Sick and wrong.

My gut is screaming at me to look away, but I can't stop.

The warm, sticky sound as she crawls out of the carcass seeps deep inside of me, making me woozy.

Tyler and the others sink to their knees before her.

She stands, towering over them, her perfect body glistening with blood and viscera in the golden glow of candlelight.

Slowly, she raises her head.

When I finally see her face, it feels like all the air has been punched from my lungs.

Chin lowered, lips slightly parted, the rise and fall of her chest.

Ali peeks out of her long, slick dark hair.

The air returns to me all at once, and I suck in a rasping breath.

The corners of her mouth curl into a seductive smile. "He's coming."

They all turn toward me, their mouths stretched open, letting out a chorus of guttural moans.

8

I STAGGER back, my head spinning, every nerve ending on fire as I take off running into the wheat.

The crops lash my arms. The night swallows me. No moon or stars to guide me, but I know these fields.

I listen for the sounds of them crashing through the wheat behind me, but they don't come. I'm trying to concentrate on the air going in and out of my lungs, the relentless pounding of my heart, but my mind keeps going back to the breeding barn— nothing but blood, limbs, and pure black eyes. I don't know what's happening, but I have to pull myself together, for Ali's sake. I have to be smart about this. I don't want to get her in trouble, but I saw her bare chest . . . her naked body. I saw her crawl out of a dead cow, for Christ's sake! I know Tyler put her up to this. He must be controlling her in some way. Whether it's drugs or some kind of prank, she's in way over her head. She needs help.

When I glimpse the light shining down from the equipment shed onto my truck, I know what I have to do. Same thing I did after I found my dad. I have to get Sheriff Ely. He and Dad were friends. He's not part of the Preservation Society. He'll have to hear me out this time.

I roll down the windows and listen closely as I ease down the drive toward Route 17. It's eerily quiet, the same way it gets right before the weather turns. No insects scrabbling over the wheat, no wind rustling the crops. It's like Mother Nature knows something's coming. I can't take my eyes off the wheat. I'm not even sure what I'm looking for . . . monsters.

THE STREETS are dead. Everything's closed up. Even the Quick Trip's dark, which means it's past one in the morning.

I pull into Sheriff's gravel driveway, in front of an old farmhouse about half a mile east of town, and lay on my horn until a light comes on upstairs. Mrs. Ely peeks through the lacy curtains, her hair all coiled up in those pink spongy curlers. I hear them bickering as the porch light flickers on. Positioning myself directly in front of his door, I wait. There's a bug zapper right next to my head. The constant low hum along with the occasional electrocution isn't helping my nerves.

"Clay?" Sheriff opens the door just a crack. "Greg Tilford's on duty tonight."

"No, not him." My voice comes out shakier than I'd like. "I need to talk to *you*."

He blinks up at me, the bags under his eyes dark and heavy. "You sleepwalking, son? Need me to call your ma, or Dr. Perry?"

"No, listen to me, it's Ali. She's out at the Neely ranch, and something bad happened to her."

His thick gray eyebrows merge together. "The Neely ranch?"

"Please." I look down at my boots for a moment before I meet his gaze again. "It's important."

"Come on in," he says with a heavy sigh, his shoulders collapsing under his worn plaid flannel robe as he shuffles down the hall into the kitchen and turns on the light.

"Wait." I take off after him. "We have to go. You have to come with me. You have to see what they're doing out there."

"*They?*" He settles himself in one of the oak chairs crowded around a small table. "I thought you said it was just Ali?"

"Ali and Tyler," I say as I pace the linoleum. "But Jimmy, Tammy, and Ben are there, too."

He shakes his head. "So this is about the Preservation Society again."

"No, it's not about that. Not really."

The floorboards above me groan, making me flinch.

"Dear," Sheriff calls. "As long as you're up can you get Clay one of those calming teas?"

I crane my neck to see Mrs. Ely hovering at the top of the stairs, listening.

The wood buckles under her weight as she comes down the stairs. She glares at me as she crosses over to the sink; her face is all scrunched up like one of those fancy Persian cats.

"Let's start from the beginning." He pushes a chair out, motioning for me to sit. "What were you doing out at the Neely ranch? We talked about this. That's trespassing."

Reluctantly, I take a seat. "Today at school, I saw this mark on Ali's neck. Tyler has the same mark on his wrist. And then Ali came over to my truck and told me to meet her out at the breeding barn at midnight."

"Hogwash," Mrs. Ely blurts. "Ali would never do such a thing. She's a—"

"*Dear,*" Sheriff interrupts. "The tea."

She purses her lips so tight you'd need a crowbar to pry her mouth open.

"Okay, Clay. Then what?"

"So, I ignored it, tried to put it out of my head, and when I got back to the combine, the calf was gone . . . just vanished."

Sheriff's eyes narrow. "Hold up. What's this about a *calf*?"

"Crazy, just like his daddy," Mrs. Ely mutters as she dunks a tea bag in a mug of microwaved water.

My jaw clenches. There's a hundred things I want to say right now, but I hold my tongue.

"Why don't you head up to bed, dear," he says gently, but the vein pulsing in his temple gives him away.

She slams the mug down in front of me, sending steaming piss-colored water sloshing over the side.

He waits until she's upstairs, the bedroom door crashing shut, before turning back to me. "Go on now. What calf, Clay?"

"This morning I ran over a calf with the combine. And then the Wiggins kid said something about it this afternoon."

"The Wiggins kid?" He glances around the room, his eyes locking on the gun belt hanging by the back door, and I know exactly what he's thinking.

"Look, I'm not crazy and I'm not doing meth, the calf was there. It was real. I don't know how . . . or why, but when I came back from school to dig it out of the cutting blades, it was gone."

He gives me an exasperated look.

"I know what it sounds like, but tonight, I woke up from a nightmare—"

"Okay, now we're getting somewhere. So, you had a nightmare."

"No, I woke up from the nightmare and when I went to shut my window, I saw a glow coming from the Neely ranch."

"A glow?" he repeats, one eyebrow raised.

"Yeah, they lit a bunch of candles in the breeding barn."

He clasps his hands tight in front of him, resting them on the table. "I know you and Ali were close at one time, and I know you and Tyler have your issues, but his daddy owns the ranch. Not against the law to entertain on your own property."

"Entertain?" I struggle to find my next words. "Ali crawled out of a dead cow's stomach . . . naked . . . covered in blood."

He leans back in his chair, which creaks so loudly I think it might snap in two. His mouth stretches into a thin grim line. "Tell you what, I'll give Ali's folks a call first."

I take in a deep breath. "That's a start."

He gets out the directory; it's painful watching him find the M's and then scan each name.

"631-0347." I call out her number, my knee bouncing up and down like a jackhammer. "And I want it on speakerphone."

Sheriff gives me a weary look, but complies. The volume's low, but I can hear each agonizing ring until someone finally picks up.

"Hello?" Mr. Miller answers, groggily.

"Charlie, it's Ely. Sorry to bother you like this, but I've got Clay Tate over here, and he claims he saw your daughter out at the Neely ranch tonight. That she might be in some kind of trouble."

"Not this again." Mr. Miller yawns. "We went to the football dinner at the Preservation Society and then she went straight to bed."

"Tell him to check her room," I whisper.

Ely shushes me. "Would you mind just checking her room for me? Put the boy's mind at ease."

"What's going on?" I hear Mrs. Miller ask in the background.

"Fine." Mr. Miller sighs as he puts the phone down. I can hear the springs creak as he gets out of bed.

I stare at the Elvis clock mounted on the wall above Sheriff Ely's head. Each sway of his hips equals a second. Each one slower than the last.

"We're wasting time," I whisper as I edge forward on my seat. "God only knows what's going on out there now. Their eyes were black and the—"

"Snug as a bug," Mr. Miller says as he comes back on the line. "Like I said, sleeping like a baby since ten."

I bolt out of my chair so fast it topples. "That's impossible. I just saw her."

"Little advice," Mr. Miller says. "Unless he's ready to join the council, you better keep him away from the Preservation Society. Kid's a loose cannon, just like his dad and you—"

"Thanks for checking," Sheriff interrupts as he fumbles to take it off speakerphone. "You have a good night now."

He hangs up and looks at me. I know that look. Pity.

"He's in on it. Don't you see that?" I start pacing again. "My dad found something. Something they don't want me to see. My dad must've said something to you. You were best friends. You have to help me."

"Clay." Sheriff stands, planting his hand firmly on my shoulder.

"I didn't want to have to tell you this, but your dad came over here ranting and raving about the same types of things on the night he died. Said he had to stop the evil before it was born. After he hacked up every pregnant cow on that ranch, he ripped off his own fingernails trying to pry open that stainless steel door to get at Neely's prize bull. Whether it was drugs, schizophrenia, or whatever, he was seeing things . . . violent things that weren't real. He kept talking about the seed, the sixth generation, a golden calf, a prophecy, and sacrifices. He kept going on about some secret room at the Preservation Society. All kinds of crazy things."

I feel the blood drain from my face. "Why didn't you tell me about any of this? I came to you before—"

"My point is"—he tightens his grip—"unless you want to end up just like him or at Oakmoor, I suggest you get your ducks back in a row. You've got your mom and sisters to look after now. Don't you think they've suffered enough?"

Feeling completely gutted, I think of Noodle in that white eyelet dress she insisted on wearing to Dad's funeral, because it was his favorite. She held my face in her hands and said, "We pick what we want to remember and I pick good."

I feel my shoulders cave. What if Sheriff's right? What if it's all in my head?

"Get some sleep, Clay," he says as he leads me out the door. "We've *all* had nightmares from what happened out there. Trust me, no one wanted to believe your dad more than I did, but it's time to move on. It's for your own good. And you heard the man. Unless you're going to join the council, you need to stay away from the Preservation Society, and like it or not, that includes Ali Miller now."

In a daze, I walk back to my truck.

"And Clay?"

I turn, waiting for some last bit of wisdom, something that will help me make sense of all this.

"Who do you think's going to win the big game tomorrow? I've got my money on Midland, but without you playing quarterback, it's going to be a close call."

I know he's probably just trying to lighten the mood, take my mind off all this, but it feels like I just got sucker punched. Who gives a shit about football at a time like this? Without another word, I get back in my truck and tear out of there.

Gripping the steering wheel, I clamp down all the hurt and anger raging inside of me. I can't go off the rails. Not now.

I know I should go home, pull myself together, but I find myself going to the one place I know I shouldn't.

9

GRABBING THE flashlight from my glove box, I sneak around the side of the Preservation Society to the wall of box hedges sealing off the back. I dive through the hedges, the prickly branches scratching the hell out of my arms.

As I make my way across the lawn to the French doors lining the back of the main house, I can't help thinking about the last time we were here as a family—Fourth of July picnic, the summer before Dad's death. I don't even have to close my eyes to see it . . . to smell it . . . the honeysuckle, the fresh-cut grass, and gunpowder from the cannon they kept shooting off. Noodle's standing on Dad's toes as he twirls her around to the music, Mom's playing Bunco with her friends from church, and Jess . . . well, Jess still looks normal. And there I am, throwing the damn football, watching Tyler steal

Ali right from under my nose. I wish I could go back in time. I'd do everything so different.

As I jiggle the door handle, trying to force it open, I realize the magnitude of what I'm about to do. I'm about to cross a very big line.

If I'm caught breaking in here, I could go to jail. I wouldn't be able to finish the harvest and Noodle certainly wouldn't be going to that private school.

But if there's something here, if they have a secret room like Dad said, I could blow the lid off this place. Clear his name.

Taking off my cap, I drag my hand through my hair. "This is crazy," I whisper.

I turn to go back the way I came, but I can't do it, I can't walk away from this. Yeah, Dad acted crazy at the end, but he was a reasonable man. A fair man. I have to believe there's more to it than him just going insane. 'Cause if it happened to him, it can happen to me, and I'm not about to go down that road without a fight.

"Screw it," I say as I wrap my cap around my fist and jab it into the pane of glass closest to the latch. I brace myself for an alarm to start blaring, or attack dogs to come chasing me back through the hedge, something to make me stop, slap some sense into me, but all I hear are the frogs singing over at Harmon Lake.

My adrenaline's so high I could lift the door right off the hinges, but I don't need to. I unlock it and it swings wide open without a hitch. Almost like it's inviting me in.

I take in a jittery breath as I step over the threshold.

My footsteps echo off the gleaming hardwood floors, occasionally muffled by one of the rugs as I walk down a long corridor lined with old photographs and glass cases full of "artifacts"—just a bunch of rusted-out farming equipment and ledgers, but this crap is like the holy grail for people in this town.

It didn't used to be this fancy, but ever since Mrs. Neely took over the decorating committee you'd think this was the White House, not the former town hall for a bunch of roughneck immigrants.

The front rooms are immaculate. So much so I'm afraid to touch anything. Can't imagine there being a secret room up here. I decide to head downstairs, where the jail used to be. They keep it set up just like it was in the old days.

At the foot of the stairs, I trip over some iron shackles attached to a dark wood beam, a couple of axes, ropes, a gallon of fake blood. Props for the justice reenactments they do during Settlers Week. That's when they break out the bonnets and covered wagons. Everybody running around town talking like hillbillies, which is dumb considering how most of the settlers came straight from Ireland.

I guess it was pretty fun when I was a kid—watching your neighbors get their hands chopped off for stealing another man's livestock, or their foot cut off for running out on a fight. They even did a mock hanging one year. Poor Mr. Timmons, runs the Tastee Freeze, they rigged him up in a harness, pulled the lever, and Mr. Timmons swayed on the rope, his feet kicking beneath him dramatically. It was all fun and games until he got a big hard-on. They made all us kids cover our eyes, but I'll never forget it. It's burned into my memory. Haven't been to the Tastee Freeze since.

I open every door I can find. Most of the rooms are full of extra plates, folding tables, linens. There's a whole room just for Christmas decorations. Nothing looks out of place, unless you count the way Mary and Joseph are stacked up on top of each other in the sixty-nine position. But there's a strange smell—similar to what I experienced at the breeding barn, like rotting meat and herbs. When I reach the end of the hall, the smell intensifies. My heart picks up speed; that same sick feeling washes over me, but I can't figure out where it's coming from. Running my hands over the paneled wall, I remember they just had the annual steak dinner. Maybe they aged the meat down here. Or maybe it's all in my head. I've heard of people smelling weird stuff right before they're about to have a stroke or an aneurism.

I shake it off and step into the cell, walking the perimeter, knocking on the floors with the heel of my boot, listening for a loose plank, but there's nothing here. Just like Sheriff said.

"What're you doing, Tate?" I whisper as I sink down on the cot wedged against the iron bars. The creak of the ancient springs sends icy chills across my skin. "This is crazy, even for you."

Just when I'm thinking of cutting my losses, I hear a car door slam shut. Jumping up on the cot, I peer through the small barred window.

Greg Tilford's out front talking to Ian Neely. Greg came back from Afghanistan even more of an asshole than he was before. Wound tighter than a cuckoo clock. After Neely donated the new computer system to the town, Tilford magically became a deputy. He was the first officer on the scene when my dad died. Threw up everywhere. I don't know if it's because I saw him lose it, or the fact that he's Ian Neely's cousin, but he's had it out for me ever since.

Looks like the two of them are arguing about something. I can make a run for it out the back, through the hedge, into the woods, but my truck's parked right out front. I'm such a dumbass. Of course they have some kind of high-tech alarm system here. What did I think would happen? I'd just break into the Preservation Society and no one would figure it out? In a town this small you can't take a shit without everyone knowing your business.

Mr. Neely's walking up the brick pathway toward the front door.

Panicking, I scramble up the stairs and rush toward the back of the house.

"Clay?" Mr. Neely calls out as he shuts the door behind him.

I stop in my tracks. I'm breathing so hard. I feel like a trapped animal.

"In my office," he says calmly as he disappears into one of the main rooms off the foyer, turning on a lamp. No doubt Neely just wants to give me an "I told you so" lecture before Deputy Tilford hauls my ass off to jail.

As I trudge down the hall to his office, I feel ashamed. Not because I got caught, but because I was wrong. Sheriff tried to warn me, but I wouldn't listen.

I step into the main office, a richly appointed room with taxidermy and football memorabilia glaring down at me from every direction.

He sits behind the desk, motioning for me to take a seat in one of the big uncomfortable leather chairs opposite his desk. I remember sitting in this exact spot right after my dad died. I can't believe it's only been a year. It feels like a lifetime.

"I'm curious." He twists the state championship ring around his finger, making the ruby flash in the light of his desk lamp. "Why'd you break in?"

I keep my mouth shut. I've seen enough TV shows to know I'm not supposed to say anything until I have a lawyer. Where the hell am I going to find a lawyer?

"The reason I ask is because you've had the key to the kingdom all along."

"The key?" I want to knock that smug look off his face. "Look, if you're going to have me arrested, just do it. Save me the sancti-monious speech."

His face softens as he holds out his hand. "Your car keys . . . it's your dad's old set, right?"

Tentatively, I dig the keys out of my pocket and place them in his hand.

"The brass one." He singles it out and slides the set back to me. "That's the key to the front door."

I feel like even more of an idiot, if that's possible. I grip my fin-gers around the key, hoping the sharp grooves cutting into my skin will take me out of this misery, but it only seems to make things worse . . . more real.

He picks up the phone and dials.

My pulse shoots through the roof. "Wait! I'll pay for the glass. I'll volunteer, I'll do anything you want," I sputter. "Just don't—"

Mr. Neely holds up his hand, then says into the phone, "I think we're all set. Clay and I are just going to have a little chat. Thanks for your assistance."

I look toward the window but I can't see a damn thing through the heavy curtains. I hear an engine start. Mr. Neely hangs up the phone and we both sit there listening as the car pulls away, the tires getting fainter by the second. I know I should be relieved, but there's a glint in Mr. Neely's eye, something that tells me I'm not out of the woods yet.

He leans back in his chair, knitting his arms across his chest. "What were you looking for?"

"Mr. Neely . . . sir . . ." I take off my cap and set it on my knee. "I've had a rough night . . . a rough year, really. I thought I saw something out at your ranch tonight. Something sick. I went to

Sheriff Ely and he'd mentioned my dad was talking about some secret room right before he died. I know I'm probably losing it, just
like he did, but I had to find out for myself. There's nothing here. I
know that now."

"A secret room, huh?" The left corner of his mouth curls up.
"Would you like to see it?"

My stomach drops.

Mr. Neely rises out of his chair, pressing on the dark wood pan-
els behind his desk. A tall, slender door pops open. It blends into
the grooves so well, you'd never even know it was there.

"No one's been trying to keep you out, son. We've been trying
to bring you in," he says before stepping inside.

I push myself into a standing position, but it feels like my blood's
been replaced with concrete. I take a deep breath, trying to prepare
myself for what I'm about to see.

Mr. Neely flicks on the overhead lights.

And it's just a room. I step inside to find an old jukebox from
the fifties, a couple of poker tables, some cowboy prints decorating
the walls, and a sprawling bar.

Mr. Neely stands behind the solid piece of oak, pulling out two
glasses. He pours bourbon, pushing one toward me. I look at it,
wondering if it might be poisoned, but Mr. Neely sucks it back
without a second thought. "Back in the dry years, this place came
in handy. Now it's just good for hiding from our wives." He chuckles to himself. "Your dad and I had some good times in this room.
You remind me of him." He scratches his chin. "He was secretive,
too . . . always holding everything inside. It's hard to ever really
know a man like that. He had a weakness for the ladies, though.
Couldn't hide that." He taps the bottom of his glass on the bar.
"Don't worry, he cut all that out by the time you were born."

I slam back the bourbon. A revolt goes off inside my body, but then a numbing warmth quickly follows.

He pours another round. "What happened with your dad was a lot more gradual than it appeared. We'd been covering for him for months. There was talk."

"What kind of talk?"

"Well, he was spending an awful lot of time down by the junkyard, if you know what I mean."

"Are you talking about the Wiggins trailer? Meth?"

"I'm not saying anything," he says as he raises his hands in the air. "All I know is in the end, he thought God was talking to him." He downs his drink. "And I think we both know it could've been a hell of a lot worse."

I rub my neck, thinking about the explosives in the shed. Did Mr. Neely know about that?

I take another shot. It goes down easier this time.

"I loved him like a brother. Sure, we fought and argued, like brothers do. We had a competitive rivalry, like you and my boy, but that's what makes a man rise to the occasion. Hell, he even gave me power of attorney if something were to happen to your mom. I'd be responsible for taking care of you and your sisters."

I grip the edge of the bar, forcing myself to listen.

"What I'm trying to say is the founding families have stuck together through thick and thin. We'd never turn our backs on your family. Not then. Not now. Not ever. But it's a two-way street. This is quite a stunt you pulled tonight, breaking in here."

I think about Noodle and Jess and Mom and my throat gets so tight I can hardly swallow. This was just another stupid move on top of a dozen other stupid moves. I see that now.

"What are you going to do?"

"The real question is what are *you* going to do?" He takes a deep breath and stares into my eyes, like he's pondering my fate.

"I don't understand."

"We've tried to give you your space, but now it's time for a little tough love. So, I'm offering you a choice. I can press charges, leave your fate in the hands of Judge Miller, or you can stop this nonsense and join the council. Start playing ball again. Let the Preservation Society take care of you and your family. You've done an admirable job. Your dad would be proud. Hell, I'm proud. You put up quite a fight, but this is getting you nowhere. What do you say?"

"I . . . I can't just pick up where I left off . . . pretend like none of this happened."

"Why? Give me one good reason."

"Because . . . everything's different now."

"Are you talking about Ali? Because she was under strict instructions to let you be. All of them were. I thought you'd come around on your own, but you're stubborn, just like your daddy was."

I wonder if that's the reason Ali hasn't talked to me all this time. Maybe that's why she was so on edge when she came over that night after my dad's funeral, because she wasn't supposed to be there.

"Don't you miss playing ball?" He stares off in the distance all misty-eyed. "I'd give my left nut to play again."

"It's a little more complicated than that."

"No one blames you for what happened out there during your last game. You were just doing your job. It's a violent sport. A man's sport."

I watch him twisting his ring and I can't help wondering if this is all about getting me to play . . . bringing home the W's for Midland.

I think about trying to explain myself, but someone like Ian

Neely would never understand what I went through. For twelve straight hours not knowing if I killed that kid or if he'd ever wake up from his coma. And I had to deal with all that on my own. No friends, no family, no coach telling me it was going to be okay. Having to bury my dad and come to terms with being the man of the family. Giving up football. Giving up my dreams. Giving up college. Giving up Ali. And the fact is, I'm a different person now.

"I just don't think I belong here anymore."

"You belong here more than anyone I can think of, son."

I wish he'd stop calling me that. *Son*.

"Like it or not, you're a pillar of this community. The Preservation Society needs you. The town needs you. Stop fighting so hard—look where that's gotten you."

He pours another shot, but I don't take it. My sweaty palm print clings to the thick glass long after I pull away.

"I'll make you a deal." He throws another one back. "You come to the Harvest Festival on Saturday night, bring your family, stand on the council, rejoin the team, and I won't mention this to anyone. It'll be our little secret." He's starting to slur his words. This could get real ugly, real fast.

"I'll think about it." I stand, thinking he's going to tell me to sit back down, demand an answer, but he lets me go. For now.

"Oh, and Clay?" he calls after me. "You know why Ali's hanging around my son, don't you? You know why he's quarterback now? Because he took it from you. I'm offering you an opportunity to take it back—all of it."

10

I WALK out of the Preservation Society a free man, but more confused than ever. I can't believe Mr. Neely was talking about his own son like that. Talking about my dad like that. I'd heard the rumors about him hanging out at the Wiggins trailer, but I never wanted to believe it. Whether it was meth or schizophrenia, or whatever else, it still didn't change the fact that he massacred a barn full of pregnant cows . . . and that didn't change the fact that he was a great dad. He was a complicated man and I may never know what happened to him, but he's gone now and I have to figure out how to live with this. How to live with myself . . . on my own terms.

As I ease down Main Street to make a U-turn, I find myself turning down Ash Street toward the historic district. I haven't let myself do this for months.

I park under a huge magnolia tree a few houses down from Ali's, a big white colonial with black shutters. Her room's the last one on the left. I wonder if our initials are still carved into the leg of her four-poster bed. I wonder if she ever thinks of me.

Tomorrow, I'll have to deal with the fallout from all of this, the whispers, the staring. I don't think Mr. Neely will say anything, at least for now, but Mrs. Ely's the biggest gossip in town. It doesn't even matter. Right now, all I want is to be close to Ali. I need to know she's okay. I feel like if I see her face, I'll know what I have to do.

And maybe I'll finally be able to let her go. Let it all go.

I'VE BEEN staring at Ali's front door so long my eyes feel welded in place. I hardly notice morning's come when Tyler pulls into her circular driveway; his car's all decked out with red and black streamers, "#6 NEELY" and "QB" painted on his windows. Pep girls must've paid him a visit. I'd forgotten all about homecoming tonight.

Ali comes springing out the front door in her cheerleading uniform, her long shiny ponytail swinging behind her. My breath catches in my throat. She looks rested, not a care in the world, her bright hazel eyes shining with excitement.

I chuckle to myself like the crazy person that I am. I'm toast. I've officially lost my mind. Imagined the whole thing at the breeding barn. Of course I did.

Tyler doesn't even get out of the car to open the door for her; he's too busy checking himself out in the rearview mirror. As soon as she gets in, he pulls onto the street with screeching tires. Ass.

For a second I think Ali sees me. I hunch down in my seat, but she looks away so quickly it's hard to tell.

I wait a couple of minutes before pulling out. I may have sat outside her house all night, but I'm not a total stalker.

The closer I get to school, the heavier my shoulders feel. Mrs. Ely must've called half the county by now. The way I see it, I have two options. I can ignore it, pretend like it never happened, or I can take the Dale approach—laugh it off, tell everyone I got wasted and blacked out. That's what happened when his mom posted that video of him twerking to that Miley song.

I pull into my spot in the back of the lot and take a deep breath. Like Dad always said, you're either a rip-the-bandage-off all at once kind of guy or the peel-it-off-slow type. Looking out toward Tyler's car, I brace myself for the stares, but not a single glance comes my way.

Confused, I get out of my truck. Maybe he just hasn't noticed me yet. Wanting to get it over with, I stretch my arms high above my head and crack my back. That should do it, but still, nothing. Except for the occasional nod from a couple of football players passing by, or the random shy gaze from some freshman girl, no one pays any attention to me.

And then it hits me—maybe no one knows.

Maybe there is a God.

I let out an unexpected laugh as I lace my hands behind my head and stare up at the sky—that beautiful endless Oklahoma sky. It feels like it's the first time I've really seen the sun in over a year.

"Interesting look, cuz," Dale says as he strolls over to my truck.

"It's a new tactic," I say as I try to smooth down my hair. I must look like crap, but I feel good. Light. "The homeless look so girls will feel sorry for you."

"Wait. Does that actually work?"

"No." I laugh. "Sometimes I worry about you."

He squints up at me. "You sure are chipper today. Does this mean you're coming out with me tonight? I heard Laura Dixon's cousins are coming in from the city—Tulsa. One for you, one for me." He leans forward. "I'll even give you first pick."

"Wow. That's generous of you, Dale, but I can't. Last harvest."

"Wheat blows." He kicks a clump of dirt off my tire. "Haven't you heard? Gluten is the Devil."

"Tell me about it." I grab my bag and start heading across the lot.

We step aside, letting a bunch of JV cheerleaders pass.

"Well, you're missing out," Dale says as he stares after the girls. "Guess I'll have to handle both of them on my own tonight."

I laugh, and not a forced laugh—a real laugh.

On instinct, my whole body starts to tense as I pass Tyler's car, but the Preservation Society pack doesn't even acknowledge me. It's like I'm invisible. Or maybe they were never looking at me. Maybe it's all been in my head—this entire year. Whatever the reason, I'll take it. Fine, I'm a delusional weirdo, but at least Ali's not crawling out of a dead cow. I almost feel normal again, like the old Clay.

As I grab hold of the frigid metal door handle to head inside for class, I glance back at Ali. She's not looking at me or anything, but it feels right, like I finally might be able to move on with my life.

NOT FIVE minutes into first period, a note comes in summoning me to Miss Granger's office. It's almost a relief. I knew I wouldn't get off this easy from my "incident" last night. She probably just needs to know I'm not going to go all Columbine on her.

I duck into her office. "Before you say anything, just hear me out."

She bolts up from her chair and shuts the door behind me.

Wow. I must really be in trouble. "Look, you were right," I explain. "It's the sleeping pills . . . it has to be. I stopped taking them last night, flushed them all down the toilet. The calf, the symbol, the dreams, Ali climbing out of the dead cow, the conspiracy theories . . . it's all just a way to deflect from the truth." My throat's knotting up, but I force out the words. "My dad had schizophrenia or he was a meth head . . . it doesn't really matter. That's on him . . . not me. There, I said it. Are you happy?"

"Clay," she says, quietly. "There's something you need to see." She slides a sheet of paper on her desk toward me with her index finger.

On the page, I find a sketch of the symbol, the upside-down U with two dots above and below. Scrawled beneath it, the words "DEVIL'S PORTAL."

"What is this?"

"The mark you saw on Tyler and Ali. It means something. It's an ancient symbol predating the Old Testament by a hundred years. They've found it throughout time carved into stones, trees, rivers . . . flesh. It's considered an invitation."

I try to play it off, but a chill rushes through my veins. "An invitation for what?"

She leans in, the smell of perfume and tea clinging to her skin. "For the Devil."

My mind slips back to the breeding barn. The dead cow, slashed down the middle—Ali, her naked body slick with blood—the whispering, the stamping of feet like hooves. I'm trying to wrap my head around what she's saying, but it can't be.

I force a chuckle. "This is some kind of joke, right?"

"I know this is a lot to take in. I wanted to do this differently, in a different way . . . but things appear to be escalating quickly."

"Seriously, don't mess with me right now. Last night was crazy. I get it, okay?"

"This isn't a joke, Clay."

I start pacing the room, looking for hidden cameras or something. "Wait . . . so let me get this straight. I've been coming to you all year long telling you something's not right with the Preservation Society . . . this town, and now that I've finally accepted things, now that I'm finally ready to put all this behind me, you're telling me this is all about the *Devil*? That there's some kind of invitation . . . in their *skin*?"

She places her hand on my arm. "I can help you, Clay. I know people . . . in the church."

I pull away. "This can't be happening. This isn't real."

"I think you're a prophet. You see things others can't see. Just like your father."

"Please stop . . . just stop . . ." I dig my fingers into my skull.

"We knew something was coming here. Something evil. We just didn't think it would happen like th—"

"Did Mr. Neely put you up to this?" I turn on her. "Is this some kind of a test? When he asked me to join the council last night, come to the Harvest Festival, get back on the team, I thought it was a suggestion. I didn't know he'd go this far. Tell him no thanks. He can send me to jail, or whatever, but I'm not playing his games anymore."

"Clay, I . . . I don't know what you're talking about."

"You're all trying to drive me insane." I stalk toward her. "Is that what this is all about?"

"I . . . I only want to help you," she sputters as she backs against the far wall, like she's suddenly afraid of me.

I snatch the paper from her desk and get right in her face. "Is this your idea of *helping* me? Helping me straight off a cliff?"

"Clay," she whispers. "You need to trust me. You're not crazy, but we need to act swiftly and—"

"I always stuck up for you. People said you were off, but I just thought they were being jerks. I'm not so sure anymore." I crumple up the paper and throw it in the trash. "I'm done talking about this. Thinking about this. I actually felt good today." Tears sting my eyes, which makes me even angrier. "I don't need you and I certainly don't need a high school diploma to plow fields."

"Clay, I know this is a tough time for you with the anniversary and the game—"

"This isn't about football!" I pull my hair back from my face in frustration. I feel so fucking confused, I don't even know what to do with myself. "Just leave me alone."

I storm out of the school to my truck. As I'm driving down Main Street, past the Preservation Society, I turn on the stereo, hoping for some relief. Instead, an evangelist shouts, "Hold your loved ones close because the Devil's coming for you. Coming for all of us."

"You've got to be shitting me!" I rip the stereo from the dash and chuck it out the window.

||

ON MY way home, I pull into Merritt's to fill up the tank. I hear a bunch of kids messing around on the side of the building by the woods.

A girl laughs; I stop pumping the gas. I haven't heard it in a long time, but I know that laugh.

Fists clenched, I stride toward the side of the building, my boots sinking into the gravel. *Please let me be wrong.*

I come around the corner to find Jess angled up against the concrete-block wall, smoking a cigarette. She's wearing skintight jeans, Noodle's favorite unicorn T-shirt, which barely covers Jess's chest, and my flannel slung low around her hips.

A boy with stringy black hair gawks up at me. "Oh, shit."

The kids take off running into the woods.

I grab Jess's arm, whipping her around. "Don't even think about it."

I'm not sure if she's on something or what, but she's staring off behind me all dreamlike. I turn to see Lee Wiggins standing at the edge of the woods, smiling at me with his split lip. It's like he's daring me to come after him. I wonder if my dad told him all that crazy stuff about the seed and the calf when he was out there buying meth. Whatever his deal is, I'm not taking the bait.

I drag Jess back to the truck and buckle her in. "What the hell are you doing out here?" She doesn't even fight. It's like she's amused by the whole thing.

"You lied to me," I yell, pulling the truck back on the road. "You told me you weren't hanging around the Wiggins kid."

"I never told you that. You just don't listen. Lee's nice to me. He listens. He knows things."

"Oh, yeah, like what? How to be a goddamn loser?"

"*Things.*" The way she says it, the way she's smiling, makes me want to crawl out of my skin. The thought of that sick kid laying a finger on my sister makes me want to turn back and pummel him to death with my bare fists. But I can't lose control again. I tighten my grip on the steering wheel. "So, what? You're skipping school now?"

"At least I came home last night."

I glance over at her and wish I hadn't. That sly smile curling the corner of her smudged red mouth.

I clench my jaw. "It's not what you think."

"Don't worry, Mom covered for you, said you must've left early to get supplies. You're still *perfect* in Noodle's eyes."

I drive past the last turn to head back into town, and Jess fidgets in her seat. "You're not taking me back to school?"

I don't answer. I'm so pissed I can hardly stand to be in the same car with her.

"Clay! What are you going to do?"

"The question is what are *you* going to do." I can't believe I just used the same line Mr. Neely used on me.

She groans. "Are you going to rat me out or not?"

"I'll tell you what, if you wash all that crap off your face, put on some normal clothes, and do something nice for Mom, I'll tell her you came home sick."

"That's blackmail." She huffs, staring out the window.

"We all make sacrifices. That's life," I say as I turn into our drive. "I can't believe you're hanging around at Merritt's . . . and in Noodle's shirt."

"Is that what's really bothering you?" she snaps. "Here, take it." She yanks it off and throws it in my lap. She's just sitting there in a black sports bra.

I shield my eyes. "What the hell's going on with you?"

She pulls on the flannel wrapped around her waist and pushes her boot against the dash, holding her head in her hand. "What does it even matter?"

I look over at her, remembering a time when everything was a lot simpler. We were just kids lying in the wheat, watching storms roll past, seeing who could hold out the longest before running back to the house. She was always braver than I was.

I pull up in front of the house and turn off the engine. Taking in a deep breath, I say, "It matters. To me."

We sit there in silence.

"I know about the school," Jess says almost under her breath.

"What?" My throat goes dry.

She leans over and pulls a letter from her backpack. It's already been opened.

I grab it out of her hands and read it.

"We are pleased to inform you that Natalie Tate has been accepted into the All Saints Academy for the following academic year.

Please remit the full deposit by November 1st."

"She's in." I exhale, my shoulders dropping a good two inches. "Noodle got in." I look over at Jess to find her glaring at me. I fold the letter and put it in my back pocket. "How long have you had this?"

"A few days."

"You know, just because you're pissed about your own life, don't take it out on Noodle. She's got a good shot at getting out of here. Making something of her life."

"And *I* don't." She picks at her already mutilated cuticles.

"I'm not saying that." I let out a frustrated sigh. "But you've done nothing to show me any different."

Jess opens the door and gets out, black tears streaming down her face. "I shouldn't have to show you. You should just know."

I want to go after her, tell her I'm sorry, but I can't. I can't deal with one more thing. I stare out at the wheat waving in the wind. All that matters is the harvest. I see it so clearly now. All of this with the Preservation Society, Miss Granger, Tyler, Ali . . . it was just a giant distraction I made up to avoid reality. I have forty-four acres of untilled wheat. *This* is my reality. Finishing the last harvest is the only thing that will help us now.

Save me.

12

I KILL the wheat. Ten acres in eight hours. A new record for me. My body aches; it's tough just prying myself out of the combine. I can hardly keep my eyes open, but that's the way I want it. I might work myself to death, but at least I'll be sane.

As I drag myself up the rickety front steps, Noodle opens the door. "We ate without you," she says as she takes my jacket and hat, hanging them up. "Just like you asked, but it wasn't near as much fun. Jess sat there like a lump, didn't say a word." Noodle pulls out her sticker bag. "Tell me when," she says and starts to place them one at a time on the board, counting out loud as she goes.

She looks up at me with wide eyes when we make it past five, and when we pass eight, she's grinning so hard I think she might explode.

I finally call out "when" at ten and she drops the sticker bag and runs over to me, squeezing me exactly thirty-four times. One squeeze for each remaining acre. "We're almost there."

"I just hope the frost will hold off a few more days."

"It will. It has to."

"Clay?" Mom calls from the kitchen. "I've got a plate for you. Special treat."

Noodle takes my hand and skips me into the kitchen. It smells amazing, like charcoal and salt and spices.

"Go on, sit down." Mom bullies me into my chair. Guess it was a triumph to get her to eat without me. Now, I just have to work on getting her to let me fix my own plate.

Noodle hops around the table, still beaming from our victory. Mom pulls the plate from the oven and presents it to me.

My stomach drops.

"We've got a baked potato loaded with butter and bacon bits and those green beans with the little slivers of almonds, just like you like," she says eagerly.

But all I can see is the big-ass steak in the center of my plate, red juice leaking from the bottom, infecting everything around it. My mind goes back to the breeding barn—my dad surrounded by calf fetuses. Ali pushing through that dead cow, covered in blood.

"Where'd this come from?" I manage to ask, bile burning the back of my throat.

"Tyler Neely brought them over," Mom says. "Last night was the annual dinner at the Preservation Society, before the homecoming game. I can't believe we missed it. Your dad must've forgot, too. We're slipping in our old age. Anyhoo, they had some left over and thought we might enjoy them."

"Tyler was *here*." I stab the meat with my fork. "And he brought us *steaks*."

Noodle looks at me quizzically, her chin resting in her hands. I want to scream—throw the steak against the wall—but I can't make a scene.

I poke at it a few times and glance anxiously at the clock. "Tell you what." I keep my voice as calm and even as possible. "Can you wrap this up for me?"

"Oh, is it not cooked right?" Mom comes over to check, but she's not really paying attention, she's staring off toward the living room.

"No, it's perfect." I force a smile for Noodle's benefit. "I just kind of feel like getting some fried chicken from the Piggly Wiggly."

"Do you hear that?" Mom asks, cocking her head at a strange angle.

"What, the clock?"

Her gaze shifts to the kitchen clock. "Oh, you're going to be late for the game. You better hurry up."

"Yeah, sure." I get up from the table, giving Noodle a sympathetic wink.

"Can I come?" Noodle asks.

"No." I tickle her under her chin. "You've got to get ready for bed. You think you get all those smarts by staying up late? And we need you as smart as you can be. Who else would keep this farm running?"

She nods. "You've got a point."

As soon as I pull onto Route 17, I reach for the stereo, only to find the gaping hole where it used to be. "Idiot!" I scream at the top of my lungs in frustration.

I know Tyler brought over those steaks just to mess with me. He must've finally heard about me going over to Sheriff's last night. About the cow.

I pull into the empty lot with six minutes to spare. I'm not even hungry, but if I come back empty-handed, Noodle might start worrying. She's been through enough. I duck in under the disapproving eye of Mr. Cox, the store manager. "Make it quick."

He coached my Pee Wee team in third and fourth grade. Last name, Cox, first name, Richard. It was just too easy. His parents must've hated his guts.

All the deli employees have already gone home. One chicken meal sits baking away under a heat lamp. Grease oozes from the container, but anything's better than Neely's steak.

I walk up to the register and pull out the bills from my back pocket. They're all tangled up with Noodle's school letter and the note she left in my shoe last night.

He turns away from the little radio broadcasting the game with an irritated sigh. "Just take it. Would've thrown it out anyhow."

"Thanks, Mr. Cox."

He glares at me, unsure if I'm making fun of him or not.

"Big Ben and Wilson are managing to hold them off, but the pressure's on—and that Neely kid's been dropping the ball all night. Can't buy an arm. Not like yours. That's a gift from God. Shame you're not playing anymore. We need a killer out there."

I look at him sharply, but he's lost in the game.

The neon lights shut off before I'm even out the door.

"Nice to see you, too, Dick Cox," I mutter as I step into the cold air.

It's dark, but I've got a little light from the Midland Stadium in the distance. If I listen real close I can hear the faint roar of the crowd. It makes my hand ache, like I should be holding the ball.

I open my truck door, setting the chicken dinner on the seat. I start to cram all the stuff back in my pocket when Noodle's note drops to the ground. I pick it up and unfold it. I could use a little cheering up. I lean forward to read it in the small overhead light.

Written in Noodle's handwriting, surrounded by sparkly heart stickers, are the words, *"He's coming."* My blood turns to ice in my veins. I start to shake so hard I can hardly hang on to the note.

I'm bracing myself against the truck, trying to catch my breath, when I hear a horrible screeching noise followed by a strange sucking sound, the same noise I heard in my nightmare of Noodle suckling from the dead calf.

I walk toward the sound, around the back of the building, and into the alleyway. My heart's pounding against my rib cage.

It's dark, but I can see the outline of the dumpsters and something large in the middle of the alley.

With each step forward, the repulsive sucking sound grows. Everything inside me wants to run, but I have to see what it is.

I take my next step, and the motion sensor floodlights come on.

In the middle of the alleyway, there's a girl in a Midland cheerleading uniform. She's crouched with her back turned to me.

"Hey, are you okay?" I step forward, but a low growling noise stops me in my tracks.

Slowly, she turns to look at me, her dark hair spilling across her cheek, blood dripping down her chin, a dead cat clutched in her hands.

"Ali," I whisper.

She drops the cat and lunges for me.

13

CLUTCHING MY jacket, Ali murmurs, "The sixth generation . . . he's coming for us," before collapsing in my arms.

"Ali?" I shake her, trying to get her to look at me, but she's staring right through me, like she's in some kind of trance. I scoop her up in my arms and carry her back to my truck. Pushing the chicken dinner to the ground, I lay her on the bench seat. Her eyes are closed now, but I can see her chest rise and fall with each breath.

"Jesus," I whisper as I back away, dragging my hands through my hair. I kick the container of rancid chicken across the dark, empty lot. What the hell just happened back there?

I know I should just go get Mr. Cox, let him deal with it, or maybe I should call Sheriff Ely, or Ali's parents. God, I can't even imagine how that conversation would go. *Hey, Mr. Miller, I just found your daughter in back of the Piggly Wiggly eating a cat.*

I peer inside the truck. She looks so helpless now, but when she turned around with the cat clutched to her mouth, she looked like some kind of feral animal. Maybe she has rabies. We saw something about that in health class a few years back, or maybe it was TB . . . I don't even know what the hell I'm thinking.

I dig my phone out of my pocket and scan through my contacts, stopping on Emma Granger. She put her number in my phone at the beginning of the year. I've never even come close to calling her before, but I can't think of anyone else.

My hands are trembling as I dial her number.

"Hello?" she answers on the first ring.

I open my mouth, but nothing comes out. It's like I can't remember how to work my vocal cords.

"Clay, is that you?"

"I . . . I need a favor."

"Anything, and I'm so sorry about today. I—"

"I found Ali behind the Piggly Wiggly." I clear my throat. "Eating a live cat."

"One Twenty-two Pine Street," she answers like she's not fazed in the least.

I slide into the truck next to Ali and shut the door as quietly as possible. Going through town would be quicker, but I don't want to risk being seen by anyone. The game will be over any minute now. Win or lose, people will be razzing me.

Using back streets, I make my way toward Route 17. As soon as I pull onto the two-lane highway, I glance down to see Ali curled up next to me, her skirt riding up over her hip. I can't tell you how many times I've fantasized about having her in my truck like this . . . well, not exactly like this.

I'm reaching over to pull the hem of her skirt down when she starts making a strange sound, nuzzling her face into my lap. All the blood rushes to the surface of my skin. But when I realize the sound she's making—that she's *purring*—I freak out. Yanking the truck over to the side of the road, I jump out and start pacing. My heart's beating so hard I'm afraid it'll burst out of my chest. *This can't be happening.* I lean against the truck, staring in at Ali. She's lying there, completely still. What if this is just another nightmare? Or maybe it's the schizophrenia kicking in.

What if none of this is really happening?

A semi thunders by, rocking some sense back into me.

I grab my toolkit out of the bed of the truck and wedge it between Ali and me as a barrier. The rest of the ride across town, I try to keep my eyes on the road, pretend she doesn't exist. But the smell of her skin, her hair, only seems to deepen the ache. I glance down at her.

Even though there's blood on her mouth, I still want to kiss her.

14

As I pull up in front of Miss Granger's house, I see her peeking through the curtains, waiting. I gather Ali in my arms. She presses her mouth into my neck and a shiver rushes through me.

Miss Granger opens the door and hurries us inside. "In the tub," she says as she directs me to a small bathroom. I know this house. Jess used to take piano lessons over here with Mrs. Wilkerson, until she got Alzheimer's.

Gently, I lay Ali down in the few inches of lukewarm water. Miss Granger checks her pulse, raises her eyelids, looks in her mouth.

I shift my weight, digging my hands in my pockets. "She's going to be okay, right?"

Miss Granger gives me a curt nod as she grabs a fresh washcloth from under the sink. "You did the right thing bringing her here. She's going to be out of it for a while."

"What's wrong with her?"

"Let me clean her up first," she says. "Can you get a nightgown from my bedroom, please?"

Reluctantly, I back away from the bathroom and make my way down the hall. My footsteps sound spongy as my boots sink into the shag carpeting.

I pass a utility closet and a small room stacked to the hilt with file boxes. The last door on the left has a bed in it. It's covered in an old-fashioned bedspread, like those doilies Mom used to make us use under our drinks when we still hung out in the living room.

As soon as I step over the threshold, it feels like all the air is being squeezed from my lungs. The walls are covered in cruci-fixes. There must be a hundred of them—all different shapes and sizes. Some are crudely pieced together with string, others or-nately carved. Where did she get all these? I close my eyes, trying to shake the memory of Dad marching off into the wheat clutch-ing the crucifix to his chest, but the image seems to be etched into the back of my eyelids.

I look around the room trying to find something to focus on, anything other than the crucifixes.

There's a photo next to Miss Granger's bed—a girl probably around Noodle's age, with a man and a woman, maybe her parents. Palm trees, sunburned skin, but no one's smiling. It makes me un-comfortable, like it's something I'm not supposed to see. There's a well-worn Bible next to the pillow, a passage underlined in ink, with handwritten additions and notes.

I lean over to read it in the dim light.

"'Blessed is the seed,' the lord said unto them. 'The seed will be chosen *and he shall be fruitful and multiply and fill the earth and subdue it and have dominion over the fish of the sea and over the birds of the heavens and over every living thing that moves upon the earth. The blood of the golden calf will set forth ten sacrifices. Only the chosen one will be allowed to care for our lord. To usher in a new age.'"*

What the hell kind of Bible is this? I'm looking for a copyright when Miss Granger calls from the bathroom, "Is everything okay?"

"Yeah." I stand up ramrod straight at the sound of her voice.

"The nightgowns are in the dresser, bottom drawer," she says.

"Sure, okay." My voice comes out strained as I force myself to move on, to focus on something else.

On top of her dresser, there's a small, framed photo of Miss Granger with some old man in a fancy robe and a weird hat, maybe some kind of priest. Looks recent. I knew she was Catholic, but I had no idea how religious she was. Come to think of it, I think Mrs. Wilkerson was Catholic, too. She was a sweet lady, but kept to herself. I wonder what happened to her.

Crouching down, I open the bottom drawer. It's filled with perfectly folded white linen garments. I pick one up. It's a simple long sheath; I guess it's a nightgown. As I'm getting ready to close the drawer, I catch a glimpse of black lace buried beneath the other gowns. I pull it out by the thin strap; it's a sheer one-piece, like something you'd see in a Victoria's Secret catalogue.

"Did you find it?"

"Be right there," I say as I bury the black lace under the gowns and close the drawer with a little too much force. I shouldn't be in here looking through her things.

I stand, and I swear I can feel every Jesus from every crucifix glaring down at me . . . judging me.

Clutching the nightgown, I escape the room.

I make my way down the hall, back toward the bathroom, but the shag carpeting seems to swallow my every step, the hall stretching out in front of me like an endless corridor.

I hear whispers, a slight trickling of water.

As soon as I reach the bathroom, I freeze.

Ali's cheerleading uniform is wadded up in the sink. Miss Granger's back is turned to me; she's using a wet washcloth to wipe down Ali's body. She squeezes the excess water from the cloth on Ali's shoulder blade. I track a droplet of water as it trickles over Ali's breast. Just the sight of it brings the same overpowering feeling I had in the breeding barn. It feels sick and twisted, but I can't tear my eyes away.

I must make some kind of a noise because Miss Granger looks back at me with the strangest expression.

I think we both know we could get in a lot of trouble for this.

She holds out her hand. "The nightgown, please."

I give it to her. "I . . . I'm so sorry, I—"

And without another word, Miss Granger pushes the door closed.

15

PRESSING MY forehead into the cool wood grain of the door, I whisper, "You're fine, Clay. Just pull it together."

My phone vibrates in my pocket. Desperate for a distraction, I step into the living room. It's just a text from Dale. *"Not too late to change your mind. I could really use a wingman."* There's a picture of him photobombing two girls at the Quick Trip. No doubt Laura Dixon's cousins. They look bored out of their minds.

Jesus, Dale, not now. I put my phone away.

Pacing the room, I notice how sparse the furnishings are. No knickknacks or personal items. Just an old brown couch covered in another one of those doily things, a couple of pillows, two hardback chairs, and a coffee table, all situated around a wall where the TV should be.

The wall has a crisp sheet tacked to it, like it's covering something up. I peek underneath. I'm expecting a weird painting or crumbling plaster, but not this.

I pull out the tacks, letting the fabric sink to the floor. The wall is covered with photos, articles, aerial maps, weather reports, and sticky notes. At first glance, it looks like a random collage, but slowly, a pattern begins to emerge. The documents seem to be arranged in six columns. One for each family of the Preservation Society. At the top of each column is a picture—Tyler, Jimmy, Tammy, Ben, Ali, and *me*.

"Can you give me a hand?" Miss Granger calls from the bathroom.

I pry myself away from the wall and tentatively open the bathroom door. Ali's still unconscious in the now-dry tub, wearing the nightgown.

My heart stutters. It looks like the same slip she was wearing in my nightmare . . . the one where I was pushing her on the swing. How can that be?

"Clay?" Miss Granger's voice snaps me back. "Can you carry her to the couch for me? I'll go make some tea."

I pick Ali up and try not to think about how close she is to me. Setting her down on the couch, I drape the doily quilt thing over her. I don't know what the hell's going on with me, but I need to get this under control.

With a soft sigh, she rolls onto her side, turning away from me.

I'm reaching out to brush her hair back from her cheek when Miss Granger comes back in the room carrying a tray. Quickly, I sit down in one of the chairs, pulling a throw pillow across my lap.

She glances down at me . . . at the pillow. *God, this is humiliating.*

I clear my throat. "What's wrong with her?"

"She'll need her rest." Miss Granger pours the tea. "Being marked for the Devil takes a lot out of you."

I let out a burst of nervous laughter, but Miss Granger stares at me, unflinching.

"You're being serious?"

"I'm afraid so." She reaches out to hand me a cup.

I want to storm out, tell her she's fucking crazy, but when I look over at Ali and think about what's happened over the past couple of days, I take the tea. Whatever Miss Granger's wacko theories are, it's a hell of a lot better than me just being a total nut job.

I take a sip, letting it scald my mouth, hoping it'll burn away the desire I feel twisting up inside of me. But I can't stop staring at Ali's legs, her tan skin peeking through the holes in the quilt.

Emma pulls an old Polaroid camera from the drawer of the side table. "Can you hold her hair back for me?"

A prickling heat rushes to my face.

"I just need to document the mark."

I set the pillow aside. But as soon as I gather Ali's long silky hair in my hands, the feelings stir up in me again—stronger than ever.

The flash goes off.

I twist her hair in my hands.

I have to force myself to let go. I take a deep breath. Whatever this is, whatever's going on with me, it's carnal . . . like a bomb has been detonated inside of me.

Miss Granger shakes the photo a few times. I settle back in the chair, watching it develop from a dark-gray mass into the soft muted colors of Ali's skin.

Miss Granger pins the photo under the Miller column.

"What is all this?" My voice hitches in my throat.

"Research." She looks back at me with a weary smile. "I've been watching all of you for some time now."

"Who *are* you?"

"I'm Emily Granger, but people call me Emma. I'm twenty-six years old. I'm from Milton, Mass—"

"No . . . I mean who are you, *really*? What's your deal, because I know you're not just some guidance counselor."

She purses her lips. "I work for the church."

"What? All Saints?"

"No. The Vatican."

"Wait . . ." I lean forward, my elbows digging into my knees. "That photo on your dresser . . . is that . . . is that the *pope*?"

A tiny smile lights her gray eyes. "We've known something was coming for a long time, we just didn't know how he would present himself."

"Who?"

"The Devil."

I choke on the tea and set my cup back down. I want to laugh it off, but deep down I know she really believes it. "And you think this has something to do with the marks, the symbol you were telling me about . . . the invitation?"

"Yes, but the invitation is only the beginning." She twists the cross around her neck. "According to the prophecy, six will be chosen."

"What prophecy? From the Bible?"

"From something much older than the Bible."

"Is that what you had in your room?"

She looks at me sharply. She knows I've been digging around in her things. "We've pieced it together over time. The original prophecy was torn into six sections." She takes down a photocopy from the wall and hands it to me.

I trace the shape of the tear marks with my finger.

"It's a pentagram. We're missing the middle section. Six have been chosen as potential vessels for the Devil, from the sixth generation of this community. But only one will be chosen above the rest, leaving five to fall . . . to usher in a new age. The question is, which one will it be?" I watch her eyes skim the photographs.

"You think the six are the Preservation Society council members?"

There's a photo pinned off to the side. A school photo of a kid with crooked teeth, crooked smile, and pale blue eyes.

"Is that—"

"Lee Wiggins, before the explosion."

"Why is his photo up here?"

"It's nothing," she says as she takes the photo down. "Just a theory I was working on. He's very disturbed."

I stand next to her to study the documents. "So the others have the mark, too?"

"I believe so."

I swallow hard. "Then why's my photo up there? I don't have it."

"You're special, Clay. You're one of the eldest sons and daughters of the founding families, yet somehow, you've been able to resist."

"The sixth generation," I whisper, the words feel like they're being scraped out of my throat with a dull knife.

"Does that mean something to you?"

"My father, before he died, he said it was the sixth generation and something about the seed. He also said, 'I plead the blood.'"

"Do you know what that means?" she asks.

"I think it's from the Bible."

"It's usually said when praying over someone tormented by

demons," she says as she studies me. "Did he say anything else before he passed? Anything at all."

The memory of his final moments slip under my skin like cold liquid steel.

She knows I'm holding something back. But some things are best left buried.

Like Noodle said—we choose what we want to remember and I choose good.

Desperate to change the subject, I glance back at Ali. "Is the Devil inside of her? Is that what made her eat the cat?"

Miss Granger lets out a careful breath. "The things you see . . . the way you see them . . . aren't always what they appear to be. The calf . . . the ritual with Ali climbing out of a dead cow . . . the cat—"

"But there was blood all over her mouth. *You* saw it." I start pacing.

"I'm not saying she wasn't bleeding, Clay."

"Then what *are* you saying?"

"Ali has a slight contusion on the inside of her lip, lining up with her bottom teeth, as if she's been struck. She and Tyler were seen arguing at half-time. She grabbed his arm and he pulled away from her, accidentally striking her lip. And then she ran off."

"So, wait . . . you're telling me there was no cat?"

"You've been under a lot of strain."

I exhale a shaky breath as I sink back into the chair. On the one hand, I'm relieved, but the thought of Tyler laying a finger on her makes my blood boil. "I'm gonna kill him." I clench my hands into fists.

"Clay, listen to me." She kneels in front of me. "I need you to focus. Keep your cool. We have more pressing matters right now."

"I know it." I bob my head. "I'm crazy."

"You're not crazy. Your father wasn't crazy. I think he was a prophet, just like you."

I look up at her, letting out a strangled laugh. "Sure. Lock up your livestock, Midland, we've got a prophet on the loose!"

"I won't let that happen to you. Your father had his own demons."

Demons. Did she know about him? His extracurricular activities?

"I can help you through this. It's a gift."

"Whatever this is, it's no gift." I lean my pounding head in my hands. "I feel like I'm losing my mind. And what does that even mean . . . being a prophet?"

"It means you may have the foreknowledge of future events, though it may sometimes apply to past events of which there's no memory and to present hidden things that cannot be known by the light of reason."

"So, you're telling me I'm seeing the future?" I dig my fingers into my skull, desperately trying to understand. "That someday Ali's going to eat a live cat?"

"No." She gently shakes her head. "I think it's your subconscious telling you that something's happening to Ali. Maybe you see a darkness lurking around her . . . a hunger. I've seen it come to people in different ways. She's in danger, but she's not lost yet. You can save her."

"You're going to have to slow down a little." I lean back in the chair, feeling dizzy again.

"I believe you're one of the many prophets throughout history," Miss Granger says. "It's an honor. You join a noble tribe. Jesus had a vision of the dove when baptized in the book of Mark. Visions of afterlife in the martyr's account of Perpetua and Felicity. Constantine's vision of Christ's sign. Even René Descartes had a series of dreams that set the course of his life in science."

"No. You don't understand." I grit my jaw. "I'm not seeing God, or light, or things for the good of mankind. I'm seeing death and destruction and blood and . . . *filth*."

"You can fight it. We can deal with it, if we know what's happening. We can find the things that trigger the visions—maybe it's a feeling that comes over you when you have them. Some people see a halo of light, some get shaky, some hear a hum. I can help you. Together, we can end this."

"How do you even know about all this?" I glance up at the wall. "The six chosen ones. The marks."

She scratches the side of her head and then fixes her bun. "Because it's happened before." She pulls out an old photo album.

"Beirut. Philippines. Prague. Belize. And most recently, Mexico City in 1999."

She turns to a news clipping: TWO MISSIONARIES AND FIVE CHILDREN ARE FOUND DEAD AFTER A BRUTAL ATTACK AT THE CHURCH OF GRACE.

"But how did you know it was coming to Midland?"

She turns the page to a set of disturbing autopsy photos. "Each child had the mark, the upside-down U with two dots above and below, on a different part of their body. The surviving child had it on their scalp. But *these* were the marks that were left on the missionaries. They weren't burns or scrapes; the lettering was raised from the inside, like someone carved the numbers from inside their bellies. A reverse etching . . . like Braille." She runs her fingertips across the photo. "There was a distinct marking—35.0264 on the man's torso, 99.0908 on the woman's."

"What do the numbers mean?"

"At first, I thought they were Bible verses. I checked every scripture—New Testament, Old . . . nothing fit. It wasn't until we were sailing from Haiti to Miami to investigate a case last year that I realized they were coordinates."

"To where?"

"Midland, Oklahoma. More specifically, the breeding barn at the Neely ranch. And when I saw the story in the news—"

"'Mooder in Midland.'" I sigh.

"I knew we'd found the place of his next attack."

"So, you're telling me Midland's the gateway to hell?" I drag my hands through my hair.

"You don't believe me, do you?"

"I do. I mean, I want to, but this is a lot to take in. You're going to have to give me some time."

"Unfortunately, that's something we don't have. Whether you believe it or not, if we don't act swiftly, they'll die. One by one, the Devil will pick off the weak, until only one remains." She takes the album away from me.

"There must be a way to stop this."

"Only an exorcism will cleanse them, stop the cycle. And in order to do that, we need information. We need proof to get this sanctioned."

"Sanctioned? What, by a priest?"

"By the Church. This isn't something we take lightly." Her gaze turns to the photos on the wall. "The demons are putting Ali and the others through their paces as we speak . . . trying to decide the best route. They're all vulnerable right now."

"How long do they have?"

"A month, a week, a few days . . . it varies, but once the cycle starts, the Devil's influence will spread like poison."

Ali stirs. We both glance back at her.

Miss Granger whispers, "She doesn't realize what's happening to her."

"We have to tell her. We have to tell everyone."

"No." She looks at me with pity. "This is bigger than you and me. He could have disciples all around us. And no one would believe you. They'll only put you away, send you to Oakmoor. You won't be able to help anyone in there. She's going to need you."

"It's hard to explain, but when I'm near her . . . when I touch her, I feel a darkness."

"We all have darkness, Clay. She's still Ali. The girl you love."

I feel an embarrassed flush creep up my neck. How did Miss Granger know about that? Was I that obvious?

"Why didn't you tell me about any of this?" I ask. All those hours we spent together . . . every day for the past year . . . you think you could've mentioned something?"

"I kept waiting for you to change . . . to join the others. I tried to tell you today, but, well, that didn't go exactly as planned."

"I'm sorry about that . . . about the way I acted."

"We all have a purpose, Clay. It's time you fulfill yours."

"Why us?" I ask, looking up at the photographs.

"That I don't know. But I intend to find out, and you can help me."

"How? What can *I* possibly do?"

"You said Mr. Neely invited you to the Harvest Festival, to take your place on the council, the team. You need to do that."

"Are you crazy?" I bolt out of my seat. "Hell, no. Especially not after all this. I'm not getting near that place."

"They think you're one of them. They've been waiting for you all this time. We need information and you're the only person who can get close enough. This town needs you. Ali needs you. She just doesn't know it yet."

I glance at Ali, sleeping so peacefully, and it's hard to believe any of this is possible, but I can feel a kernel of truth buzzing under my skin. The artifacts in the Preservation Society . . . the family Bibles, everything my dad said to me about the sixth generation . . . the seed. There's something to this. Maybe my dad discovered the truth. Sure, he went crazy at the end, but maybe he was just desperately trying to stop this from happening.

I swallow hard. "What do you need me to do?"

"Tomorrow, meet me at All Saints in Murpheyville at 11:00 A.M. Bring Noodle for a tour. It will give you an excuse to be there. While they're showing her around, we'll present our case to the priests."

"Noodle . . . I almost forgot . . . the note." Frantically, I dig through my pockets. "I had this terrible nightmare the other night . . . and then I found this." I pull it out and hand it to her.

She unfolds it. "I don't understand."

"Look what it says."

She glances up at me with a puzzled expression. "It's a gas receipt."

I snatch it back from her. "No, this wasn't it. There was a note from Noodle that said, 'he's coming.'"

She reaches out for my hands to steady them. "Clay, whatever you saw . . . whatever you *think* you saw, it's your subconscious mind. The nightmares . . . the visions . . . it's just your fear taking over. You're afraid for Noodle, for Ali, for your entire family, which is perfectly normal."

Ali murmurs something.

"You should go." Miss Granger crosses the room to check on her.

"But shouldn't I be the one to take her home? If she wakes up and she's alone with you in some weird nightgown and—"

"I've been Ali's counselor for a year now. She won't be afraid. It makes sense that she would come to me after what happened at the game."

"What? Why didn't you tell me?"

"I didn't know if I could trust you."

"Why is she in counseling?"

"She mostly talks about you. The Preservation Society forbade her from speaking to you until you were ready, but she misses you. She's worried about you. You have to remember, in her eyes, you're the one who's changed. You're the one who abandoned her."

It feels like someone just kicked me in the gut.

All this time I could've been with her, watching out for her.

I take a step closer, but Miss Granger stops me. "Don't worry," she says as she leads me to the door. "We have God on our side."

16

THE HOUSE is dark and quiet—same as any other night, but everything's different now.

More sinister.

My body's exhausted from all the adrenaline pumping through me, but my mind's wired. I go into the kitchen to dig around in the fridge. I'm suddenly starving. I grab an apple, rub it against my shirt, and take a giant bite out of it as I check out my options, but all I see is that bloody leftover steak. And just like that, my appetite's gone.

I scrape the plate into the dog bowl. As I'm washing up, Hammy miraculously appears through the dog door just long enough to grab the steak and take it back outside.

"Traitor," I say, shaking my head.

I'll never understand that dog. He's got a nice warm place to sleep. Hell, Noodle'd probably let him sleep in her bed if he wanted to. Instead, he stalks the perimeter of the wheat all night long like he's looking for something . . . waiting.

I write a note for Jess on the back of an envelope from some college in Texas that's still trying to recruit me.

We're all going to the Harvest Festival tomorrow, 6pm—look normal. You owe me.

As I swing around the banister to head upstairs, a fly buzzes past me into the living room. I stuff the note in my back pocket and grab the flyswatter hanging from the nail in the kitchen. The fly lands on the stark white wall where the crucifix used to hang.

There's a dozen of them buzzing around, big and slow, like they've been trapped in here for weeks. I haul back the swatter.

"Don't." Mom's voice startles me.

I let out a jittery breath and turn to see her sitting on the couch in the dark, staring at the wall.

"They'll die soon enough . . . all on their own," she whispers.

I can tell the pendulum has swung in the other direction. She remembers everything now. I can feel the pain seeping out of her.

I lean the swatter against the fireplace and take a seat next to her on the couch.

We watch the flies.

It's strangely mesmerizing, how they land for a few seconds and then buzz around a little before landing again in a different spot. Over and over again, like they've been choreographed.

I want to tell her everything I've learned about Dad, the Preservation Society, Miss Granger, the marks . . . but I can't. I'm still not sure what's really happening, what I believe. Maybe when this is all over, when I know we're all safe. But for now, I need to put her at ease. And more than anything, I want to give her a little bit of hope.

"Everything's going to be okay," I say as I pull the acceptance letter from my pocket and hand it to her. "Tomorrow, I'm taking Noodle to look at All Saints Academy in Murpheyville. She got in."

She studies the paper. "Can we afford that?"

"I've been saving up. Dad would want this. She deserves a fresh start."

Mom grabs my hand, squeezing it so hard I can feel her entire body tremble with the effort of trying to hold in her emotions. Tears slip from her eyes and I look away. She wouldn't want me to see her like this.

"And tomorrow night we're going to the Harvest Festival. The whole family. I talked with Mr. Neely. I'm taking my place on the council."

Unable to hold it back any longer, she lets out a gasping breath as she pulls me in for a hug. I haven't hugged her in so long. I don't think she's hugged anyone since Dad died. It hurts. Her sharp shoulders cut into me. I can't believe how thin she's gotten.

"I'm scared," she whispers in my ear.

"Why are you scared?"

"Do you hear them?" She grips onto my shirt.

"Hear what?" I pry myself away.

She just stares at the wall . . . at the flies.

"You should get some sleep." I help her to her feet and lead her up the stairs to her room. "We've got a big day ahead of us."

Before I can even pull the quilt over her, she's out cold.

I thought she was getting better, but since the anniversary she seems to have lost her footing again. Maybe she can sense what's happening here . . . that something evil's coming.

"Soon, this will all be over," I say as I gently close her door.

Taking the envelope from my back pocket, I slip it under Jess's door and then peek in on Noodle. It's brighter in her room because she leaves the drapes wide open, like she doesn't want to miss anything. She looks like an angel when she sleeps, with those long dark eyelashes, pink cheeks. She smiles in her sleep. I don't know anybody else who does that. As I pull up the covers, I notice the mangy baby doll she's clutching. It's not some family heirloom. A lady gave it to her at Dad's funeral. When I asked her why the sudden interest, she said she was practicing. All the more reason for Noodle to go to All Saints. She's capable of so much more than that.

I know Noodle doesn't like people messing with her hair, but I don't know how she can sleep with those lopsided pigtails. As I go to take out the elastics, I notice the decrepit doll's eyes are open, staring right at me, pure black orbs, glistening in the dark.

I stumble back a few feet, my heart pounding against my ribs. Its eyes were closed a second ago. I'm sure of it. And then I remembered Miss Granger's explanation about the prophet stuff. Maybe it's all in my head, my fear manifesting in some weird way. I clench my eyes shut for a second and take a deep breath.

Something hits the floor.

There's a dragging sound.

I feel a dark presence all around me.

I open my eyes to find Noodle has turned over on her stomach, the doll at my feet. I nudge it over with my foot to find its eyes closed. I let out a burst of nervous air. It must've fallen off her bed when she rolled over. I feel a little bad for doing it, but I kick it under the bed. I know she loves that baby doll, but I'm hoping it's an out-of-sight, out-of-mind thing.

I close Noodle's door and start for my bedroom, but I can't make myself go in. I might be delirious from lack of sleep, but I know the moment my head hits that pillow, I'll dream. And I can't face another nightmare. Not tonight.

Being mindful of the creaks, I ease down the stairs and slip on my boots and jacket.

I walk across the wheat to the harvester, to the only peace I can find.

17

By 9:00 A.M., I've cleared out another seven acres, cleaned myself up, and told Noodle we're going on an adventure. Just the two of us.

"Wear something nice," I tell her as I head outside and wait for her in my truck. I can't bear to sit in the kitchen, watching Mom desperately try to rally with that haunted look in her eyes. She's like one of those willow seeds clinging to my windshield wipers, teetering on the edge, waiting for one stiff breeze to blow her into oblivion. I watch the seed drift away toward the Neely ranch. Maybe seeing her old friends tonight at the Preservation Society, her old life, will do her some good.

Noodle comes skipping out of the house wearing her purple and pink fairy costume—wings and everything. I pull my cap down low and try to hide my grin. I know I should probably tell her to go in and change, but this is the nicest outfit Noodle can think of for herself. Why spoil it?

"You look perfect," I say, as I hop out and let her in the truck.

"Thanks." She slides over to the passenger seat, carefully placing her wand next to her.

As we drive down Route 17, across the county line, Noodle finally asks where we're headed. I get the feeling she doesn't even care as long as we're together. That's how it's always been between us.

"I'm taking you to Murpheyville."

"To the auto parts store?" She pulls the map out of the glove box. She doesn't even seem slightly disappointed at the prospect.

"Nope. I'm taking you to All Saints."

"The place with the big steeple? Wow. What for?"

"Well . . . ," I say as I dig the letter out of my pocket and hand it to her. "You, Miss Natalie Anne Tate, have been accepted as a student."

She smooths the paper on her lap, fiddling with the edges. "Did I do something wrong?"

"No, nothing like that. It's a school for smart kids. Like you."

She swallows hard. "You're not leaving me there, are you?"

"Of course not." I reach over and give her arm a squeeze. "I'll take you every day and pick you up."

She studies the map. I can tell by the way her eyes light up that she's doing math in her head. "But that's forty-six miles each way."

"It'll give me time to think. You'll be doing me a big favor. It's not all good looks, you know. I've got a lot going on up here." I tap the bill of my cap.

She giggles. "Like thinking about Ali Miller?"

I can't believe it was just last night that Ali was lying here in my truck, right where Noodle's sitting. On pure instinct, I reach for the stereo, forgetting that I ripped it out a couple of days ago.

"What happened here?" She touches the wires.

"Broke." I squint into the sun.

"You know, Ali'll be at the Preservation Society tonight, the Harvest Festival."

"Yeah, I know."

"You should dance with her."

"You think?"

She nods her head emphatically.

"And who are you going to dance with?"

"Maybe Mom." She shrugs her shoulders. "Jess, if she'll let me."

"Don't pay any attention to Jess. She's going through a phase. Best if we let her alone."

"She's just sad 'cause Dad died."

I feel a tiny stab in my heart. Maybe Noodle's right. I should probably cut Jess some slack. She may look grown up, but she's still just a kid. I need to remember that.

Noodle rolls down the window, carving her hand through the air like it's a paper airplane, and smiles over at me. All it takes is something simple like this to make her happy. I hope she can stay like this forever.

"Do you want me to sing for you?"

"Sure." I chuckle.

Noodle starts singing a tune I recognize. It's this weird counting song she made up when she was little. I can't believe she still remembers that.

With the sun in her hair, her fairy wings flapping in the wind, and that toothless grin, I feel something I haven't felt in over a year. Hope.

As I pull off the highway into Murpheyville, the church comes into view. It's all dark-gray stonework surrounded by a grove of old oaks and pines. I've never really looked at it before, but it's imposing, like something straight out of a history book—something you'd see in the English countryside, not some hick town in Central Oklahoma.

"Look, Miss Granger's here." Noodle leans up on her knees and waves at her as we pull into the parking lot.

"I didn't know you've met Miss Granger."

"Sure, silly. She's always at Oakmoor when I help out Mrs. Gifford on Saturdays. She makes the best Rice Krispies Treats. And she came to Dad's funeral, remember?"

I don't remember her being there, but then I don't remember a lot about that day. It's weird to think she's been watching me all this time. Watching all of the Preservation Society kids.

"I like her," Noodle says. "She's nice."

Miss Granger waves back. She's standing in front of the chapel with two nuns. She's wearing a blue blouse that I saw hanging in her closet with a slim tweed skirt, her hair pulled back in its usual tight knot.

"I like her, too," I say, feeling a little embarrassed about rummaging through her things last night.

We get out of the truck and Noodle practically drags me across the lot like a Clydesdale to meet them. I've never seen a nun in real life. They're pretty intimidating looking, but Noodle doesn't seem fazed in the least.

"This is Sister Agnes and Sister Grace," Miss Granger says.

"Hello, Natalie." Sister Agnes smiles down at her warmly.

"It's Nood—," I start to say, but she steps on my foot.

"Yes, I'm Natalie Tate." She reaches out to shake their hands.

Fresh start. Maybe she's been craving it, too. *Natalie.* That's going to take some getting used to.

"Are you a good fairy or a mischievous fairy?" Sister Grace asks.

"I count things."

"Oh, well that's a very useful fairy skill, indeed," Sister Agnes chimes in.

"I'm not a *real* fairy. It's just a costume. I like your costume, too," Noodle says, as she admires their black robes. "Do you have wands?"

"Afraid not," Sister Agnes replies.

"I can make you one if you want. I can teach you my counting song, too."

"That would be lovely. Let's show you around, a private tour."

I start to follow, but Miss Granger holds me back. For a second, I forgot why we're really here.

Miss Granger leads me up the steps to the chapel. She opens the heavy carved door and my stomach coils up in knots. I peek in to see two grim-faced priests dressed in fancy robes and weird hats standing at the end of a very long aisle.

I glance back to give Noodle a reassuring wave, but she doesn't need it. She's skipping along with the nuns, holding their hands, her head held high.

Miss Granger pulls me inside the chapel and bolts the door behind me, shutting out all the natural light.

18

THIS PLACE is over the top—carved mahogany pews, frescoed ceilings, marble floors, a gold pipe organ. Hundreds of candles line the sides of the cathedral, casting an eerie red glow on the stained-glass windows.

This looks like a place God would live.

Nothing like Midland Baptist. All we've got are plain rickety oak benches, an upright piano, and dusty windows cluttered with decorations some kids slapped together at Sunday school.

As we walk down the center aisle toward the priests, I try to match my heartbeat to the steady sound of Miss Granger's heels clacking against the marble floor, but the closer we get, the quicker her footsteps become.

She's nervous, too.

"May I present Cardinal Machiovini and Archbishop Antonia."

Their names and titles all blend together in my head.

"Hey, I'm Clay Tate." I stretch my hand forward to greet them, but they don't move a muscle. They just stare down at me from the altar like I'm some kind of disease.

They're all decked out with massive rings on their fingers and heavy gold crosses around their necks—they've got more bling than any rapper I've ever seen. Reverend Devers, over at Midland Baptist, he always wears the same suits he got from Sears twenty years ago. The only jewelry he owns is the tarnished wedding band he still wears, even though his wife took off with an oil rigger a couple of years back.

Miss Granger stands up even straighter than usual. "As we've discussed, I believe Clay is a prophet. He had a vision of the golden calf. It appeared to him, freshly slaughtered, and then disappeared. He's also had a vision of the rebirth ceremony of the dead."

The priests begin to whisper in another language . . . Latin maybe.

"What's going on?" I sidle next to her.

"They're deciding how to proceed."

"Don't forget the cat," I add.

Miss Granger shakes me off. "I believe he's one of the six, but he's been able to resist. He's special."

The priests continue to talk among themselves like I'm not even in the room. Their voices become more agitated with each pointed stare.

"What is it? What's wrong?" I ask.

Her brow furrows. "They think it's too risky."

"Couldn't agree more."

Miss Granger shakes her head. "Not too risky for you . . . for *us*."

The priest with the tallest hat says something final sounding and they turn their backs on us.

"I'm willing to stake my career on this." Miss Granger steps forward.

The priests turn, eyes searching.

"He's the one." Miss Granger holds her ground. "He can save them all. We have a unique opportunity to study them from the inside. Clay can help us get the proof we need to sanction the exorcism before a single life has been taken."

This seems to get their attention.

The priest with the reddish beard looks at me, and it's like he's staring straight into my soul. *"Tu autem casus?"*

"What?" I ask. I have no clue what he's talking about, but he's making me seriously uncomfortable. I look to Miss Granger for help.

"He's asking if you've been chaste." A deep blush creeps up over her collar. "If you've . . ."

"What . . . if I've had *sex*?" I drag my hands through my hair. "What does that have to do with anything?" They just stare at me stone-faced. "Wow . . . okay . . . that's really personal, but no."

As the priests begin to confer again, my eyes veer toward the exit. I had the same feeling in Miss Granger's bedroom surrounded by all those crucifixes. I just want to get out of here.

They finally say something to Miss Granger. She nods, shooting me a tight smile.

"What's happening?"

"They've agreed to baptize you."

"I'm already baptized. They did it when I was a baby . . . in the river."

"The Catholic Church doesn't recognize a Presbyterian baptism."

"I'm not a Presbyterian. I'm a Baptist."

"In the eyes of the Catholic Church, it's the same thing," she says.

The priests crowd around what looks like a birdbath, murmuring some kind of prayer.

"I don't know about this."

"Clay, please." Miss Granger looks up at me. "It won't take long." She presses a robe into my hands and leads me to a flimsy screen on the left side of the altar.

"I can't believe I'm doing this," I say as I duck behind the screen and take off my shirt and pants. I put on the robe. It's not soft like those ones you see in fancy hotel commercials. It's thin and scratchy and smells weird.

I step out from behind the screen. Miss Granger blocks my path. "Socks and underwear, too."

"Seriously?"

She looks at me pleadingly. "Ali needs you . . . *I* need you."

With a deep sigh, I maneuver out of my boxers from under the robe and pull off my socks.

She brings me to the center of the cathedral, where the light's streaming in through the stained glass.

The priests step down from the altar, carrying small silver bowls, forming a circle around me.

"Time to disrobe," Miss Granger says.

"What? No way." I cross my arms across my chest awkwardly.

"Clay, they have to check you first . . . make sure you don't bear the mark."

"Well, I can assure you I don't have it. I take a shower every day . . . sometimes twice a day—"

"I believe you, but it's the only way." Miss Granger places her hand on my arm. "Keep your eyes closed if that helps. Think pleasant thoughts. I won't let anything happen to you."

I let out a deep sigh, close my eyes, and untie the robe, letting it drop to the ground.

"Hold your arms out, please," Miss Granger instructs gently.

I do as I'm told and try to hold still, but my insides are trembling. I can feel her warm touch on my wrist. I can feel her breath on my skin, running from my fingers all the way up to my left shoulder. "Clear," she whispers.

The priests chant a prayer. Something cold and wet splashes on my skin. I suck in a startled breath.

"It's just holy water," she whispers. "To protect you."

They do the same thing with my right arm.

Miss Granger then steps behind me, running her fingers across my shoulder blades, down my spine; my skin prickles up in goose bumps. But it's not just from the cold or the shock of water on my skin . . . it's her touch, and that's the last thing I want to feel in this moment. Miss Granger is a beautiful woman, but she's still my guidance counselor. The holy water splashes across my back.

Miss Granger moves in front of me. I hear the priests's robes swishing against the gleaming marble floors as they switch positions. I feel a hand slip between my knees and I practically jump out of my skin.

"It's just me. Can you step apart, please," Miss Granger's voice soothes. My quad muscles flex under her touch.

I try not to think about her being so close to me, her warm fingers pressing into my skin, but my imagination is getting the better of me.

I open my eyes, hoping the scenery will squash this feeling building inside of me, but when I see her kneeling on the ground in front of me, I catch a glimpse of the black strap of that negligee peeking out beneath her blouse.

I clench my eyes shut again. *Jesus. Not now, Clay.* I try to think of something else—anything other than that black strap against her skin. The calf caught in the cutting blades. The cow ripped down the middle. The metal crucifix covered in blood. Ali with the cat clutched to her mouth. But it's too late.

The room goes deathly still. It's like we're all holding our breath.

The priests splash the holy water across my chest. I take in a shuddering breath. *"In nomine Patris et Filii et Spirtus Sancti,"* they say in unison.

Miss Granger drapes the robe over me. "It's done."

I keep my eyes trained on the ground as I head back behind the screen. I can't look at her. I can't look at any of them. As I put my clothes back on, I will my body to calm the hell down.

I take a few deep breaths before I step out from behind the screen and bolt for the exit. My head is spinning. I try to open the door, but it won't budge.

Miss Granger comes up behind me. "Let me," she says, as she unlatches the door.

I still can't look her in the eyes.

The fresh air hits my lungs and I finally feel like I can breathe again.

"I have something for you." She reaches out to pin a gold cross on my jacket.

"I don't want it." I try to pull away, but she hangs on to me.

"It's not what you think. It's a camera . . . a recording device."

"What?" I stare down at it.

"See that tiny jewel in the center? That's the lens. All you have to do is press the top of the cross and it will record whatever you're seeing."

"Why? What's this for?"

"Tonight at the Harvest Festival. Wear a tie. We need you to document the marks on the others."

"Wait . . . except for Ali and Tyler, I have no idea where their marks are. How do you expect me to do that? It's not a pool party."

"I have faith in you." She steps in close, pinning it on my jacket. "You should know, Ali whispered your name last night before she woke up. She dreamt you saved her. Do whatever you have to do to get close to her. You're the only one who can protect her now."

Noodle slips her hand into mine and I flinch.

"Did I scare you?" She giggles.

"No . . . no, 'course not," I stutter and force a smile.

"See you tonight," Miss Granger says as she walks back up the steps and disappears inside the heavy chapel doors.

Noodle and I walk back to the truck, hand in hand. The sun doesn't feel as bright as it did before, like there's something hanging over us. Hanging over the world.

It feels like judgment day.

19

I CAN'T stop tugging at the navy-blue tie around my neck; it feels like a noose.

We haven't dressed up like this in ages—not since Dad's funeral. Mom keeps checking herself out in the rearview mirror, smearing her coral lips together. Noodle's on Mom's lap counting the number of stitches on the hem of her dress, while Jess is crammed against the passenger window, like she couldn't get far enough away from me if she tried.

For the millionth time, I glance down to adjust the gold cross pin on my tie. I still can't believe it's a video camera. I feel like some kind of hillbilly James Bond.

"Watch it," Jess snaps as the gravel on the shoulder of the road kicks up, smacking the side of my truck.

"Sorry," I murmur, as I swerve back into my lane.

I try not to make a big deal out of it, but I'm stunned at how Jess looks. Her dress is a little short for her now, but she looks nice. Normal. There's none of that crap on her face. She even took off the black nail polish and brushed her hair out of its usual rat's nest. She's always had such nice hair, not a towhead like Noodle, or like I was before mine turned dark blond. Jess's hair's the color of roasted chestnuts. She just came out that way.

With everything that's going on I feel stupid even thinking about it, but I can't help wondering what will happen with Ali tonight. Will she just start talking to me now that I'm "one of them"? Could it be that simple? And how the hell am I going to get their marks on video? If I go in too eager, they're going to be suspicious. Worse than that, what if they accept me, no questions asked, and try to brand me? Miss Granger didn't prepare me for anything like that.

By the time we pull into town, the pit of dread in my stomach has turned to straight-up doom. Main Street is packed with cars on both sides. Everyone who's anybody is here. It's one of the few events put on by the Preservation Society that's open to the public. In the old days, it started out as a fair, a place for people to trade their goods when the crops came in, but now it's more like a carnival.

There's music, some old-fashioned games, but the big attraction is the Hell House. Midland Baptist puts it on every year. It's like a haunted house, only they lead you through a bunch of huge canvas tents presenting little plays on whatever hot topics they think are pulling people away from the church. Meth. Abortion. Gay sex. Satanism. Video games. It's really just a chance for people to show off, get some attention. I was in it when I was a kid; I got to play a skeleton in the afterlife. It was pretty fun, jumping out at people and scaring the bejeezus out of them. Another grand tradition around here.

I let out a shaky breath as I get out of the truck. I've kept my family in seclusion, away from everyone for the past year, and for what? Here I am dragging them straight into the Devil's lair. I can't believe I'm spying on the Preservation Society for the Catholic Church, gathering evidence to sanction an exorcism. It sounds fucking crazy, even to me.

Just as I'm thinking about getting everybody back in the truck, hightailing it out of here, Noodle grabs my hand. She doesn't even flinch at how sweaty it is.

"Doesn't it look so pretty?" She squeezes my hand, like she knows how tough this is for me. "Just like a fairy tale."

"Yeah." I swallow hard.

It's all lit up with gas lamps and jack-o'-lanterns, a maze made from bales of hay set up on the front lawn. Just like last year, and the year before that. Probably looked this way a hundred years ago. Hardly anything ever changes around here.

I was so ticked off last year when they went ahead with the homecoming game. And after I nearly killed that kid, they went ahead with the Harvest Festival. But this town has a way of turning a blind eye like nobody's business. After news of my dad's slaughter spread, a handful of reporters descended on Midland like a bunch of turkey vultures, but they couldn't find a single person in this town to give them an interview. Mom felt real grateful, but it weirded me out more than anything. What did they have to hide?

A string of little kids rush in front of us, their faces painted up like tigers and princesses, laughing their heads off as they disappear into the maze. Reminds me of why I'm here. If there's even a nail's head of truth in all this Devil business, I have to do everything I can to stop it. For my dad. For my family. For the future.

While all the other guests have to walk around the main house and use the side gate to get to the back lawn, we're Tates. The founding families use the front door. It's our privilege. It's what's expected. Even stepping over the threshold feels like a commitment, like I'm a part of this now, whether I like it or not.

I notice Jess having some trouble with the clasp of her necklace.

"I can help," I say as I step forward.

She lets me.

As I'm securing the locket around her neck I say, "Keep an eye on Noodle for me."

Noodle looks back at me like she's about to give me a piece of her mind, but I give her a sly wink and she simmers down. She gets it.

Noodle takes Jess's hand and leads the way down the long hall toward the festivities. Mom follows, clutching her purse in front of her like it's the last life preserver on the *Titanic*.

I keep my eyes trained in front of me, but I can feel my ancestors and the rest of the founding families staring at me from the portraits lining the hall. Even though they're trapped behind glass, it feels like they're watching . . . waiting.

With every step, my heart's pounding double-time.

As we head out the French doors lining the back of the building, I notice the window's already been fixed, like it never happened. For a second I wonder if it ever did. I wonder if this is how Dad felt at the end, questioning every little thing, but when Mr. Neely steps forward to greet me, bracing my elbow with a firm grip, I know it was real.

"Welcome home, Clay," he says. There's a sanctimonious glint in his eyes as he leads me to the edge of the patio so everyone can get an eyeful.

I glance around nervously. They're waiting to see what'll happen next. Even though I hate myself for doing it, I reach out and shake Mr. Neely's hand. And it's almost like I can feel the entire community take a deep breath.

As if on cue, the bluegrass band strikes up a raucous tune. Couples start two-stepping; kids are running around all high on Kool-Aid and sheet cake. Strands of tiny white lights are strung overhead, twinkling like low-lying stars.

Mrs. Neely quickly ushers my mom over to the other women of the founding families. They seem to welcome her back into the fold without a hitch, but there's something about Mom, a distance, like she's not all connected. I wonder if they can see it, too. God, I hope not.

The only one who hasn't changed is Noodle. And with any luck, she'll never have to. People are fawning all over Jess, telling her how pretty she looks. A boy asks her to dance—Ben Gillman's little brother. He's a good kid, decent QB at Midland Middle. Maybe this is just what Jess needs, a reminder of how things used to be, how they should be.

And just like that I find myself getting caught up in it all. It'd be so easy to slip back into this life, into ignorance, like cattle being led to slaughter. I guess that's the Devil's plan—it may look like a Wyeth painting, but it's really the gateway to hell.

I take a deep breath, trying to get control of my nerves. *Just stick to the game plan, Clay. Get the video and get the hell out of here.*

I lock eyes with Tyler, who's hanging around the patio with Tammy, Ben, and Jimmy. He doesn't look surprised to see me. Mr. Neely obviously told them I'd be coming tonight.

As much as I want to just walk up to them, get this over with, I know I have to let them come to me. I circle around the party, acting as normal as possible. All anyone wants to talk to me about is football, and for the first time, I'm grateful for it. I head toward the buffet tables lining the center of the lawn, chock-full of casseroles. Mr. Miller has his smoker all set up. The whole place smells amazing, like hickory and spices, butter and caramel. There are metal troughs full of giant blocks of ice with all kinds of pop, kegs of beer. Kids are hiding out under the red-and-white-checked tablecloths, trying to sneak some, just like me and Dale used to do. Don't have to sneak it anymore. If you play ball, you can get away with murder in this town. I fill up a cup with beer and slip it under the table to them.

"Thanks, Fifty-four. You're the best!"

"No way. Clay Tate's here?" A kid with freckles for miles peeks his head out. "Will you throw the ball to us, a real spinner, see if we can catch it?"

"Sorry boys, not tonight," I say as I scan the crowd, looking for Ali.

I spot her with her parents. Our eyes meet and she quickly looks away. If I didn't know any better, I'd swear I saw her blush. She looks good. Painted-on Levi's with a lacy tank top and a plaid shirt on top. Cowboy boots. A turquoise buckle. Her hair's loose and shiny, grazing the middle of her back. Tyler sees me watching her and practically races across the lawn to put his arm around her shoulder, but she shrugs away from him. I'm glad for it. I don't want him touching her. Especially after what happened at the game last night. I still can't believe he hit her, even if it was an accident. Tyler was always a loose cannon. He's one of those guys that gets so jacked up before a game he has to throw up. I want to kill him, but I can't draw attention to myself. I have to gain their trust and work my way into the inner circle.

I notice Miss Granger enter the party through the side gate. The Preservation Society kids are watching her as she makes her way to the patio. I wonder if they suspect something about her, if they can sense her connection to God or something creepy like that.

If what Miss Granger is saying is true, the chosen one could be any one of them. As soon as the Devil chooses, takes root, the others will fall. At least that's what happened back in Mexico. I need to protect Ali until the exorcism. As soon as that happens, she'll be cleansed of all this. Miss Granger says it will be like it never happened—just a bad dream.

Miss Granger's wearing a fitted navy blue dress. It matches my tie. Mr. Neely, Deputy Tilford, and Dr. Perry are all over her like a tick on a coon dog. My first instinct is to go over there and give her an out, but I have a feeling Miss Granger can handle herself. And I can't let on that she's behind this in any way. Maybe she's doing this as a distraction, so I can make my move.

I start fiddling with the gold cross pin on my tie, making sure it's in place, when Dale sneaks up on me. I flinch.

"Jesus, Tate. You gotta relax." I can see he's already plenty relaxed. "Want some?" He opens his coat and I see the silver flash of his dad's flask.

"I'm all good."

"I'm just on a break. Hell House duty. Hey, did you see Mrs. Neely?" he says, as he gives the air in front of him a good humping.

"Dude, that's Tyler's mom."

"And?" He laughs.

I shake my head. "And that's just wrong."

"That's so right it *hurts*," he says as he takes another sip. "Speaking of fine-looking ladies . . . someone can't take their eyes off you."

I follow his gaze to see Ali, standing alone now, on the edge of the dance area.

Dale pushes me toward her. "Go, you dumbass."

I take a deep breath and start the long walk across the lawn. People are slapping me on the back, shaking my hand, calling me out by my number. I just smile and nod. I don't hear a word they're saying. I don't even care. The only thing I care about is getting to Ali. Feels like I've been waiting for this moment my whole life.

20

"Hı, Clay." Ali's voice is so soft it takes me aback. *Is this really happening? Is she seriously talking to me?*

"Hi." I hold back a grin as I put my hands in my pockets and rock back on my heels.

She pulls her hair over her shoulder. "I know you don't like to dance."

"I do," I blurt a little too eagerly. "I mean . . . I'd like to dance with you . . . I mean, that is, if you're asking?"

A smirk lights her eyes as she takes my hand, leading me to the center of the dance floor. All eyes are on us, but I don't care. Ali Miller is holding my hand. A slow song comes on, an old Hank Williams tune. It's like they're playing it just for us.

She steps in, lacing her hands behind my neck. I tentatively place my hands on her waist and we sway to the music.

"So, Clay Tate's finally decided to grace us with his presence?"

I can hardly concentrate on what she's saying because of the way she's casually stroking the ends of my hair.

"And he's finally talking to me again?" she adds, lifting her chin so she can look me straight in the eye.

"Me?" I know I'm supposed to play it cool, but I can't help myself. "You're the one who ran out on me that night."

She lowers her voice. "I wasn't supposed to be there."

"Since when do you do everything the Preservation Society tells you to do?"

She looks at me sharply, but doesn't reply.

"Besides . . ." I take a deep breath. "After that, it seemed like Tyler was always around."

"Since when have you been scared off by Tyler Neely?"

"Since it seemed like you wanted to be with him . . . instead of me."

"Is that what you think?"

There's a wall of tension between us that doesn't belong there and I don't know how to break it down. I don't know how to fix this.

"To be honest, I was afraid," she says.

"Afraid of what?" My breath catches in my throat.

"Of this," she whispers, running her hand along my collar, down the length of my tie, straightening my pin. "Being this close to you."

My heart picks up speed as she touches the cross. Maybe I've seen too many monster movies, but I'm pretty sure if the Devil was inside of her she wouldn't be able to touch it. She must not be that far gone.

"But you're not afraid anymore?" I ask.

"I don't know what I am anymore."

And there's this tiny moment, a wisp of sadness that passes over her face, making me wonder if she knows what's happening to her. If she's trying to tell me something.

"Are you thirsty?" Ali wets her lips.

"Sure," I reply.

"Let's get out of here." She leads me across the lawn toward the main house.

I glance back at the party to check on Mom, Jess, and Noodle, but all I see is Ian Neely smiling at me, raising his glass.

21

ALI LEADS me inside the Preservation Society, down the long hall back toward Ian's office. It's dark and quiet. We're alone. The urge to tell her what's really happening, to warn her, is too strong to ignore. "Ali, I need to—"

"Shhh . . ." She presses her finger to my lips and an entirely different urge rises inside of me.

Ali pushes the wood panel behind Ian's desk and the wall pops open.

"Surprise!" A bunch of people yell from behind the bar—Tammy, Ben, Jimmy, and, unfortunately, Tyler.

"Welcome to the council." Tyler holds up a bottle of booze, but it's not a warm welcome. He glares at Ali and then back at me.

"Man, it's good to see you." Ben lumbers forward to greet me, clamping his enormous hand over my shoulder. "We've been waiting for you all year."

"Hey, Clay," Tammy half-whispers as she passes by, never taking her eyes off the ground in front of her. "Welcome to where all the magic happens," she says completely deadpan.

I can't help but laugh. I never knew Tammy was funny. Maybe no one knows because they can never hear her.

Jimmy lets out a nervous burst of air, kind of a cross between a laugh and a cough, and then hunches back over the bar, almost like he's trying to disappear back into the oak. He's always been an odd one.

"Are you surprised?" Ben nudges me.

"Yeah, I mean look at this place." I scan the room, my eyes settling on Tyler. More than anything I want to tell him his own dad brought me in here the other night and told me to take his son down. It'd serve him right, his stupid smug ass, but I hold my tongue. Now's not the time.

For a split second I almost forget why I'm here, but as Tyler pours a round of shots—tequila—I see he's got his sleeves rolled up just enough so everyone can see the brand on his arm. I mean, who rolls their sleeves up like that? He must've seen it in some stupid men's magazine.

I pretend to adjust my tie, pressing the small button on the top of the cross. I feel skeevy recording all this, but Miss Granger's right. No one else would be able to get this close to them. And the sooner I get proof, the sooner I can get out of here, and the sooner we can be done with this.

"So, what kind of mark is that?" I ask as I pick up one of the shot glasses. "Is that the Chinese symbol for asshat or something?"

Ben starts laughing so hard he spurts tequila everywhere.

"Yeah, you're hilarious, Tate," Tyler says as he refills Ben's shot glass. "Don't worry. You'll find out soon enough."

I look toward the exit, making a mental plan. If they try to brand me, I swear to God, I'll tear this place to the ground.

"To us. The sixth generation." Tyler raises his glass.

I take the shot—liquid courage.

Everyone sets their shot glasses back down on the bar. Tyler refills them.

"What does that even mean . . . 'the sixth generation'?" I ask. I pretend to be interested in the photos on the wall, the jukebox, but I'm really just checking everyone out, searching every bit of exposed skin, looking for the mark. I don't see anything on the others. What if Miss Granger's wrong? What if Tyler and Ali are the only ones who have it? What if all this is just some weird coincidence? A mistake?

"The sixth generation will inherit the earth," Tyler says as he spreads his arms out wide.

"Or at least this Podunk town." Tammy winces as she slams another shot.

"It's pretty cool our parents are stepping down this early," Ben says. "Who wants to rule when you're all old and shriveled up. Might as well get some fun out of it."

"Oh yeah?" I ask. "And what's fun about it?" I look at the five of them stationed around the room like barflies. "What do you actually *do*?"

"You're pretty much looking at it," Tammy says as she leans against the bar.

"We have meetings every once in a while, but we usually end up getting hammered," Ben says as he downs another shot. "No one can even remember what we talked about."

It's like this is all one big joke to them. It makes me wonder if they have any idea what's really happening.

"But there's girls," Tyler says. "Lots of girls who want to be with someone on the council. Even little Jimmy's getting some of our leftovers."

"Don't listen to them," Ali says as she slides her shot over to Ben. "It's for the town. There's always been a council. Always will be. It's tradition. Loyalty, family, community."

"And don't forget football." Ben raises his glass.

"Amen to that." Tyler squares his shoulders.

"And God," I add.

The room goes deathly still.

"Sure." Tyler closes the distance between us. "None of this would even be possible without *God*." He raises his hands as if in fake praise.

Jimmy snickers, but the rest of them stand perfectly still, staring at me, like I just walked in on some kind of inside joke. It gives me the creeps. Or maybe it's just my imagination. So far, it's just a bunch of people getting drunk. Nothing satanic about that or you'd have to give this whole town an exorcism.

As much as I want to bolt out of there, I've got a job to do.

Strolling over to the card table, I run my hand over the worn green felt. It gives me an idea.

"We should play."

"Poker?" Tyler scoffs. "We don't play for wheat, Tate. How much money you got?"

"Let's raise the stakes," I say with a casual shrug.

"I'm liking the sound of that." Ben takes off his jean jacket and rubs his hands together. "What'd you have in mind?"

"Strip poker."

"Hell yeah!" Ben slaps me on the back and takes a seat at the table, shuffling the deck.

"This won't be weird at all," Tammy says as she takes a seat.

Ali studies me. "I'm game."

"Come on, Jimmy." Tyler pries him away from the bar and pushes him over to the table.

"What are we . . . thirteen?" Jimmy mumbles into his shot glass as he slumps down in the chair next to me.

Tyler's the last one to sit down. He's checking me out. He doesn't trust me yet. "Five card draw. Two fold max," he says.

Ben deals the first hand.

As we all look at our cards, there's a tension in the room, like the feeling in the air right before lightning strikes.

Tyler smirks. He's so easy to read, shows his emotions all over his face, in his body . . . always has. Obviously, he thinks he's got a good hand. I learned how to control all that playing ball. I swear, half of it's a mental game. Especially for the quarterback; it's all about the fake out. Even though I've got a flush, I shift in my chair, lean forward, rub the back of my neck. I need everyone to think they've got me nailed.

Tammy's got nothing, not even a pair of deuces, but she doesn't complain about it. Without taking her eyes off the table, she slips out of her dress.

Tyler and Ben start snickering.

She pushes her glasses up like she doesn't care, but I can see the flush spread up her neck. I don't want to look, but I have to—that's why I'm here. I spot the mark right above the pink elastic band of her underwear on her left hip. Just the sight of it raises the hair on the back of my neck. It's really true then. Miss Granger was right. It's the sixth generation—they've all been marked.

"Take a picture, it'll last longer," Tammy says to me.

Everybody starts cracking up. Even Jimmy.

All I want to do is wrap her up in Ben's jean jacket and tell her I'm sorry, but I bury it behind a fake grin. *Two down, two to go.*

While Tyler's bluffing up to his eyeballs, probably dying to take something off just so he can show us his abs, Ben's got his hands crossed over his chest, like he'd rather keep his clothes on. As a kid, Ben was on the husky side. People used to tease him, tell him he had bigger tits than his sister. They wouldn't dare tease him now.

Tyler's watching me out of the corner of his eye. And I feel that competitive streak coming back. I thought I'd buried it along with my dad, but I can feel it taking over every cell in my body. I want to beat him at any cost, teach him a lesson. I wouldn't mind losing a hand, either. I might not be training with the team anymore, but farm work is no joke. I'm cut and I know it. The only thing I can't take off is my tie.

I win the next hand. Ben's got nothing. He opts to drop his khakis, revealing a droopy pair of green plaid boxers. Everyone whistles and hollers at him as he spins around to give us the full view. I spot the mark on the back of his calf.

Knocking my cards to the ground, I crouch under the table so I can give the camera a good long look. His mark looks fresh and raw, almost like I can still see the heat coming off it.

Tyler leans under the table, glaring at me. "You all right down there, Tate?"

"Yeah, fine." I bump my head against the bottom of the table and then settle back in my seat.

Ali loses the next hand with a pair of sixes. She stands up and I don't have to pretend to be interested. She has my full attention, but I don't want her to take anything off, not in front of everyone. Especially not in front of Tyler. She unbuckles her turquoise belt and my heart starts hammering in my chest. Just the sound of the thick worn leather swishing through the loops sets off something inside of me.

She coils it on the table.

"That's it?" Ben teases.

She lifts an eyebrow. "Accessories count for girls."

"Wuss," Tammy says under her breath. I can't help but crack a smile.

Jimmy's the only one left. He's already folded twice. His number's up and we all know it. As soon as he gets his cards, I can tell how irritated he is. Tiny beads of sweat dot his furry upper lip. He's going down. He shows his hand and he's got zilch. I can see him struggling, trying to decide if he should take off his shirt or his pants. He opts for the shirt. He's always been a weird kid, but I feel sorry for him. His skin's pale and smooth like a baby's. I can see every rib poking out along with a half dozen chest hairs spread out in the worst places. He folds his shirt over the back of his chair and I get a glimpse of what I think is the mark on his lower back. He shrinks back into his seat too quickly to be sure. I can tell he just wants to be left alone, but I have to record it. He's the last one. Just one more and I can get the hell out of here.

I don't want to do it, but I start baiting him, razzing him, trying to get him to stand back up. I pretend to shield my eyes. "Jimmy, man, maybe you should put it back on."

Tyler and Ben quickly join in.

"Don't want to scar the ladies for life."

"If you take anything else off, we're all going to be sterile."

Jimmy looks around the table at everyone but me. They're all trying not to crack up, but the harder they try, the worse it gets, until they're all cackling like hyenas.

"Screw you, guys." Jimmy throws down his cards. "I should've known better than to play with you jocks." Without getting up, he reaches for his shirt.

He's not going to stand up. Damn. This could be my only chance.

"Six," I yell as I look to my left. "Forty-two," I yell as I look to the right. "Hut!"

The three of us tackle Jimmy to the ground.

Ben and Tyler are laughing their asses off as they roll to the side. I flip Jimmy onto his stomach. He's kicking, spitting and hollering, trying to get out from under me, but it's no use. I trap his hands under my knees and jerk down his pants. There it is, on his lower back. I can't believe they gave him a tramp stamp. I pretend to adjust my tie, making sure the camera has a good view.

As I get off him, Jimmy grabs his shirt and crawls into the corner like a wounded animal. His cheeks are ruddy and damp. Nobody pays him much mind. Tyler high-fives me and my stomach drops. It reminds me of that last game. Tyler did that after I beat the shit out of that kid. If Tyler high-fives you, you know you've probably done something rotten. I feel awful, but it had to be done. Jimmy took one for the team and he doesn't even know it.

"Nobody humiliates me like that anymore." Jimmy staggers to his feet. "Nobody!" he screams and storms out of the room.

"Jimmy," Ali calls after him.

"Leave it," Tyler says.

I think about going after him to apologize when Tammy grabs a bottle of bourbon from the bar. "How about a different game?" she whispers, laying the bottle on the card table.

"How many times do I have to tell you to speak up," Tyler says. "No one understands a word you're saying."

"I think she wants to play spin the bottle." Ben grins. "Tammy, I had no idea you cared."

Tammy rolls her eyes.

"I'm in," Tyler says, as he sinks back down in his chair. "But for the record, I'm not making out with Tate."

"You wish." I tuck in my shirt, trying to regain my composure.

"Hell, I'm so happy you're back, I might." Ben slaps my back as we take our seats.

Ali spins the bottle, never taking her eyes off me.

I hold her gaze. I want the bottle to land on me so badly. I don't think I can bear watching her kiss someone else.

Please let it land on me. If you're up there, give me a sign. You owe me this.

When it lands squarely on me, I can't help the grin spreading across my face.

Tyler acts like he's not bothered by the whole thing, but I can see the rage creeping into his jaw.

Ali grabs the bottle and walks toward me. The way she moves, the glint in her eyes, stirs something in me.

A smile eases across her lips as she sits on my lap.

I try to play it off, but every nerve ending in my body is firing . . . reaching out for her.

"Oooh!" Ben's egging us on.

Ali takes a swig from the bottle and then laces her fingers through my hair, pulling me toward her. She presses her perfect lips against mine, her tongue pushing warm liquid into my mouth, forcing me to swallow. She gives my hair a final tug before getting up. My body feels liquid now, my lips numb and tingling. My head is spinning; it feels like I'm soaring, like I'm not even touching the ground. I want to pull her back for a real kiss, but I have to admit that was the sexiest kiss I've ever had.

As she walks back to her seat, everyone's talking, laughing, but I can't see anyone but her anymore.

Ali puts the bottle back on the table and slides it over to me. "Your turn, Clay."

I take a deep breath and give the bottle a hard spin. I can't take my eyes off her mouth. And she knows it. She licks a corner of her lip and I find myself getting sucked in to every movement, like I'm disappearing into her, into her skin.

Everyone groans as the bottle points to Ali.

"Lucky bastard," Ben sighs. "You know what that means."

"Seven minutes in heaven," Tammy whispers as she slips her dress back on.

"This is bullshit." Tyler snatches the bottle from the table to inspect it.

Ben's cracking up as he yanks the bottle from him, taking a deep swig. "Game on. Just like old times."

I'm excited and nervous. The last time I played spin the bottle with her—ninth grade—this same thing happened. Seven minutes in heaven. We sat in Jane Rodgers's closet and I ended up talking to her about turtles or some stupid shit like that. I told her we didn't have to do anything. I wanted her to tell me that she wanted to, but she never did.

"It's not like anything's going to happen." Ben slaps Tyler on the back. "It's Virgin Clay with Virgin Ali."

I perk up. *Virgin Ali.* All this time I thought she and Tyler . . . but obviously, that's not the case. I try and play it cool, but I feel a million times lighter. I know it shouldn't matter, but it does.

She's still . . . Ali. And I'm still me. I breathe easier. There's still a chance.

"You have seven minutes." Tyler glares at us. "Don't make me come find you."

Ali grabs my hand and we slip out the door.

22

ALI AND I run down the front steps, spilling onto the lawn. I want to pull her into the hay maze and kiss her like I should've done years ago, but she leads me toward the Hell House.

"They won't be able to find us in here."

"But the line is huge and Tyler said we only have seven minutes—"

"Forget Tyler. If he wants to try and find us . . . let him."

We head to the front of the line where Ali says something to Mandy Johnson, the girl working the entrance.

"Official Hell House business," Mandy announces as she pulls back the rope to let us in.

The crowd groans behind us.

The first tent is packed with a group of twenty or so people huddled around a bunch of medical equipment. Laura Ridgefield's weeping on a gurney with bloody blankets stuffed between her legs. "My baby . . . my baby . . . what have I done?" she howls into the spotlight.

Ali takes my hand, squeezing it tight, like she's scared.

"Hey, are you okay?" I wrap my arm around her.

"I don't like this," she says.

"Do you want to move on?"

She nods and we sneak into the next tent, full of crazy zombies.

I know this one—they do the same thing every year. Meth.

Ali screams as some scrawny guy in a ripped-up flannel, waxy flesh dripping down his chin, darts forward to tickle her.

"Back off." I push him away. Ali clings to me a little tighter, nestling her face into my chest.

"Dude, it's just me." Dale laughs. "You've really got to lighten up."

"Call me" he mouths as we duck into the next tent and find ourselves standing in the middle of a makeshift rave. "Oh, crud, is it time already?" Mr. Brett, our seventh-grade math teacher, yells out over the techno music. "They were supposed to walkie-talkie us before they sent in the next group."

"No, we're just passing through. It's Ali . . . and Clay," she says as she squeezes my hand.

"Thank the good lord," Mr. Brett says as he continues oiling up one of the Pine twins. He looks a little too enthusiastic about the whole thing.

"The next group's still in abortion. You've probably got another four minutes until they catch up," Ali adds.

The Pine twins, Charlie or Chip, I can never tell them apart, are wearing matching speedos, but the one who steps forward's got fake sores all over his body and a set of rotting teeth.

"Tate? Is that really you?" He shields his eyes from the glare of the disco ball. "It's Charlie."

"Yeah, hey." I let out a nervous laugh. "What are you supposed to be, anyway?"

He shrugs. "AIDS, man."

"That's seriously not right," I say. "You know, you don't have to—"

"Red rover in three," a voice spits over the walkie-talkie.

"Showtime, boys." Mr. Brett rubs his hands together and puts on his leather cap.

"I can't watch this," I say to Ali.

We back into the next tent where we catch up to one of the tours. The room is dark except for the flashlights the choir members are shining up on their faces while they chant some kind of made-up Latin. An over-the-top goth kid pulls a normal-looking kid out of the choir and into the spotlight.

"Come over to my house, Jerry," the one with the fake green Mohawk says stiffly. "We can play violent video games and listen to heavy metal music. It'll be fun."

"But isn't that dangerous?" The normal-looking one gives an exaggerated shrug.

"Not at all." Goth kid eases a large plastic silver pentagram necklace over his head. "You look cool now. You're one of us."

Clearly, we've entered the Devil worship room, but they have no clue what the Devil's really like, what he's capable of.

That he might already be *here*.

I look at Ali and she pulls me away from the group into a narrow passageway.

The walls are made out of soft black stretchy fabric. Midway

146

through the tunnel, she stops and turns to face me. Standing on her tiptoes, she whispers in my ear, "You didn't forget me."

There's something in her eyes, a softness I haven't seen since she came over to my house the night of my dad's funeral. "I could never forget you," I say as I place my hand on her waist, my thumb brushing a bare sliver of skin between her top and her jeans. The feeling I get when I touch her makes every muscle in my body tense. It's like I'm a live grenade and she's got her finger on the pin. One tiny movement, the smallest gesture, and I'm not sure I'll be able to hold myself together. She moves closer. I can feel the heat coming off of her . . . or me . . . or both of us. Eyes glistening in the dark, lips parted, I lean down to kiss her, when "Welcome to hell" booms over the speakers, followed by strobe lights and heavy metal music blasting through the tunnel. The fabric walls cave and bend all around us. People's hands are pawing at us, faces pressing into the fabric like souls trying to get out of hell. Ali grabs my hand, pulling me through the rest of the tunnel away from the group pushing in behind us.

We emerge into an all-white room with harp music playing. Reverend Devers is standing up on a narrow ledge of a giant wood cross, taking a huge bite out of a Rice Krispies Treat. Ali clears her throat and he stuffs the rest of it into the pocket of his white robe.

"Welcome to salvation." He spreads his arms out wide, quickly slipping his hands through the rope loops on either side of the crucifix.

Ali tries to stifle a laugh. "Hey, Reverend. We're not part of the group . . . but you've got some, um, marshmallow? On your nose."

"Heavens to Betsy." He chuckles as he wipes it with his robe. "Is that Clay Tate with you?"

"Hi, Reverend." I give him a sheepish nod.

"I heard you were here. I hope this means you're back on the team. I don't mean to cast stones, but Tyler sure did make a mess of things with the homecoming game last night. We could sure use you."

"Well, I don't know about that . . ."

"Nice wig." Ali saves me from having to come up with a coherent response.

"Oh, this old thing?" He shakes his long brown hair. "Got it from my hippie costume from last Halloween. Jesus was a hippie." He shrugs with a goofy smile. "But we still love him."

"Well, the next group should be coming in any second," Ali says as she pulls me toward the exit.

"Clay?" Reverend calls out. "Don't be a stranger. Come see me at the church anytime. Miss Granger was telling me how well you're doing. We could just chitchat or talk ball. Whatever you want, son."

"Yeah, sure, okay."

As we head outside, Ali says, "I know a place where no one will find us."

"Where?"

She pulls me up the front steps, back inside the Preservation Society. "The secret room."

"Yeah, but Tyler and the others are in there."

"Not that one." She leads me down the hall past Mr. Neely's office, stopping in front of the basement door. "The real one."

23

I'm FOLLOWING Ali down the dimly lit stairs when I hear a girl moaning.

It's not a pleasant moan. There's something about the tone of her voice that hits me right in the gut. I run down the rest of the stairs to find Jess sprawled across the cot in the cell, Jimmy Doogan standing over her.

"What the hell's going on?" I rush forward, but Jimmy slams the cell door shut.

"I'll get Tyler," Ali says as she runs back up the stairs.

I grab the cold rusty iron bars, shaking them with all my strength. "Jess, are you okay? Jess, talk to me."

She tilts her head back and stares at me. Her pupils are so big. "Hi, Dad," she whispers.

My skin explodes in goose bumps. "It's me, Jess . . . it's Clay."

"I know . . . but Dad's standing right behind you."

I whip around, but there's no one there. Hallucinating. "What did you do to her?" I turn my attention back to Jimmy. "What did you give her?"

"She was just looking for a good time, isn't that right, Jessica?" He kicks the cot, making the springs rattle. "Don't get all roiled up, Clay. Everyone in town's had a ride on that bicycle. You're lucky anyone will touch her after Lee Wiggins."

"Don't talk about her like that," I spit. "I'm going to get you out of here, Jess. Just close your eyes."

"For fuck's sake, Jimmy, open the door," Tyler says as he ambles down the stairs, Ali, Ben, and Tammy following close behind.

"Good, you're all here," Jimmy says. "No one humiliates me like that anymore. I'm a member of the council. We're *supposed* to be equals now." His voice cracks. "And Clay needs to learn his lesson." Jimmy's eyes look pure black, like staring into a bottomless pit of hatred. And I wonder if this is it—the demon taking over.

"Open this door." I rage against the bars. "Open this goddamn door!"

"Get my dad," Tyler says to Tammy. She runs up the stairs.

"Jimmy, listen to me," Tyler says as he steps forward. "He's one of us. That's Clay's sister. We don't cross our own."

"Then what happened back there? Huh, Tyler? Why didn't you stop him? Why didn't you defend me? He doesn't even have the mark yet. Until the seed is chosen, we're all equals. Maybe it's me. Maybe I'm the chosen one. The blood of the calf has set me free."

"What's he talking about?" I ask.

"No clue," Tyler says as he stares him down. "He's obviously drugged out of his mind."

I step away from the cell, pacing the wide-planked floors. "Jimmy, I swear to God, if you don't open this door—"

"You'll what?" Jimmy says as he edges forward. "What are you going to do about it?"

One more step . . . just one.

"That's what I thought." He laughs. "Look who's in charge now, bit—"

I lunge for him. Stretching my hand through the bars, I grab hold of his shirt and yank him toward me, head-butting him with such force his head lolls back, his knobby knees buckling under him, but I don't let go. Blood's gushing from his nose as I get my hands around his throat, holding him clean off the ground. His limbs are flailing around, desperately trying to find something to latch on to.

"Please," he grunts as his lips turn blue, blood vessels bursting in his sallow skin. I glance over at Jess lying there and it only makes me want to squeeze tighter. I'm about to crush his windpipe when I'm jerked back, Tyler and Ben fighting to get control of me.

Jimmy's on the ground in the fetal position, coughing and spitting up blood, when Mr. Neely comes downstairs, calmly sorting through the keys until he finds the right one.

As soon as the cell door pops open, I charge forward. I almost reach him when I feel hands on me, from every direction. "Stop it, Clay," I hear Ali say.

I want to fight, shake them off, but I don't want to hurt anyone . . . especially Ali.

Ian Neely steps in front of me. "We'll take care of this, son. You don't need another incident on your record."

Jess stirs. "What's going on? What are you doing down here?"

I go to her, pushing her hair back from her face. "I'm so sorry, Jess."

As I pick her up, carrying her out of the cell, Ian and the others close in around Jimmy.

Mr. Neely takes off his belt.

The sound of the leather strap hitting Jimmy's flesh follows me until we're safely outside of the Preservation Society.

The scariest part is that it sounds good.

24

As I carry Jess outside, the fresh air seems to slap us both in the face.

"I would've been fine," she murmurs as she struggles to break free of me, wavering on her feet.

"You don't know what you're talking about." I try to help her to my truck, but she pulls away from me, staggering across the lawn.

"You still don't get it." She laughs, but it doesn't reach her eyes. "It's too late. No matter what happens, no matter what you do . . . he's coming."

"What are y—"

"Clay?" Miss Granger hurries across the lawn.

Jess stares at her for a moment, her face softening into a winsome smile. "You're here," she says as she stumbles forward into her arms.

"I'm sorry." I shake my head. "This is my sister Jess."

"It's okay," Miss Granger says as she strokes her hair. "I heard there was an incident. Are you okay? Is *she* okay?"

"Jimmy fucking Doogan," I say, the rage coming back to me in a flash of heat. "I don't know what he gave her."

"It was only a little Special K," Jess says, slurring her words.

"Ketamine." Miss Granger checks Jess's eyes, her pulse. "She'll be fine. It's fast acting. She just needs to sleep it off."

"Don't make me go with him," Jess pleads. "I want to go with you. I'm ready now."

"I'll tell you what," Miss Granger says as she nods toward her Volvo parked on the street. "Why don't you wait for me in my car and I'll take you home."

Jess starts heading over to Miss Granger's car when I grab her arm. "She's coming with me."

Jess shrieks like a wild animal caught in a trap.

"Clay, you should take some time to cool off," Miss Granger says as she pries my bloody hand away. "I know you're upset, but you're only scaring her more." I let go and Jess takes off, getting into the passenger seat of Miss Granger's car, locking the door behind her.

"I'll make sure she gets home okay. Your mother and Noodle, too. Your mom had a bit of an episode at the party."

"Now what?"

"It's nothing really. She started talking about flies."

"Oh God." I drag my hands through my hair.

"She's better now, but I should get her home. Clay, do you hear me?" She squeezes my shoulder. "Everything's going to be fine."

"You don't understand . . . Jimmy," I say, my eyes veering back toward the Preservation Society. "Something happened to him back there. Something evil. His eyes turned black. He said something about being chosen. And something about the seed."

She grasps my trembling hands. "I hate to even ask, but did you get what we came for?"

"Yeah, here . . ." I push the top of the cross to stop recording and take it off. "I got all the marks, but you might see some things you . . . well, things you shouldn't—"

"The marks are the only thing we're interested in. Don't worry. I'll delete the rest."

I can't believe how dirty I feel. I can't believe I got caught up in all this. If I'd left right after the poker game, none of this would've happened.

"Because of you we might be able to save them in time. Save the whole town . . . the world."

"You better hurry," I say as I dig my keys out of my pocket. "Because if Satan doesn't kill Jimmy Doogan—I might have to."

25

I NEED a beer . . . or twelve.

Quick Trip is too risky this time of night. Dale's probably staking the place out and the last thing I want to do is rehash tonight's events with him. Merritt's is still open, and nobody decent hangs out there anymore.

As I pull up, I notice a beat-up ten-speed out front. I think it belongs to that girl in Jess's class. She's always hanging around here, chatting up the clerk, Nick. He must be pushing thirty by now . . . no good reason to be hanging out with a thirteen-year-old.

The broken bell on the door clatters when I walk in. The girl's sitting on the counter, dangling her legs over the side, her beat-up sneakers skimming the candy bars.

Nick's wearing a tank top, probably just so he can show off those stupid sailor tattoos. Doubt he's ever even seen the ocean.

I grab a six-pack of Shiner from the cooler and bring it up front.

"Aren't you in my little sister's class?" I ask the girl.

"Yeah. Jess, right?"

I look from her to Nick and back again. "Isn't it a little late for you to be out on your bike?"

"No worries, my man. I'll drop her home." Nick winks at her as he rings me up.

"That's *exactly* what I'm worried about."

"Okay, *Dad*." He gives me a sarcastic salute and the girl laughs.

I slap a ten down on the counter and walk out. This town. I swear. No wonder the Devil picked Midland. We're already halfway to hell.

As I cross the lot, I see Lee Wiggins standing beside my truck holding a two-by-four.

I burst out laughing, beer dribbling down my chin. I wipe my mouth with my sleeve. "Believe me . . . you don't want to mess with me tonight, Wiggins."

He slams the plank into my taillight, busting it clean out.

"You little shit." I drop the beer and he takes off running into the woods behind Merritt's.

It's so dark, there's a thick mess of clouds covering up the moon and the stars. I'm weaving in and out of the pines, straining to hear him moving through the brush, but I can't hear a thing over my heaving breathing.

"I'm done playing games with you," I holler.

"Too bad, 'cause I'm just getting started with you," a low voice says behind me.

Before I can turn, something smacks me in the back of my head. I stagger forward a few steps, like a bear that's been hit with a tranquilizer gun.

Warmth oozes down my neck. I'm so dizzy I can hardly get my bearings, but my body refuses to go down. I twist around to see Lee standing there with the two-by-four, that sick smile stretched across his scorched skin.

"You think you're better than me. You got the name. You got the looks. But you're dead wrong. It could be me."

Dropping to my knees, I tip over backward, my sticky head resting in the debris. My eyes are wide open, but everything's gone hazy.

"Poor Clay," I hear Noodle say.

"He's not dead, is he?" Jess's voice hovers over me.

Even though I know I'm slipping into unconsciousness, I want to call after them, plead with them to help me, but my lungs won't work. Darkness creeps over me like a lead coffin.

I'm walking through the wheat.

The setting sun is an intense red-orange, making it look like the crops are on fire. Even the sound of the wind moving through the wheat makes it sound like it's sizzling. The sky is a sheet of solid gray. No break in the clouds, like it's trying to cover something up. The row in the wheat begins to narrow, bending in all around me, leading me to a hollow. I hear a soft humming noise—one of Noodle's songs, an old one. My heart starts pounding in my chest; my palms are sweaty. Each step fills me with dread. The smell of musty iron and sweet decay fills my nostrils, like rotting meat and candy. As I get closer, I see Noodle kneeling next to the dead calf. That decrepit baby doll is nestled into the calf's split-open belly. Noodle's holding something in her hands. Whatever it is, it's dripping blood.

At first, I think it's a piece of meat, maybe an organ from the calf. She looks up at me. "It's all for the chosen one," she says with a childish lilt as she shows me the gift.

I WAKE in the woods, retching up the contents of my stomach. Pine straw and bile stuck to my face. I sit up and all the blood rushes from my head. It's pounding so hard, I feel like I've got to hold it together or it'll crack right open. I feel the back of my head; I've got a pretty good knot. It's sticky with blood, but it's not bad. Nothing an ice pack won't fix.

I think about searching the woods for that little prick, but I'm not even sure what happened last night. The dreams are so real now. And life sometimes feels like a dream. It's all mixing together into one fucked-up mess.

Making my way out of the woods next to Merritt's, I shove my head under the hose. The water's freezing, but it jolts me out of my stupor.

I go to my truck and pull out my cell phone. I try Miss Granger, but it goes straight to voice mail. I call home. Noodle picks up.

"You must've gone out real early this morning," she says. I can hear every breath, like her mouth's pressed flat against the receiver.

"Yeah, I had some errands to run. Hey, is Jess there?"

"Still sleeping." Noodle sighs. "But Miss Granger gave me a present, a really neat outfit that I'm supposed to wear to school. It's not as fancy as the nun's costume, but it's nice. There's a skirt and a shirt and a coat thing and there's even a matching outfit for—"

"That's great, Noodle." I glance at myself in the rearview mirror and wince. Man, I look like hell. "Show it to me when I get home, okay? I'll see you in a bit."

"Okay. Bye," she yells into the receiver. I rub my temples.

I know I should go home, try and piece together what happened last night, but I really need to talk to somebody—an adult—before I lose my mind. Sheriff isn't an option, and Miss Granger's unavailable. The only person I can think of is Reverend. He said I could come and talk to him anytime. Pretty sure there's a confidentiality thing. He's a man of God . . . so he must believe in the Devil, too.

26

I PULL into the dirt lot at Midland Baptist. The only car is Reverend's old maroon Buick parked out back by the little apartment he lives in. I wonder why he didn't park in his garage. His car's got an I LOVE JESUS sticker along with the mandatory I LOVE MIDLAND HIGH PIONEERS. God and football—one and the same in this town.

I glance at the clock on my dash: 7:42. He must be getting ready for his sermon by now. I heard he downloads them straight off the Internet.

I sit on the front steps of the church and wait for him. It's so different from All Saints. There's no extravagance or mystical outfits. What you see is what you get, from the rotting wood steps to the chipped white paint. The founding families built this with their bare hands. We don't have some fancy baptism font—we go down to the creek that spills over from Harmon Lake for our baptisms. People might call us backwoods, but it seems more honest in some way. The people in this town might whoop it up on a Saturday night, get in brawls, cheat on their spouses, go down to the old trailers near Ted Bannon's junkyard looking for meth, but they'll always show up here on Sunday morning to make amends.

I don't even know what I'm doing here, what made me come here. Maybe it was Reverend dressed as Jesus last night. I know it sounds stupid, especially because I don't really believe in that anymore, but there's a part of me that wants to. Maybe he can help, not with Ali or the others, but help *me,* with my soul. "Lay your burdens down." That's what they're always singing about in those hymns. I want to lay them down and leave them here. Part of me thinks we should've gotten out of Midland when we had the chance, but I've seen enough horror movies to know you can't run from the Devil.

"Clay Tate!" Reverend swings around the corner. "What a nice surprise."

He's got a mug full of milky coffee that smells more like candy than coffee, his Bible tucked under his arm. "Sorry to keep you waiting. Couldn't find my dang keys. Had to dig around for the spares." He yanks up his collar, but not before I spot the hickey on his neck.

I glance back at the garage. He must have company. I wonder who it is.

"From the looks of you and me, I think it's safe to guess we both got a little carried away last night. I'm a sinner, Clay, but I think the big guy will forgive me. Praise the lord," he says with a nervous laugh.

He goes to unlock the door, only to find keys already dangling from the lock. "That's strange," he murmurs. He turns the knob and pushes the door open.

The odor hits us like a brick wall.

Like rotting meat and herbs. The sound of flies buzzing around.

At the front of the church, directly in front of the pulpit, is Jimmy Doogan. Stark naked, kneeling at the altar.

"Guess we're not the only ones who had a fun night." Reverend laughs. "Son, you better skedaddle," he calls out to him. "Folks are going to start showing up here any minute and unless you want them to see your—holy mother of God." He gasps as he drops his coffee and Bible.

I step around Reverend; I feel drawn to the altar. Jimmy's eyes are open. Pure black. His pale white skin looks like it's made of marble. His mouth's agape, like he's getting ready to tell me something. There's a bloody knife next to him. In front, the symbol, the upside-down U with two dots above and below, smeared in blood. I can't tell what he's holding, but his hands are cupped in front of him, on his lap, just like Noodle from my dream.

I crouch so I can feel for a pulse. As soon as I make contact with his neck, I know he's dead. I know the feel of dead flesh. I glance down at his cupped hands. He's holding something smooth and sticky with dark blood. It takes a while for my brain to catch up to what I'm seeing. And when it hits me, hot acid rises in my throat.

I stagger back, knocking over the American flag on a stand and bashing into the upright piano, my fingers slamming down on the keys. I careen outside to see the lot filling up. People smiling, greeting each other. Ladies carrying casseroles, men straightening their ties. I see the sheriff and his wife get out of their car. Ely's eyes lock on mine; I feel my insides crumble.

"Clay, what is it?" Sheriff says as he steps toward me.

Unable to produce a sound, I slump down on the steps, my hands trembling.

"Help!" Reverend yells from inside the church. I put my hands over my ears. I can't stand to hear his voice. "Help," he yells louder and louder like a cranked up siren, gaining strength with every rotation of breath.

Sheriff gives me the strangest look before he hurries into the church. People are rushing in from every direction. Someone calls an ambulance. There's weeping and throwing up. I peer through the chaos, across the lot, to see Ali, Tyler, Ben, and Tammy leaning against the back of Tyler's car. They're just staring at me, like they're not surprised in the least. Could they've had something to do with this?

"Clay." Miss Granger grabs my arm, pulling me away from the church. I didn't even see her pull up. She's wearing the same clothes from last night. She looks a mess, like she hasn't slept a wink.

"He's dead," I murmur. "It's starting, isn't it? I dreamt about this last night. Jimmy's the first one to fall. We need to warn the others, we need to tell Sheriff Ely."

"Clay, look at me," she says forcefully. "You can't tell them you had a premonition of Jimmy's death or they will lock you up at Oakmoor. Believe me, that's not a place you want to be right now. You have to trust me on this."

Sheriff steps out of the church, pushing everyone back.

"I need you to go home," Miss Granger pleads as she leads me to my truck. "Go about your normal Sunday."

"But . . ."

"If anyone comes to talk to you, you know nothing. Do you understand me?"

I look back at the church to find Sheriff staring right at me, like he knows.

She nudges me into the truck.

As I pull out of the lot, I can feel the eyes of the Preservation Society kids on me like I'm a moving target. I can't believe how calm and collected they are. Is this punishment for what Jimmy did to Jess? Is that what this is about? Did they do it for *me*? Tyler threatened him last night, but so did I, and I have no alibi for my whereabouts last night. I was in the woods, alone, having a prophetic dream because I'm a goddamn prophet. I grab my cap off the dash and pull it down low. I look down at my hands, the dried blood under my fingernails, and I wonder, could I have done this myself?

27

I HEAD straight for the combine. I can't bear to go inside the house and face Mom, Noodle, and Jess—not after everything that's happened.

I try to call Miss Granger again, but it goes straight to voice mail. "Damn it," I yell, as I shake my phone. I feel like I'm going crazy. Of course Dale's called like a million times. I guess he hasn't heard about Jimmy's death yet, because all he wants are details on Ali. Heard we got caught making out in the Hell House. I swear, this town . . . nothing stays buried for long.

As I crank up the combine, I try to erase the image of Jess on that cot, staring back at me like she knew what was coming and she didn't care, like she'd already given up on herself . . . and me. Jimmy kneeling at the altar . . . Noodle giving me the "gift" in my dream . . . the doll . . . the calf. . . . the clouds . . . the sound of the combine grinding through the wheat . . . the feel of the wheel in my hands pulsing like the tendon in Jimmy's neck—everything seems to be a reminder.

The wheat has always been an escape for me, a sanctuary, but now it feels like a prison, like it's closing in around me.

As I near the fence line of the Neely ranch, I make a wide turn. I'm working my way back toward the house when I spot a cloud of dust moving down our drive. Hopefully it's Miss Granger, because we really have to talk. I'm nearly back to the equipment shed when I spot a tan cowboy hat bobbing up and down through the wheat. My heart withers in my chest. I know that hat. Belongs to Sheriff Ely. And it's not some fake nod at being country—he *is* country.

I turn off the combine and wait. I try Miss Granger one last time, but she doesn't pick up.

Pushing my hair back from my face, I readjust my cap, trying to remember what she told me at the church. *Act normal. Don't say anything.*

"Looking good," Sheriff says as he scans the crops. "You're not using the same pattern as your dad."

"Nope." I try to act casual, like it's a perfectly normal thing to have the sheriff standing on my land, shooting the shit after I just fled a murder scene. "Just using the force, I guess."

"Is that right?" He puts his boot up on the tread of the combine, and all I can think about is the calf. I wonder if there's any blood spatter underneath that tread. "I just wanted to come over here . . . chat a bit." He looks up at me, eyes like a coyote, luring me into some kind of trap.

"It's terrible what happened to Jimmy," I say, as I reluctantly climb down out of the safety of the combine.

"Yep. Never seen anything like it." He breaks off a shaft of wheat, sticks it in his mouth, and walks around the combine until he's facing the Neely ranch. "Not the worst thing I've seen. You either." He glances back at me, trying to size me up. "But this was strange. We had that case a few years back when Mrs. Timmons tried to give her husband that botched vasectomy after he'd passed out from another night of tomcattery. But never seen anyone do it to themselves before."

"What?" My throat goes bone dry.

I can feel him studying me, which makes me even more self-conscious. "Coroner came, said Jimmy did it himself. And his prints were all over the keys. Must've swiped them from the reverend at the Harvest Festival. Damndest thing." His steely blue eyes dig into me. "Do you know what might make Jimmy Doogan do something like that?"

I swallow hard, thinking about him standing over my sister, my hands around his throat last night squeezing the life out of him. "No." I look down at the decimated wheat under my feet. "Can't imagine."

"Hmm . . ." There's a long pause, but I don't dare look at him. "See, I heard there was a little scuffle at the Preservation Society last night."

I press my lips together so I won't blurt out anything stupid.

"Heard he was getting fresh with your sister—"

"Who told you that?" A flash of anger rises up inside of me. I don't want to bring Jess into this. Don't want anybody talking about her even more than they already did.

"Doesn't matter." Ely shrugs, but he's still watching my every move. "You're not in any trouble, Clay. Neither's Jess. I'm just trying to get the full picture."

"A lot of people were pissed at Jimmy last night," I say as I pretend to check the tires.

"Including Tyler Neely. Am I right?"

Shoving my hands in my pockets, I look out over the wheat shivering in the wind. My eyes veer toward the breeding barn . . . the blood . . . the flies. I clear my throat. "I'd love to sit and chat, but if you don't mind, I have a harvest to finish."

Sheriff lets out a deep sigh. "All right, Clay." He pats me awkwardly on the shoulder. "If anything comes to mind, anything at all, I want you to call me."

I give him a curt nod and climb back into the combine.

I don't even wait for him to leave before I rev up the engine, feeling the earth tremor beneath me. I know he can feel it, too, but he doesn't move a muscle.

Grinding the gear into place, I make a sweeping arc around him, hoping he gets a good pelting by the discarded wheat stems. Sheriff needs to keep his nose out of this if he knows what's good for him. Whatever made Jimmy do it, it's strong enough to stop Sheriff in his tracks. That much I'm sure of.

The Devil is here.

Sheriff Ely doesn't know it yet, but he needs saving, too.

28

MONDAY MORNING rolls around and I can't even imagine the spectacle of what today will bring at Midland High—news cameras will probably be set up everywhere, people crying, talking about what a great guy Jimmy was.

But as I pull into the lot, I'm stunned to see it looks just like any other day. No cameras, no armbands, no tears. The only difference is there's one less set of eyes staring at me from Tyler's dickmobile.

I turn off the engine and glance down at my hands. I can't stop thinking about them around Jimmy's throat. I might've done it, too—killed him right then and there if they hadn't pulled me off of him. So if the Preservation Society had something to do with his death, why'd they stop me?

Dale backs up against my window, his arms wrapped around

himself pretending to make out with someone. "Oh, Clay, don't stop. You're such a big strong man, Clay."

I open the door, jabbing into his body, making him stagger forward.

"Real funny," I say as I grab my backpack.

"Why didn't you call me back?" he asks.

"If this is about Jimmy Doogan, I don't know anything—"

"Forget Jimmy Doogan."

I look at him sharply.

"What? He was a little prick. But that's a pretty gnarly way to kill yourself."

"How'd you know he killed himself?"

He shakes his head. "Dude, it's Midland. Anyway, I heard he's been in counseling for months with Miss Granger. Maybe you should think about getting a new counselor."

I try to play it off, but I can't believe Miss Granger didn't tell me. I know she said she'd been keeping an eye on all the Preservation Society kids, but why wouldn't she have told me about it when we were talking about Ali being in counseling? She said she didn't tell me because she didn't know if she could trust me. Does she still not? It makes me wonder, what else is she keeping from me?

Dale's snapping his fingers in front of my face. "Earth to Clay."

"What?" I bat his hand away.

"I need the *real* dirt . . . you and Ali?"

I glance over at her. She's leaning against Tyler's car with the others. She smiles at me, but not in a creepy way. Her face is soft, almost wistful. It's hard to believe she'd ever be mixed up in something like this.

She's wearing a Pioneers T-shirt with a pair of faded Levis.

"Hey, that's my shirt," I murmur. She stole it from me a couple years back to use as a sleep shirt, but I've never seen her wear it in public. It has my number on it and everything.

"That's a sign, you dumbass," Dale says, as he stands next to me. "She's basically saying she wants you all over her body."

Maybe it *is* a sign, but not like Dale thinks. Maybe she's trying to give me some kind of secret signal.

"So, you're just going to stare at her from across the lot? That's pathetic, man. Even for you. You better check yourself before you wreck yourself," Dale says as he takes off after some freshman girls, clucking at them like a chicken. For some godforsaken reason they seem amused.

As I make my way over to Tyler's car, I'm thinking about what I'm going to say to Ali—to any of them—but it turns out I don't have to say anything at all.

"Get in." Tyler swings his door wide open, blocking my path.

"What? Now?" I look around. "First bell's about to ring."

"Let's call it a sick day." Ben comes up behind me, slapping me hard on my shoulder.

"We just want to talk," Tammy says as she gets in the backseat, never once taking her eyes off the ground in front of her.

I look to Ali. She gives me a reassuring smile.

"Yeah, okay . . . sure." I swallow harder than I'd like. "Just let me put my bag in the truck."

As soon as I turn away from them, a shuddering breath escapes my lungs. Sheer panic starts taking over—my eyes are watery, my throat's bone dry. I clutch the keys in my hand, the metal notches digging into my palm, and I'm thinking I could just take off . . . get in my truck and keep going. But where could I possibly go? Everything I love, everything I am, is right here in Midland.

I lean in my truck, pretending to stash my bag under the seat, while I frantically text Miss Granger. *They want me to go with them. In Tyler's car. What do I do?*

As I'm waiting for a response, I peer up at them over the steering wheel. My heart's pounding in my chest. There's a part of me that's telling me, screaming at me, to keep my distance until the exorcism. I did my part, now it's time to let the church take care of this . . . but there's Ali. I don't think I have the strength to walk away from her.

I text Miss Granger again. *Why won't you answer me? I need your hel—*

"You won't be needing that where we're going," Ali says as she slips in behind me, turning off my phone. "No cell service."

I'm not sure if she saw the text or not, but as I follow her back to Tyler's car, it feels like a death march.

I get in the backseat—Tammy on one side, Ali on the other. Tyler's driving, Ben's riding shotgun.

As we pull out of the lot onto Main Street, I can't help wondering if this is it. If this is the last anyone will ever see of me, or if I'll come back different . . . branded.

29

TYLER SLOWS down as we near the Preservation Society. All I can think about is the secret room. The real one Ali told me about before we found Jess and Jimmy in the cell. Is that where they're taking me? I lean back in my seat, running my sweaty palms down the front of my jeans. Tyler smirks at me in the rearview mirror, like he knows exactly what I'm thinking, and then revs the engine, racing down Main Street, toward the outskirts of town.

I have no idea where we're going, but for the first time in my life I'm thankful for Tyler's stupid techno music. It's covering up my rapid breathing.

When we pull onto the axis road, out by the old silos, I finally figure out where we're headed—the fairgrounds. Tyler and I used to do Junior Rodeo out here, but I haven't been here in years. He whips into the dirt lot next to the ring and cuts the engine. As soon as Tyler opens his door, I spring from the car, inhaling the manure-filled air.

"What are we doing out here?"

"Thought this would be a good place to talk," Tyler says as he goes to the back of his car and opens the trunk, pulling out a big black duffel bag. "Maybe blow off a little steam."

I don't know what's in that bag, but it can't be good.

Tyler eyes me. "Sure are nervous, Tate."

I pull my damp hair back from my face and scan the grounds. I'm looking around for a witness, but it's deserted. I wonder if they'd ever find my body out here. "You know, everyone saw me leave school with you."

"Yeah . . . I made sure of that," Tyler says as he dumps the duffel at his feet with a dull thud.

"Seriously, Tate." Ben stands next to Tyler, crossing his arms over his chest. "We're the ones who should be scared of you."

"Me?" I balk.

Tammy and Ali close ranks and that's when it dawns on me—they think I had something to do with Jimmy's death.

"You've got to be kidding me." I exhale. "Is that what this is all about? You seriously think I did that?"

"No." Ben wrinkles up his nose. "But someone must've made him do it. Someone he was scared shitless of."

"And you think that was me?"

"All I know is it took five of us to pull you off him."

"We all wanted to kill him," I say, in my defense.

"Then where were you that night?" Tyler steps toward me. "'Cause we know you didn't go home."

"Oh yeah?" I square my shoulders. "And how would you know that?"

Tammy nudges Ali.

"I went to your place after the Harvest Festival," Ali says, her voice soft, her eyes full of sympathy. "I waited for you all night."

"Just to talk," Tyler adds through gritted teeth.

"And Nick, up at Merritt's?" Ben clears his throat. "He said you came in all agitated. Said you were bustin' his balls over some girl and then took off into the woods, left your truck there till morning."

"Look." I let out a deep sigh. "I didn't want to say anything, but I had a run-in with the Wiggins kid."

They all look at each other, an uncomfortable silence hanging in the air.

"I'm not a meth head, if that's what you're thinking. It's personal—has to do with Jess. He was waiting for me when I came out of Merritt's. Hit me in the back of the head with a two-by-four, knocked me out cold." I bend my head down so they can look.

Tammy steps forward to inspect. "There's nothing there," she whispers.

"What?" I lurch to Tyler's car, tilting the side mirror. "It must've already healed," I say as I run my fingers over the base of my skull.

"Or it never happened." Tyler stares me down.

"You think I'm lying?" I advance on Tyler and Ali steps between us.

"Clay, we know about what you thought you saw at the breeding barn," Ali says. "We know about the calf. We know you've been *seeing* things."

"I can't believe this is happening," I say as I pace the dirt.

"When Sheriff came to talk to us—"

"Wait . . . did you tell him I wasn't home?"

"Hell no." Ben juts his head back. "We didn't tell him jack shit."

"That's what we're trying to tell you," Ali says. "You can trust us."

"We've got your back." Ben slams his hand on my shoulder. "You're one of us now."

"You don't understand." I pull away from him and continue pacing the lot. "There's a lot more going on here."

"Like what?" Tammy asks.

"Like Jimmy. Jimmy wasn't himself. You saw . . . you saw his eyes. They were black. Pure black. And he was saying all these creepy things about the seed—"

"They were both high as kites." Tyler raises a brow.

"The thing is, no one would even blame you if you told him to do it." Ben rubs the back of his neck. "What happened with your sister . . . what Jimmy did was way out of line."

"It's not like that," I say, completely exasperated. "You have no idea what you're talking about."

"Then tell us," Tyler says. "Tell us how it is."

Ali steps toward me. "Please . . . help us understand. Because we're trying."

"You're trying? Trying to what?"

"We're trying to protect you, Clay. But we have to know the truth."

"The truth?" I say with a hysterical chuckle. "You want to talk *truth*? Okay . . . then tell me about the marks . . . the brand. I know you all have one. And I know what it means."

"What, this piece of crap?" Ben laughs as he pulls up the leg of his Wranglers. "When we all stepped up to the council, we thought we'd get tattoos, for the Preservation Society—"

"But Ali's afraid of needles." Tammy rolls her eyes.

"So we figured a brand might be good," Ben continues. "If it's good enough for the OU football team, it should be good enough for us." Ben gives the upside-down hook-'em-horns sign.

"Tyler used a coat hanger," Ali explains. "Bent it up to make it look like the Preservation Society symbol, you know . . . the bull with the two horns and hoofs."

"But we got *wasted*." Ben laughs. "Mr. Miller's rye is no fucking joke."

"I don't care what you guys say." Tyler rolls up his sleeve to show me. "I still think it's cool. It looks tribal or something."

"It looks like a demented smiley face, or frowny face, depending on how you look at it," Tammy says under her breath.

"I heard that, Tammy," Tyler snaps, but then a slow smile spreads across his face. "Fine. Maybe it wasn't my best idea."

Ali smooths her hair down. "I'm just glad I had enough sense to put it somewhere I could cover it up. But do you guys remember Ben that night?" She tries to stifle a grin. "Ben wanted it in the middle of his forehead. Can you imagine?"

They all start cracking up at the memory and I can see it in their faces—they're telling the truth, or what they *believe* is the truth. I mean, who knows what really happened . . . they all just admitted they were wasted. Maybe they don't know what's really happening to them.

"Hey, Tate," Ben says as he dries his eyes. "I'm just curious. What'd you think it meant?"

I could make something up, laugh it off, but this could be my shot. Tyler's always been so easy to read. If they've been marked for the Devil, and they know about it, maybe I'll be able to tell.

"The mark," I say as I drag my heel in the dirt making an upside-down U with two dots above and below. "It looks really similar to this ancient symbol called the Devil's Portal."

"The Devil, huh?" Tyler smirks, but there's something in his eyes, an intensity, that doesn't match his casual appearance. "If I didn't know any better, I'd say you've been spending a little too much time with Miss Granger."

"Miss Granger?" I narrow my eyes. I can tell by the way he's leaning against his car, the careful way he's holding his body, that he's trying to sell me something, but what? I decide to take the bait. "And what would that have to do with Miss Granger?"

"You don't know about her?" Ali pulls on her fleece jacket, rubbing her arms.

"Seriously, Clay?" Tammy rolls her eyes. "I know you're a football player, but do you have to be such a cliché? You think we just happened to get an Ivy League counselor . . . in Midland? Please."

"I don't understand."

Ben shakes his head. "She's been spoutin' off that Devil shit for years."

"Years? But she just moved here last year."

"Or just got out," Tammy murmurs.

"Out? Out of where? College?"

"Oakmoor," they answer in unison.

"What? That's impossible." I whisper, but there's something about it that registers on the back of my neck, something about it that rings true. I remember that look in her eyes when she told me not to tell anyone about this or they'd send me to Oakmoor, like she knew firsthand what that was like. "I thought she was just a volunteer over there."

"Checked herself in two years ago, right after Harvard," Tyler says as he looks at himself in the side mirror and then pops it back in place. "But I'd still do her."

Tammy and Ali smack him at the same time. "What?" He laughs. "She's hot."

"How do you know all this?" I ask.

"We overheard the council talking about it last year, debating whether they were going to take her on . . . give her a chance at rehabilitation."

"That's why all of us have had to go to counseling this year," Tammy says.

"It's a charity thing." Ben cracks his neck. "But I had no idea Jimmy actually needed it."

I think about everything Miss Granger told me. What if it was all a lie? Nothing more than the ramblings of a crazy person. And what does that say about me that I was more willing to believe the town was possessed by the Devil—that I was a *prophet*—over facing the reality that my dad was probably schizophrenic and I might have it, too? I mean, what proof did I actually have of any of this? The marks, sure . . . but like they said, they were drunk. Their story makes sense. And Jimmy killing himself. People kill themselves all the time. It doesn't mean the Devil's in town. No one really knew him. He was a weird kid. Maybe he felt so guilty about what he did to Jess that he couldn't live with himself.

Or . . . maybe Miss Granger checked herself into Oakmoor as a way to infiltrate the community. Maybe this is exactly what she wants them to think. Maybe this was her plan all along.

Anything's possible at this point.

Ali reaches out for my arm, breaking my train of thought. "I don't mind going to see Miss Granger for counseling. She's helped me a lot this year."

I study her, trying to figure out if she's talking in some kind of code. Maybe she's trying to tell me she knows about it, too. Maybe I'm not alone in all this.

"Have you guys ever noticed the way Miss Granger's always scratching her head when she gets nervous?" Tyler asks.

"Oh yeah." Ben crams a big wad of chew in his bottom lip. "I just thought it was dandruff."

Ali pulls her hair over her shoulder. "One time she caught me staring at her necklace, and she started scratching her head so hard, she drew blood. I felt really bad."

"Self-mutilation." Tammy pushes her glasses up on the bridge of her nose. "Maybe that's why she has to keep her hair up like that. To cover it up."

"Did she tell you the Devil's going to take over the town or some stupid shit like that?" Ben blurts.

I don't know what to say, so I just stand there, staring down at the tiny patch of clover trying to push up through the dirt.

"Wait. You didn't actually believe her, did you?" Tyler laughs.

They're all staring at me, waiting for an answer.

"No . . . I mean, I don't know . . ."

"It doesn't matter," Ali says as she stands next to me. "All that matters is we're here. Together. And it's a beautiful day."

"Beautiful-ish," Tammy whispers up at the gray sky.

Ben rests his arm on my shoulder. "You're all kinds of messed up right now, Tate, but we're going to make you right. The Preservation Society will make you right again."

Tyler glares at him. It's a miniscule moment, a tiny whisper of warning, but I've got my eyes wide open now. Miss Granger and I might both be crazy, but Tyler's up to something. He brought me out here for a reason. And I'm going to have to play along a little longer if I want to find out what it is.

"How about we put all this behind us and have some fun?" Tyler cracks his knuckles. "Agreed?"

Ali wraps her pinkie around mine for a brief moment. It gives me the courage to nod.

Tyler crouches to unzip the bag, revealing bull riding gear. "Now . . ." He looks up at me with a smug grin. "Who's ready to ride?"

30

ALI PLUCKS a rich brown Stetson from the bag and fixes it on my head. "There," she says, looking up at me with those big doe eyes. "You look like a real cowboy now."

I want to ask her what she meant back there when she said that about Miss Granger helping her this year, but Tyler's watching my every move. Or hers. I can't help wondering if that's what this is all about—Ali.

Ben opens the barn door and a bull comes charging into the chute. "Holy shit," he hollers. The bull's pure black, like he's made up of a thousand crow feathers, with horns sharp as razors.

"What's his name?" I ask, watching him rage against the bars.

"Diablo." Tyler grins as he struggles to get him roped up.

"Of course it is." I take a deep breath.

"Are you sure you want to do this?" Ali sidles next to me at the fence. "No one would blame you if . . . well, you don't have to do this."

"Oh, I think I do." I reach out to tuck a stray piece of hair behind her ear and she smiles up at me, like she understands everything. And that's the way it used to be between us. Half the time we didn't even need words.

Tyler clears his throat and I pull my hand back. I can feel him staring a hole in my head, his rage matching the bull's. Pretty sure he was thinking I'd wuss out, but I'm not backing down. Not anymore.

"How 'bout we make this a little more interesting," Tyler says as he hops down from the chute and pulls out his wallet, placing a hundred-dollar bill on top of the fence post. "A hundred bucks apiece to whoever can stay in the ring the longest."

"Ease up, Tyler Trump." I try and make a joke out of it, but I can't believe he has a hundred-dollar bill in his wallet, like it's no big deal.

"Yeah, that's a little steep for my blood, too," Ben says as he digs around in his pockets.

"Fine." Tyler sighs. "Whatever's in your pockets then."

Ben puts down sixty. I put in what I've got.

"Twenty-two bucks?" Tyler laughs. "I almost feel bad taking this from you, Tate. *Almost.*"

He dusts off an old horseshoe and places it on top of the money. "Your winning streak is over," he says, as he brushes past me to put on his gear.

Ben slaps me on the back. "Just like old times, huh, Tate?"

"Something like that." I force myself to smile. Tyler might have the custom-made chaps, the best training money can buy, but we're not playing for points here. What I lack in style, I make up for in heart. And all I have to do is hang on the longest. I'm good at hang-ing on to things.

I watch Ali leaning up against the fence, talking to the bull, trying to soothe it, and I know she's innocent in all this. I'll do whatever I have to do to protect her.

Tammy comes out of the brush with three blades of onion grass. We draw to decide the order. It's Ben, then Tyler, then me.

As Ben's pacing next to the chute, trying to psych himself up, I'm thinking I lucked out. They don't call him Big Ben for nothing. Hopefully, he'll tire Diablo out a bit so I can get a decent ride.

Ben climbs onto the bull and gives the signal—at least I think it's a signal. Either that or he's changed his mind and he's trying to get off.

Tyler opens the chute.

The bull spins hard to the left, does a belly roll, and that's all she wrote. Ben lasts all of 1.4 seconds before he's thrown off. He's scram-bling over the side of the ring to throw up before we even have a chance to jump in and distract the bull.

"Sexy," Tammy mutters.

"Oh man!" Ben dusts off his jeans. "I swallowed my chew."

Tyler's up next.

Back when we used to do Junior Rodeo together, he had all sorts of weird little rituals he copied from the pros. He'd kiss the bull, take off his hat, and give thanks to God . . . anything for the attention. All show, no substance, but the judges loved that crap. I see things haven't changed much. Tyler climbs onto the bull and makes a big show out of just putting on his gloves. He's pounding his fist on the flat braided rope, which makes Diablo even more pissed. I wait for the signal. As soon as Tyler tips his hat, I open the gate. The bull bursts from the chute with a fury I feel underneath my skin. He's spinning and bucking and sunfishing so hard, I'm shocked Tyler's able to last the 4.2 seconds he does. Ben jumps in to distract the bull, but Diablo pays him no mind—he's laser-focused on Tyler. The bull's got his head low as he stamps his hoof in the dirt, his tail twitching violently.

"Tyler!" I shout as I climb up on the fence. "You need to get out of there."

But Tyler just sits there in the dirt, staring at the bull, completely transfixed. He pulls a knife from the sheath in his boot and the bull rears back to charge.

The flash of silver. The snorting breath. Something snaps inside of me. I jump in the ring, diving in front of Tyler's body.

I hear the grating sound of hooves skidding in the dirt. I shut my eyes, bracing for impact, but all I feel is the hot rancid breath of the bull breathing down on my neck. Tyler scrambles out from under me. I hear the others helping him over the side of the ring.

"No way," Ben whispers behind me.

I open my eyes, and grasp onto Tyler's knife lying next to me. Peering through the settling dust, I face the bull. He's kneeling right in front of me, one of his horns pressed against my chest. All he has to do is lean in and it'll go straight through my heart. As soon as I meet his gaze, something goes off inside of me, a lightning bolt of recognition.

This is the same bull from the breeding barn. The same bull my dad tried to kill that night. Suddenly, there's no one else here. I don't even see the ring. It's just me and the bull.

He blinks his big dark eyes at me and in their reflection I see my dad's final moments playing out before me. I want to turn away, but I can't. Whatever truth I tried to bury that night wants to be heard, wants to come back to the surface.

I force myself to watch.

"I have sinned . . . against my own seed. I killed him. I thought it would stop all this. I thought I could protect you, but I was wrong." His face contorts in agony. *"I still feel it. Can you feel it? I have to stop the evil before it's born. Please forgive me."*

He clasps his blood-slick hands around my throat, and squeezes with every ounce of strength left in his body. I'm struggling for breath, but I don't try to fight. It could be madness or drugs, but he knows exactly what he's doing in this moment. He knows it's me.

"I plead the blood," he whispers, a wet death rattle ringing in my ears, right before his entire body goes slack.

Tears are searing my cheeks now, but I don't bother wiping them away. "He tried to kill me that night. He wasn't afraid for his soul. He was afraid of *me*. Of what I would become," I say as I tighten my grip on the knife, holding it to the bull's throat. But still, the bull doesn't move. He's kneeling in front of me. Somehow we're connected in all this. The two of us. It's something I feel all the way to the marrow of my bones. "What are you trying to tell me?" I ask, my hands trembling.

"He's losing it," Ben says, jarring me back to the present.

"Please," Ali cries. "We have to help him."

"No." Tyler holds them back. "Let him be."

And that's when it hits me. This is what Tyler wants. He knew exactly what he was doing by bringing me here. He knew this was the same bull from the breeding barn. He wanted me to lose it in front of the others . . . in front of Ali. But I refuse to give him the satisfaction. I don't know what they saw, what they heard, but the show's over.

Ripping through the rope with the blade, I free the bull from the tether. I get up and turn my back on him. I know he's not going to hurt me. We have an understanding. We've both seen enough carnage for one lifetime.

I climb over the fence and grab the pile of cash, knocking the horseshoe to the ground. "I'll be taking this." I stuff the bills in my pocket.

"But . . . but you didn't even ride," Tyler stammers.

"Whoever lasts the longest in the ring. That was the bet." I stab his knife into the wood post right next to him, watching his Adam's apple depress. "I guess my winning streak continues. Oh, and you're welcome for saving your ass."

31

IT'S DUSK by the time we head back into town.

Tyler drops everyone off first before taking me back to my car at Midland High.

I know he's got something to say to me, but I'm not about to give him any help.

We pull into the empty lot. I get out and start to close the door when he says, "That stunt you pulled with the bull, making him bow to you. It doesn't mean shit. You're nothing but a dead end to her. We don't even need you on the council."

"I think your dad has a different take on all that," I say, drumming my fingers on the door.

"My dad's an old fool. Besides, Tate blood's not hard to come by in this town."

"What'd you say?"

"You heard me."

I lean in. "I don't know what you're getting at, but if you come near Noodle or Jess, I swear to God, I'll kill you."

A smirk lights his face. "You still don't know, do you?"

I reach in to grab him but he jams on the gas, fishtailing out of the lot and onto Main Street.

I get in my truck and check my phone. No calls or texts from Miss Granger. Maybe she got what she needed and she's busy making plans for the exorcism, or maybe it's all in her head, some fucked-up fantasy. All I know is I feel like that beat-up pinball game down at the rec center. I keep running around, reacting to everything, and maybe that's exactly what they want me to do. Maybe I'm playing right into their hands and I don't even know it.

I take a deep breath, running my hand over the dash. This was my dad's truck, his dad's before that. I refuse to let that last memory of him in the breeding barn ruin everything we had. Like Noodle said, you choose what you want to remember and I choose good, but that doesn't mean I turn a blind eye, either. I have questions that need answering. My dad always told me in times of trouble, the answer was in the land.

I go home to the wheat.

Where I don't have to think.

I don't have to dream.

All I have to do is plow.

32

THE MOON is full and red, like a bloated tick. I hear heavy breath, discarded wheat stems being crushed underfoot . . . and a song. A nursery rhyme from long ago. It lures me deep into the wheat and when I finally see the source of the music, I freeze in place. It feels like my heart might burst with fear, with awe, with reverence. The bull stamps forward, with Noodle on his back. He isn't bucking and kicking for control; he's as docile as a pony. Noodle strokes his head as she sings her counting song. She's barefoot and wearing the white eyelet dress she wore to Dad's funeral, her hair's down, but there's something dark and wet on the side of her head. Noodle leans down to hug the bull's neck, and that's when I see the blood spurting from its throat. The bull staggers forward into a kneeling position and when Noodle sits up, I realize it's not Noodle at all, but Tyler.

"Look," Tyler says with a grin. "I got him to kneel, too."

I WAKE with a jolt on the moving harvester. I slam on the brake and check the gauges.

I'd like to think I was only asleep for a few minutes, but the tank's nearly empty. It must've been running for hours.

I scramble out of the cab to see how much damage I caused, but I'm still in the same patch of wheat as when I started.

I can't understand it. I've heard of sleepwalking, but sleep-plowing? And it looks like I've been going over the same pattern in the wheat over and over again, like a crazy person.

As I head back to the house, I keep listening for hooves in the wheat. I know it was only a dream, but it seemed so real to me. My heart aches. It's more than melancholy . . . more than dread . . . it almost feels inevitable, like the first frost has settled into my blood. Trying to rub the goose bumps from my arms, I head inside.

I walk as quietly as possible into the living room and pull a quilt over Mom. I realize she's only pretending to be asleep, but I don't have the strength to deal with her tonight . . . or the flies.

I check in on Noodle. She's all snuggled in. Still no sign of her gross doll. I'm walking by Jess's room when I see a shadow moving back and forth under her door, like she's pacing.

"Jess?" I knock. The pacing stops. I don't know what to say to her. I know she's probably still upset about what happened at the Harvest Festival. I keep thinking I should tell her about what happened to Jimmy, but I don't want to make things worse.

"You're up late," I say, and then shake my head. That was a stupid thing to say. "I mean . . . I just want you to know, I'm here for you. If you need to talk, or anything."

She doesn't answer, but I can hear her breathing, like she's got her face pressed right against the keyhole.

I start to leave and then double back. "Oh, and I wanted to give you this." I pull the wad of money from my back pocket and slide it halfway under her door. "There's a hundred and eighty-two bucks there. For those clothes you wanted. And for the record, I don't care if you cut holes in them."

I wait for a reply—a thanks, a fuck you, anything, but all she does is pull the money in.

It brings an unexpected smile to my face. That's a start.

"'Night, Jess." I back away from her door to go to my room.

I don't want to sleep, because I don't want to dream, so I sit by the window staring out over the wheat. I glance down to see Hammy doing the exact same thing.

Whatever's happening, it all leads back here. I have to finish the last harvest, before it's too late.

The first frost is coming.

I can feel it.

33

As I'm heading to school, I make a last-second turn onto Hammond Street. It feels like Old Blue knows where I'm going before I do—Oakmoor. I park a few blocks away in front of the Miller lumber yard and head over on foot. I don't want anyone knowing my business.

There's a couple of abandoned wheelchairs out front. A man sitting under a tree, rocking back and forth, while a nurse stands over him. The front of the building's painted yellow, which seems like it would be cheerful, but it looks more urine-stained than anything else. A little chime goes off as I open the cracked glass door.

"Be with you in a second, hon," Mrs. Gifford calls out. "I gotta go, it's Clay Tate," she whispers before hanging up. "Did you bring that precious girl with you?" she asks as she puts her dangly banana earring back on and peers over the counter.

"Nope. Just dropped her off at school."

"Well, she's a ray of sunshine," she says, as she unwraps a grape Jolly Rancher and pops it in her mouth. "The patients just love her. She works miracles with the hospice patients. Most kids would be afraid, but not Noodle. She holds their hands and sings that little song. She's our sweet angel around here, easin' them right on through to the other side."

"That's nice to hear."

She pats my hand. "What can I do for you, hon?"

"I came about Miss Granger—"

"Are you trying to make an appointment for *Jess* . . . or your *mom*?" She says their names, like they're dirty words.

"No . . . I just—"

"Oh, I'm sorry, that was plain rude. I just heard about what happened over at the *Harvest Festival* and. . . . never you mind."

"It's fine, I just—"

"Doesn't matter anyway. Emma hasn't been taking any appointments. Hasn't been in for months. Ever since she had her last appointment with *L.A.W.*" She whispers the letters.

"Law?" I ask. "What, with Sheriff Ely?"

"That'll be the day." She chuckles. "That man's as solid as a cement house. No, *Lee Aric Wiggins*," she says. "The boy with all the *burns*."

L.A.W. The same initials written in the margin of the family Bible . . . written all over the bank ledger. Could my dad have been giving money to that scumbag? For what? For meth?

"She'd been meeting with him every Saturday for the past year. They had no problems whatsoever, and then something happened.

She came out of the room like she'd just seen a ghost. She was real scared like. Kinda how you look right now, hon," she says, as she pushes the plastic candy dish over to me. "Here, have one. Just don't eat the grape, those are my favorite. And the next thing I know she's asking me for his birth certificate . . . acting real different. She even started scratching her head so hard it was bleeding. I thought maybe she was fixin' to call the sheriff, report him for something, but I never heard another word about it. Oh, did she send you for her things? I've been on her to pick up that box for months now."

"Yeah, if you don't mind." I force myself to meet her eyes. I feel terrible lying like this, but I'm desperate.

"You bet, hon. I just have to get it from the storage room. Would you mind answering the phone for me? If it's someone calling about Mr. Pinner, well, he died last night, I guess you best leave that to me. Back in a jiffy."

I hear her shoes squeaking against the linoleum and then disappear into the carpeting of the back offices. I hop around the counter and move the mouse around the screen. She's got a *Dr. Quinn, Medicine Woman* screen saver. Figures.

I scan through the files for patient records and pull up Emily Granger. Bam. Sure enough, Tyler was telling the truth. Checked herself in almost exactly two years ago. Self-pay. She was here a little under a year. PTSD. Religious ideology. Delusions of grandeur.

She's still not back, so I type in Lee Wiggins. Fetal Alcohol Syndrome. PTSD. Burn trauma. Claims father tried to kill him night of accident, but Devil saved him for higher calling. Prescribed: Lithium. Zoloft. Hydrocodone.

As soon as I hear Mrs. Giffords's squeaky soles hit the linoleum, I wipe the history and hop back over the counter.

"Is it hot in here?" she asks, as she sets the box on the counter.

"See, I'm a little chilly, but you're all sweated up. Hope I'm not coming down with something."

I inspect the box. "But this says Mrs. Wilkerson on the side."

"Oh, they belong to Emma now. Mrs. Wilkerson left her everything. The house, too. Lucky duck. Those Catholics sure stick together."

"She passed?"

"Last year. I think that's why Emma stayed with us so long. She didn't need to be here. She was smarter than Dr. Flannigan, that's for sure. I think she just needed a rest and she wanted to be here for her friend when the time came. It was an odd thing, though . . . how she died."

"What do you mean?"

"Emma was holding her hand, saying some kind of prayer in Catholic—"

"You mean Latin?"

"Sure, I guess, and Mrs. Wilkerson went all rigid. The look on her face was like something out of a nightmare. Like she just forgot the Thanksgiving turkey in the oven. And then she said something real funny . . . something about a blood creed or a creed of blood."

"Was it . . . 'I plead the blood'?"

"Yes! That was it." Mrs. Gifford puts her finger on the tip of her nose, like we're playing a game of charades.

It feels like all the blood is being drained from my body.

"They said it was a massive heart attack that made her lock up like that. That's why they couldn't do an open casket down at Newcomers. Her face was stuck like that."

"Like what?" I manage to ask.

"Like this." She opens her mouth as wide as it'll go, her eyes bulging, the tendons in her neck flaring.

It gives me the chills. That's the same look my dad had in the end. His same words. What does it mean? What's the connection?

The phone rings. She holds up a finger and takes off her earring.

"Oakmoor, this is Janelle, how can I help you?" she says in a sickening sweet voice, as I watch the hard candy bash against her teeth. "Oh, hold on a sec." She puts the receiver to her chest. "Listen to me jabbering on," she says. "You must be late for school. Want me to call over there and tell Miss Granger you're on the way?"

"No . . . no, I'm good," I say as I turn for the exit.

"Clay," she calls out. "The box?"

"Yeah," I murmur as I head back and grab it.

I think she says something else to me, but I can't hear anything over the buzzing in my ears, like the flies . . . like something terrible is about to happen.

34

I SIT in my truck for hours combing through the box. There's nothing of real interest, just a bunch of knickknacks and half-used toiletry items. But I can't stop staring at the photo of Mrs. Wilkerson. The Lucite cross around her throat. *I plead the blood* is usually said when praying over someone tormented by demons. I wonder if Mrs. Wilkerson was afraid of Miss Granger in the end, like my dad was afraid of me? And what's the connection between Miss Granger and Lee Wiggins? Why were his initials in our family Bible and all over our ledgers? If my dad was buying meth from Lee, would he seriously be recording it in the bank ledger? I thought going over to Oakmoor would give me the answers I was looking for, but I only ended up with more questions.

When I hear the bell ring for fifth period, I take the box and head over to Miss Granger's office. I keep my head low, moving through the crowd with precision.

Everything I need to say, everything I need to talk to her about has been building inside of me. I burst into her office without even knocking.

"I don't know what your deal is, but you need to come clean. You're ignoring my calls and something's going on . . . with you . . . with them . . . or with me . . . but the dreams are getting worse and—"

"Clay?" Miss Granger flashes a tense smile. "I believe you know Sheriff Ely and Deputy Tilford."

I follow her gaze to see Sheriff sitting in my chair, Deputy Tilford leaning against the back wall.

"What's this about a dream, Clay?" Sheriff asks.

"Nothing really." I clench the box to my chest.

His eyes flash like he's just caught me in a lie. "I was just telling Miss Granger here how surprised I was to see you at church on Sunday." He leans forward, the worn leather of his cowboy boots creaking. "Haven't been in over a year. Why the sudden religion?"

"Just trying to take your advice." I force a smile. "Put it all behind me." I can tell by the way he's looking at me that he knows something's up. I don't know how much longer I'll be able to hold him off.

"And now I hear you've been palling around with Tyler Neely and the rest of the Preservation Society kids. That's nice, I suppose." He puffs out his bottom lip like it's full of chew. "Ridin' bulls, huh?"

"Just blowing off a little steam."

"That's funny." His eyes narrow on me. "Tyler said the *exact* same thing to me this morning."

"Oh yeah?"

"It's a shame about what happened out there at the fairgrounds."

"Meanest bull in the tristate area. Worth a lot of money," Tilford adds.

"What're you talking about?"

"Haven't you heard?" Sheriff adjusts his hat. "Didn't your new buddies tell you? Someone went out there last night and slit that bull's throat."

"He's dead?" I whisper, feeling the floor buckle beneath me. *My dream.* I can't get that image of Tyler out of my head. *Look, I can make him kneel, too.* I humiliated him out there and he wanted to make me pay. I'm so angry, I can hardly breathe.

"Tyler said something strange happened out there in the ring. Said you put a knife to that bull's throat. Said you were having some kind of flashback."

"I cut the rope loose. That's all. Ask the others."

"Yep. They all backed up your story." Sheriff pinches the bridge of his nose. "But I'm thinking maybe you had unfinished business with that bull."

"You're thinking wrong." I feel a trickle of sweat running down my temple.

"Sheriff"—Deputy Tilford steps forward—"are you seriously going to listen to this—"

"So let me get this straight." Sheriff holds up his hand, signaling for Tilford to back off. "In the past few days you've joined the council, returned to church. Next thing I know you'll be suiting up again."

It gives me an idea. I know I said I'd never step on that field again, but Tyler's trying to set me up for all this and I'm not going down without a fight.

"As a matter of fact, I'm late for practice now," I say as I dump the box from Oakmoor on Miss Granger's desk. "Guess I'm full of surprises."

Miss Granger eyes the box on her desk, her thin eyebrows pulling together.

"Am I excused?" I look to her and then Sheriff Ely. "You wouldn't want to keep me from football, now would you?"

"'Course not." Sheriff seems mildly amused.

Deputy Tilford looks like he's about to blow a gasket. "But—"

Sheriff shakes him off.

Miss Granger gives me a quick nod as she twists the Lucite cross around her neck, but she can't keep her eyes off the box. Off the photo of Mrs. Wilkerson.

"Oh and Clay?" Sheriff Ely calls out. He's got a smile on his face, but I can feel his eyes digging into me like razor blades. "We'll be watching you out there."

35

I PACE the hall in front of the locker room a hundred times before I head in.

Yeah, I want to hit something. Tyler, in particular, and that scares me a little, but I'm smarter than that. I can go on that field and wipe his ass with it without ever touching a hair on his head. I can take it from him. Just like Mr. Neely said. From now on, I'm calling the shots.

Everyone's already on the field so I take my time putting on my gear. Can't believe they left my locker untouched, all my gear inside, like they knew I'd be back.

It feels strange lacing up again. Not strange in that it doesn't feel right. It feels *too* right. Like this last year never even happened. As much as I want to forget, I can't afford to do that. As much as it hurts, I've got to hang on to the past. It's the only thing keeping me grounded right now.

Heading out to the field, I half-expect to see my dad standing on the sidelines. His weathered face, cap pulled down tight over his wraparound shades. Most people had a hard time reading him. Not me. I knew when he was proud—chin raised, the way he clenched his jaw trying to hold back any kind of emotion. But when he had his chin lowered, teeth gritted, he was pissed, at me or the ball or the wind or Coach—but he never interfered. He wasn't one of those yellers, either, one of those dads who stood on the sidelines telling you what to do. He kept quiet, almost like he was praying. I guess this *was* his true church . . . mine, too. Hell, probably this entire town's.

Stepping out of the locker room, into the sun, feels euphoric. Like everything's moving in slow motion. The players stop the drills. The cheerleaders drop their pom-poms to their sides. I swear I can feel the turf cradle every step like it's been waiting for me all this time.

Ali smiles at me—the way I remember her—the way she remembers me.

I pull my helmet on for the first time in over a year, and I feel something rush through me, a sense of calm and assuredness, like nothing can touch me.

Ben beams the football at me and I don't even have to think about it. I reach out and snatch it out of the air. The feel of the ball thumping hard against my chest makes me feel . . . *alive*.

Coach's whistle pulls me back. "I was hoping I'd get a shot at you," he says, as he slams his hand down on my shoulder pad. He doesn't look much like a coach. Too clean-cut, like he's just been released from a toy package. *Texas*.

"Neely?" Coach yells at Tyler. "Go run some drills with Garrison."

"What?" Tyler yanks off his chin strap. "But I'm—"

"Don't argue with me." Coach shakes his head. "Your daddy promised me when the time came this wasn't going to be a problem."

Tyler looks toward his dad on the sidelines. Ian gives a stern thumbs-up.

"This is bullshit," Tyler says, as he stalks off the field.

I know it's immature, but I glance over to make sure Ali's watching. She is.

"Tate, you're QB one. Captain," Coach barks.

"But I haven't touched a ball in over a year."

"You just did, son." He shoves the ball back into my hands. "It's like riding a bike. I've seen your tapes. You were born to do this. I'll let you call it."

I stand there, stunned. I was ready to fight for it, to prove myself. It feels wrong to get it this way, but I can't get hung up on principle anymore. You can't win in this town if you play by the rules. If I want to figure out what's going on, stop this, I'm going to have to get my hands dirty. And nothing will put me in this town's good graces faster than bringing home a W. Always been that way, always will be.

As I take center field, I notice Sheriff and Miss Granger have come to watch. Seems like half the school's gathered around the fences now.

The guys huddle around me; I make eye contact with every single one of them, feeling my adrenaline spike, everything coming into sharp focus.

"I think this calls for a Miracle Whip special," Ben says with a wide grin before he puts in his mouth guard.

Ben and I have been running that play since Pee Wee. He might be Big Ben now, but he can run, too.

I nod. "Let's show 'em how it's done."

"Yeah!" the team hollers in response.

"On four." I call the play and everything goes from zero to sixty in a matter of seconds. Along with the beat of my heart thrumming in my ears, I hear cleats digging into turf, the shifting of pads, helmets crashing, grunts of determination as guys scramble for ground.

I dodge a tackle and pump my arm, searching for Ben. He's sailing down the field, hugging the right line. Just like we used to do it.

I let go of the ball. And I swear I can hear it sing as it leaves my hand, reverberate all the way up my arm, through my whole body.

Ben's already there. Waiting. Watching. We're in perfect synchronicity when his stance suddenly goes slack. He turns toward the fence. It looks like he's staring straight at Sheriff Ely and Miss Granger. The ball sails right over his head. Coach's whistle screams. People are laughing on the sidelines, jeering him, but still, Ben doesn't move.

I take off my helmet so I can figure out what the hell happened, when Ben slowly turns to me. I swear his eyes are black, pure black. I'm looking around to see if anyone else can see it when Ben starts stalking toward me like a dangerous animal.

Tyler jets out onto the field, trying to hold him back, talk some sense into him, but he seems hell bent on putting the hurt on me. Some of the players try and stop him, but he plows right through them like a freight train. I put my hands out in front of me, bracing myself for impact. "Ben . . . hey, Ben . . . I don't know what's going on, but let's talk about this. . . ."

He pounds into my shoulder. "It could be me," he screams. "I could be the one!"

I stagger back. He comes at me again and again like a charging bull. It takes six guys to get him off me. Finally Tyler grabs on to his helmet, forcing Ben to look him straight in the eyes. He whispers something and I see Ben's eyes go back to normal, his muscles start to relax.

Coach starts riding his whistle as he barrels through the crowd. "All right, all right, let's all cool off. This is football, boys, not a brawl!"

Ben's calm now. Just sitting on the ground, staring off into the woods as Tyler talks to him. I don't know what the hell just happened, what made him turn on me like that.

Noodle tromps onto the field, says something to Ben and then kicks him in the shin before running to meet me. "I gave him a piece of my mind."

"It can get a little heated out here," I tell her. "Nothing to worry about. Hey, how'd you get here?"

"Bobby Gillman said you were playing, so he walked me over. You're not mad, are you?"

"'Course not."

Tyler helps Ben to his feet and they head back in.

I look for Miss Granger. We really need to talk, but she's walking away with Sheriff.

As the crowd disperses, I see Lee Wiggins peering through the pines on the edge of the field, that sick smile stretched across his mangled excuse for a face.

Noodle waves.

"Why're you waving at him?"

"He looks sad," Noodle says. "And who knows? He might wave back."

When he does, I take her hand and we walk off the field together.

36

BETWEEN PRACTICE and the wheat, I'm bone weary by the time I head back to the house.

It's past bedtime, but Noodle's waiting for me at the front door in her Strawberry Shortcake pajamas.

I hold up three fingers, but she just grabs ahold of my hand, not even bothering with the sticker bag.

"Where is everybody?" I ask.

"Mom's . . ." She points to the living room. "And Jess's . . ."

The floor creaks above us, followed by a dragging sound. It sounds like she's rearranging her furniture or something emo like that. What happened at the Harvest Festival was seriously messed up, but I could sure use some help around here.

"I know three acres isn't much," I say as I take off my work boots. "But it's from the back parcel."

"That's tricky land back there. You did real good," she says as she tightens her lopsided pigtails.

I can't help but crack a smile. I swear, all I have to do is look at her sometimes and all the sorrow seems to dissolve like sugar left out in the summer rain.

"Ready for bed?" I swoop her up in my arms.

"But I have so much to tell you." She tugs on my ear. "I looked through the All Saints handbook and did you know nuns can ride bicycles and eat powdered donuts and they already knew my counting song and we did tongue twisters and . . . 'night, Mommy," she whispers as we pass the living room.

I stop and turn to see Mom's silhouette. She still hasn't moved from the couch . . . the flies.

Noodle doesn't even seem bothered by it, which makes it worse. This has become normal to her. Sometimes I wonder if Noodle even remembers what it was like before Dad's death. There's a heaviness hanging over the entire house now. Or maybe it's always been like this and I just never noticed it before.

"Why don't you go up and brush your teeth, hop in bed."

She gives my neck a hug and hops up the steps like a bunny.

As soon as I step into the living room, it feels like the atmosphere has changed. I sit next to Mom on the couch.

"I'm doing my best, but you have two girls who need you."

Her chin begins to quiver.

I reach out for her hand. It's cold.

"I don't know what to do . . . how to help you. Do you want me to call Dr. Perry?"

Her mouth contorts into a grimace as fresh tears spring to her eyes. "I hear them all the time now, the flies . . . it's like they're in my ears, like they're trying to tell me something."

"What do you think they're trying to tell you?" I ask.

"He's coming," she whispers. "He's coming for all of us."

AFTER I finally get Mom and Noodle settled down, I go to my room and pull out the family Bible, tracing the initials written in the margins of the family tree. L.A.W. There's definitely a connection, but I'm still not getting it. And what about his initials in the bank ledger? Did Dad know about Lee and Jess? Was he trying to pay him off, get rid of him? The longer I look at the words, the more they start to look like nonsense, just a jumble of letters and symbols. I'm so tired.

I only plan on closing my eyes for a second, but when I open them, everything's different.

I prop myself up on my elbows and peer out the windows. The garbage bags are gone and the sky is bloodred. "Not again," I whisper, hoping to snap out of whatever crazy shit is about to happen.

The door to my room opens, the light from the hall creating a hazy silhouette.

"Don't you dare fall asleep on me," Ali's soft voice beckons. She's wearing a Midland Pioneers jersey . . . and that's all. She walks over nice and slow, her long tan legs stretching out in front of her, like a dangerous animal on the prowl.

I let out a nervous laugh. "Fine, subconscious, lay it on me. This is one prophecy I wouldn't mind coming true."

Ali climbs onto my bed. There's just a thin sheet separating us. I run my hands from her ankles to the top of her thighs. She feels so real.

"Don't stop there." She smiles.

She leans over me, her long hair tickling my bare chest. I can see down the jersey. I can see everything. She raises my chin. With heavy lidded eyes, she kisses me. My hands move up her thighs.

"Blessed is the seed," she whispers, but it's not Ali's voice. I pull back to look at her face.

It's Miss Granger.

But I don't push her away or try to get free.

She smiles as she takes my hand. I'm trying to find the will to wake up, but the warmth, the way she's moving against me . . .

"Do it, Ben," she whispers.

Ben?

"Wake up, silly," Noodle says from the doorway. "He wants to show you something."

I wake with a jolt—my hand hanging over the side of the bed, Hammy licking my fingers.

"Oh, hell no." I jump out of bed. Hammy whimpers as he scoots out of the room.

What the hell's wrong with me? I look at the clock. It's only 2:00 A.M. and I'm sure as hell not going to sleep after that.

That was seriously messed up, but maybe it's my subconscious telling me it's time to talk to Miss Granger. She owes me that.

37

I PARK on her street, a few houses down, just to be safe. The last thing I need is people saying they saw me at her house in the middle of the night.

I knock on the door, soft, but insistent. When she finally cracks the door open, her cheeks are flushed, her hair's down. It takes me aback. I've never seen her with her hair down before. It's pretty.

As if reading my thoughts, she takes the elastic from her wrist and twists it up into the usual tight knot. "What are you doing here?" she whispers.

"We need to talk," I say as I barge past her.

"Clay, you can't—"

"I know you were a patient at Oakmoor. I know about Mrs. Wilkerson," I say as I pace her living room. "Guess who told me . . . *Tyler*."

"I'm sorry you had to find out that way, but coming to Midland, checking myself into Oakmoor was all a part of the plan. It was my way into the community."

"See, I knew you were going to say something like that."

"Because it's true."

"And Mrs. Wilkerson? Did you just forget to tell me she died just like my dad? The exact same words . . . the exact same expression."

"She had the sight like your dad . . . like you . . . but I'm not going to let that happen to you."

"What else are you hiding from me?"

I see her glance at the wall. There's a sheet tacked up over the photos and documents.

I rip it down to find Lee Wiggins's photo has replaced mine. My photo has been moved to the center of it all with SEED written beneath it.

"What is this?" I ask as I yank my photo down, staring at the word. "And what does Lee have to do with all this?" I drag my hand through my hair. "Are you in on this together? And this whole seed thing . . . is that something you just made up? Something you took from the Bible and twisted up in your sick little brain?"

"I'm sorry," she says as she takes the photo away from me. "But you can't be involved in this anymore."

"Why? Because I'm on to you now? Because I'm messing up your fantasy world?"

"There's been a disturbance at the church," she says as she tacks the sheet back in place, like she can't bear to look at it anymore. "I'm sorry, but the priests don't trust you anymore."

"That's a good one. Is that why this mysterious exorcism hasn't taken place?" I advance on her. She backs up against the wall, like she's afraid of me. "Did you get your kicks with that little video I took for you? Was that fun making me take my clothes off at the church?"

"Clay, this isn't a good time—"

"Maybe you're just some pedophile. Am I going to find all this on the Internet someday?" I take a deep breath. "If you're crazy, tell me now. I don't even care. I just need to know."

I hear a creaking noise coming from somewhere down the hall. I listen closely. It sounds like bedsprings.

"Is someone here?"

"I'm sorry, Clay, but I have . . . company." She crosses her arms over her chest, over the flimsy silk robe.

It takes me a minute to understand what she's saying. "*Company?*"

I back away from her and look around the room. The covered up wall. The candles lit on the coffee table. Two open beer bottles. A denim jacket hanging on the back of the chair.

"Like I said, it's not really a good time." She rewraps the silky robe tighter around her waist. The fabric clings to her body and I can tell she's not wearing anything underneath. I think about the dream, and I feel so dirty and confused. She looks up at me and for a split second I wonder if she knows what's going through my head.

She reaches out for me and I pull away.

"Just stay away from me. I'm done. Do you hear me? Done."

"Clay," she calls after me, but I don't look back. I can't.

38

I PARK front row, center. *Fuck Tyler Neely.*

Grabbing a work blanket from my truck, I head up to the scoring booth, the last safe haven I have. As I lie there staring at the cobwebs clinging to the damp corners, I try to clear my head. I try to remember what it was like before any of this happened. Before my dad went crazy—before the Devil supposedly came to town—but I'm drawing a blank.

I'm trying to make sense of all this, but I feel so stuck and confused.

Miss Granger tells me all this crap and then cuts me off. I mean, if this is so important to all of mankind, why's she having "company"? Why haven't they done the exorcism? I've given her every opportunity to come clean and she just keeps feeding me more bullshit. What does that even mean, "a disturbance at the church"? "The priests can't trust me anymore"? They never even said a word to me . . . not in English. Come to think of it, how the hell do I even know they were priests? I feel completely insane right now. A part of me thinks I should just check myself into Oakmoor and be done with it, but what if they're all just fucking with me? What if this is all some elaborate scheme to get me to lose it? Maybe that's exactly where they want me, where I can't get in the way. All I know is that I can't handle this on my own anymore.

I dig my phone out of my pocket and call Sheriff Ely before I have a chance to change my mind. There's no answer. I leave a message. "It's Clay. Clay Tate. We really need to talk. In person. If you get this, I'm at Midland High. On the field."

As soon as I hang up, I feel a sense of relief. I know I'll be exposing Miss Granger, exposing myself, but I need help with this.

I must've dozed off a little waiting for Sheriff to show or call back, because the next thing I know the sun's starting to rise. I have to get out of here before the groundskeepers start showing up. Don't want to add more fuel to the rumor mill around here.

I get up and stretch my arms above my head. As I stare out over the field, I catch a glimpse of a strange silhouette on the goal line, like something's floating between the goalposts.

I know I can get in deep shit for this, but I crank up the stadium lights. The deep hum of ten thousand volts of electricity permeates the air, but that's not what makes my hair stand on end.

Hovering between the goalposts is a person. I clench my eyes shut and open them again, hoping it's just another dream or a vision, but the wind blows in my direction carrying the sharp metallic scent of blood, and it hits me like a Mack truck. This is real.

I run down to the field and stumble toward the goal line.

The turf is damp, dark red seeping into my white socks, like slow-spreading poison. A dull dripping sound forces me to look up. There, strung up in a tangled mass of ropes, is Ben Gillman, wearing his uniform, blood dripping from his helmet, piss-stained pants, his black eyes bulging. With his arms suspended to his sides, his feet dangling over the metal bar, I have a flash of the reverend at the Hell House, the priests staring down at me from the altar at All Saints, the crucifixes lining Miss Granger's bedroom, my father walking into the wheat.

Ben Gillman looks like he's been crucified. A surge of bile races up my throat, my eyes are blurry with tears, but I can't unsee it.

Feeling dizzy, sick and powerless, I drop to my knees.

Someone puts their hand on my shoulder. I whip around to see the groundskeeper's face. "What's troubling you, son?"

Something's off. Something's very wrong. I focus in on him. His eyes are pure black, like endless pits of nothingness, just like the calf's . . . just like Jimmy's . . . and now Ben's.

I try to scream, but my tongue feels thick, like it's choking off my air supply. My head lolls back as a mass of gray static overtakes my consciousness and just like that . . . I'm gone.

39

I COME to, a mask over my mouth and nose, beeping noises and a strange jostling beneath me. I try to sit up, but something's holding me down—wide canvas straps.

"Hey, there, Clay." A doughy face comes into focus as the mask is slipped off my mouth. It's Larry Parker, former Midland High guard. Calls himself an EMT, but really he just answers the phone down at the courthouse and drives the meat wagon around town. "He's awake," Larry hollers over his shoulder.

"Wait!" I crane my head back toward the field. "Ben. What about Ben Gillman . . . that wasn't real, right?"

"'Fraid so," Larry says as he pulls up the gurney, locking it in place. "Shame. He was the only decent tight end we had."

"Well, look who finally decided to join us." Deputy Tilford leans over me with a smug look on his face.

"What's happening?" I ask, gripping the freezing metal bar next to my hand.

"I should be asking you the same question," he says.

"Excuse me . . . pardon me . . ." Miss Granger pushes through the crowd. She's got dark circles under her eyes. "I'm here, Clay."

Larry fumbles with the blood pressure cuff. "Hey there, Miss Granger."

"We need to get him off this field, to the hospital."

"I don't need to go to—"

Miss Granger cuts me off by resecuring the oxygen mask.

"No way." Deputy Tilford steps in front of the gurney. "Sheriff wants him close by for questioning. Besides, he probably just passed out. He's fine."

"What if he has a concussion? What if he's in shock?" Miss Granger asks.

"She's got a point," Larry says.

Greg glares at both of them. "Nearest hospital is an hour away. If I didn't know any better, I'd say you're trying to tamper with my witness."

Larry's looking around like he's not sure what to do next, sweat running through his curly mullet.

"How about this," Miss Granger says. "We take him to Midland Clinic, get him checked out, and then he's all yours. It's a ten-minute drive. You and Sheriff can come over as soon as you're done here. Better safe than sorry."

Larry's nodding like one of those demented bobbleheads. "That seems reasonable enough to me."

Greg gets right in Larry's face. "If he takes off—"

"I don't understand," Miss Granger interrupts. "Is Clay under arrest?"

"Not yet, but—"

"Then I suggest you back off and let Larry do his job."

Greg stands up straight as a cattail, like Miss Granger just threw a bucket of cold water in his face. But he steps out of the way.

"You're doing the right thing." Miss Granger pats Larry on the arm.

Larry cracks a dopey smile and then puffs out his chest as he pushes the gurney across the field, toward the ambulance.

I spot two men, dressed all in black, standing against the fence, like a strand of those spooky paper dolls Noodle makes out of crepe paper. They're dressed differently than they were before, none of that bling or weird hats, but I'd know their faces anywhere—the priests from All Saints.

Miss Granger gives them a tight nod as we pass.

Larry gets the gurney in the ambulance; Miss Granger climbs in with me.

"I'm just gonna phone ahead, tell them we're on our way," Larry says as he digs his cell phone out of his jacket and steps away.

I'm trying to say something, but it's muffled by the mask. Miss Granger pulls it away from my face. "Get me out of here," I gasp.

"That's exactly what I'm doing. This is our best option right now. Just stay calm." She tries to hold my hand, but I clench it into a fist.

"Stay calm?" I push against the straps. "Are you fucking serious?" Tears sting the corners of my eyes when I think about Ben strung up there for everyone to see. I want to kill someone, I'm so pissed. "I'm not even sure I believe you anymore . . . if any of this is real.

You said we could stop this. I did my part. What the hell have *you* done?"

"I'm sorry I didn't tell you about Oakmoor, or Mrs. Wilkerson, but this is very real. The second has fallen. Things are escalating a lot faster than I anticipated."

"Is that why the priests are here? Are they here to do the exorcism?"

"They're here because I needed them to see this with their own eyes. Ben's death was clearly a direct message to the church. They can't deny it now. This is exactly what we needed to happen in order to move forward with getting the exorcism sanctioned."

"So you were just waiting for another one of them to die?"

"A small sacrifice for the greater good."

"It's not small. These were my friends . . . people I grew up with."

"Small in comparison to what will happen if the Devil succeeds."

"All set," Larry says as he lumbers back in the ambulance. "It's getting nuts out there. They're still trying to figure out how to cut him down," he says as he resecures the oxygen mask. "Hang in there, bud."

As Larry goes to shut the door to the ambulance, I catch a glimpse of Sheriff Ely and Deputy Tilford in the distance. They're staring straight at me as the chaos swirls around them. They think I had something to do with this—with Jimmy, too. And they're not going to let this go.

40

I WANT to walk into the clinic on my own two feet, but Greg Tilford got inside Larry's head, made him all nervous that I might take off, like some kind of fugitive.

"As soon as I get you settled in a room, I'll take off the straps, but you can't leave until you've talked to Sheriff Ely and Dr. Perry gives the clear."

"Dr. Perry?" I ask. Miss Granger and I exchange a nervous glance. The last thing I need is someone from the Preservation Society in my face right now. "But he's a family practitioner. He doesn't even work at the clinic."

"He's the team doctor and you're back on the team now," Larry says, as he pulls the gurney out of the ambulance. "Only the best for our star quarterback. Enjoy it while it lasts." He flashes a crooked smile before he wheels me inside and goes off to figure out where I need to go.

"Noodle!" I blurt as I try to sit up. "I need to be there for her—"

"All taken care of." Miss Granger pushes me back down. "Ali went to check on them this morning. She'll get her to school."

"Okay, good." I let out a sigh of relief.

Larry comes back like an overeager hunting dog who's bit through the prey. "They've got you all set up in room two," he says as he wheels me down the hall. "Dr. Perry should be here any minute."

As he finally takes off the straps and transfers me to the examining table, Larry clears his throat. "Miss . . . I mean, Emma . . . I was thinking you might want to go to the Sizzler with me on Friday night before the game. All you can eat. I'd love to help you put some meat on your bones."

"Really?" I sigh.

Miss Granger flashes a controlled smile.

"That's lovely, Larry, but I have mass on Friday nights." She twists the Lucite cross around her neck. "I'm Catholic, very devout. You'd have to convert."

He stands there for a good ten seconds, like he's seriously considering it. "Maybe another time," he murmurs, before hunching over the gurney and leaving the room.

As soon as Miss Granger closes the door, I say, "I don't know what to do. Deputy Tilford is all over me. He's going to be a problem. And Sheriff . . . I called him last night . . . told him to meet me at the field."

"Why would you do that?" She turns on me.

"I . . . I needed someone to talk to."

"Believe me, or don't believe me, it makes no difference, but no good will come of you getting yourself locked up in Oakmoor.

You'll be trapped inside while your friends die around you. While *Ali* dies. Is that what you want?"

"I don't want any of this. But if the prophecy thing is true . . . if I'm the sixth, they need me for something. Maybe it's better for everyone if I'm locked away until this blows over."

"Unless it's not *you*," she says with a pointed stare.

"Clay Tate," Dr. Perry says as he saunters into the room, wearing his golf clothes. He barely acknowledges Miss Granger as he thumbs through a bunch of papers on his clipboard, which is weird because I saw him talking to her at the Harvest Festival the other night.

"Heard you had a bit of a shock this morning."

"Ben died," I say through gritted teeth.

"I heard." He blows on his stethoscope. "Teen suicide is a serious matter. You'll let me know if you're feeling depressed, won't you, Clay?" he says, a little too chipper, as he checks my heart. "'Cause I can give you something for that."

I hold Miss Granger's gaze. What did she mean, *unless it's not you*?

"But why would you be feeling down?" He says, as he checks my reflexes. "You've got the tiger by the tail, huh, QB?"

QB—just hearing him say it makes my blood pressure spike.

"Don't worry, this shouldn't affect your game on Friday."

"Wait . . . they're not canceling the game?"

"It's tragic, but life goes on. *Football* goes on. Ben would want that. You need to give this town something to believe in . . . something to celebrate. And give *yourself* something to celebrate, too. I don't know what your love life's like, but that might be just what the doctor ordered," he says with a wink.

Sheriff Ely barges in and Dr. Perry lets out a heavy sigh. "We're in the middle of a medical exam, Ely."

"He won't mind, will you Clay?" He gives me that easy grin, but his eyes are blazing.

I stare down at my feet, at the blood-stained socks from the field, and I start feeling dizzy again.

"I just need a few minutes with him and then I'll get out of your hair." Sheriff Ely leans against the wall.

They're all staring at me, waiting for a response. I just nod; that seems to be enough.

"We'll be right outside," Miss Granger says as she steps into the hall.

Dr. Perry follows. "Five minutes, Ely," he says as he shuts the door behind him.

"I came as soon as I got your message," Sheriff says in a hushed voice. "You need to tell me what the hell's going on, because this doesn't look good, Clay."

A part of me still wants to spill my guts, but Miss Granger's right. She may be lying about a hundred other things, but if I'm locked up, I'll never be able to discover the truth. Sure, there's a chance Ely might believe me, even help me, but I can't take that chance. Protecting my family, protecting Ali, is the most important thing right now.

"I don't remember anything."

"If it were up to Tilford, you'd be locked up right now." Sheriff narrows his eyes. "Talk to me, Clay. I know when someone's hiding something from me."

"Look . . ." I wipe my sweaty palms against my jeans. "There are bigger things going on here. Bigger than you and me."

"That's strange." The right side of his mouth twitches. "That's the same thing the Wiggins kid said to me when we pulled him out of the flames. You know, their trailer blew up hours before your dad went to the breeding barn that night. Even so, Lee told us what your dad was going to do. Told us it was too late, that the Devil was coming for him. Coming for all of us. That we needed to prepare for his coming and rejoice in the blood of the golden calf."

I try to stay expressionless, but I can feel the blood drain from my face. How the hell would Lee Wiggins know about any of that?

"Does that mean anything to you, Clay?" Sheriff Ely digs.

I shake my head, but I can't meet his eyes.

"You came over to my house in the middle of the night, talking about cows and blood and the Preservation Society. You said you ran over a calf with the combine and I got to thinking . . . maybe all of this is connected somehow. Is that why Jess is hanging around with the Wiggins kid out in the woods behind Merritt's? Are you in this together?"

"I don't know where you're getting your information, but you're dead wrong. Jess isn't hanging around him anymore."

"You sure about that?" Ely says. " 'Cause I just saw them together on Sunday night."

"Jess's been home in bed since the Harvest Festival."

"No offense"—Sheriff adjusts his hat—"but I'm not the one who's been seeing things, now am I?"

I shift my weight and the paper crinkles beneath me.

"You know, you can talk to me." Sheriff softens his tone. "I can help you through this, no matter what it is. I was always there for your dad."

"And look what happened to him," I say as I look out the dingy window, at an old man putting flyers on people's cars.

I hear Sheriff take in a deep breath through his nose. "I watched the tape from the field, Clay."

I look at him sharply.

"You didn't think Neely'd be keeping an eye on his precious new stadium? You pull in at 3:18 and head up to the scoring booth."

"I didn't break in . . . I have a key."

"3:24 you call, telling me we need to talk. 3:46 Ben Gillman climbs the goalpost and strings up the ropes. It took twenty-two men to figure out how to get him down. The ropes were strategic . . . almost like a puzzle. One wrong knot, one wrong length of rope and none of it would've worked. Ben Gillman was tough as nails, but not the sharpest. Now, you on the other hand could figure something like that out. You aced geometry, right?"

I try to force some words, even a grunt, but nothing comes out.

"Now, the whole time Ben's doing all this, he's staring up at the stands, crying. It's almost like someone's giving him instructions. The rope around his neck was so tight, it cut right through his skin, right through his artery. His body's jerking around, there's blood spurting everywhere, but you're asleep. And then two hours later, you run onto the field acting like you're in shock, like it's the first time you've seen him."

"It was . . . I did . . . because it's true. I had no idea. I must've fallen asleep."

"Don't you think it's *awfully* suspicious that you're the one to discover two bodies in the past week?"

I let out a ragged breath. "What . . . you think they called me up, told me when and where they were going to kill themselves, and I decided to watch?"

"Or maybe you're the one making them do it."

"I got here as soon as I could," Ali says as she enters the room. "Oh, I'm sorry. Dr. Perry said I could come in."

I've never been happier to see someone in my entire life. "Is Noodle okay?"

"She's great. I went by your house, took care of your mom, talked to Jess for a bit, and made Noodle breakfast, took her to school. Oh, and I brought you a change of clothes," she says as she places the bag in my hands. "I heard what happened at the field," she says to Sheriff. "It's so awful. Poor Ben. Poor you." She hugs me.

Sheriff clears his throat, but Ali still doesn't let go.

"When you're ready to talk," he says as he heads for the door, "well, you know where to find me."

41

I TAKE my time in the shower, getting dressed. Classic stalling move and for once it seems to work. The only person waiting for me is Ali.

"You look nice," she says as she inspects my collar and then loops her arm around mine. These are the clothes she picked out—a pair of khakis, a plaid button-down with a white T-shirt underneath, and some tennis shoes. It's strange thinking about Ali being in my house this morning. Can't imagine what she must be thinking with Jess barricaded in her room like that, and my mom with the flies, but that's the least of my worries right now. Jimmy's gone, Ben's gone, and all I can think is, who's next?

We walk outside and I can't believe how dark it is. It's not even noon, but the sun's being blocked by a slab of wet cement-colored clouds. The air is stagnant, too, like everyone's holding their breath. Or maybe it's just me.

"Can you take me to my truck?" I ask.

"Sure." Ali nods toward her mom's Cadillac. "Come on."

"Man," I say as I settle in the front seat. "I haven't ridden in this car in so long."

"Remember how we used to sit in the back and blow spit wads at everyone?" she says as she eases out of the lot.

"Yeah." I smile at the memory. "Your mom would get so mad at us."

And for a split second, I forget about everything. It's just me and Ali and nothing but open road. But as we approach the school, everything starts to narrow. I can feel reality crushing back down on me.

"Looks like the lot's still taped off," Ali says as she slows down. "But Sheriff's here. Do you want to see if they'll let you take your truck—"

"No," I blurt a little too forcefully. "I mean . . . no. It's fine. I can wait."

She pulls over on the side of the road, directly across from the school.

"At least they had the decency to cancel class for the day, put the flag at half-mast. It's more than Jimmy ever got. And look at all the flowers and teddy bears lined up against the fence. It's so sad," Ali says.

I try to keep my eyes off the field, the goalpost, but I can't help myself.

"I was in the booth when it happened." I nod at the field. "I was fifty feet away from him. I could've stopped him."

"You can't stop someone from killing themselves," Ali says

matter-of-factly. "Remember my Uncle Ricky? Sure, my mom stopped him a few times, but eventually he got his way."

"But what if there's more to it than that? What if Sheriff's right? What if I'm the one who made him do it? Jimmy, too. Is it possible that I could be doing all this and not even know it?"

"No way." She gives me a lopsided smile. "He's just trying to rattle you. I know you, Clay. You couldn't hurt a fly."

"We all know that's not true." I lean my head against the cool glass, staring at the field.

"If you're talking about what happened at homecoming last year, that doesn't count. Football is a violent sport. Everyone knows that. You're supposed to tackle each other . . . that's the whole point."

"Not like that." I run my fingers over my knuckles. "I was out of line. Excessive force."

"Which is perfectly understandable. Your dad just died," she says as she turns toward me. "Look, I want to smash my pom-poms into Julie Harron's face almost every day at practice."

I crack a smile. "But you don't."

"And neither do you, Clay. People make mistakes. When I look at you, I see the same boy who used to make his dad stop the car so he could help a frog cross the road. And you put up with Dale, which basically makes you a saint. If you don't trust yourself, trust me. I've known you your whole life and you're gentle and good."

"That's what Noodle says, too."

"Well, then it's true. Noodle's the wisest person I know. And for the record, she told me she thinks we should get married."

"Oh God. I'm sorry." I feel my cheeks go up in flames.

"Mostly for my pancake-making skills, but I can live with that."

The maintenance guys step on the field, their arms piled high with fresh sod. I don't know why it surprises me. They're going to cut out the sections soaked in Ben's blood and replace it . . . just like that. Like it never even happened.

"What is it, Clay?" Ali reaches out for my hand. There's nothing I want more than to feel the warmth of her touch, but I pull away, clenching my hand into a fist.

"There's something happening here in Midland. Something I can't explain."

"I feel it, too." She leans back in her seat, curling up her legs. "Like Jimmy and how he acted at the Harvest Festival."

"And Ben, the way he turned on me at practice."

"Then there's Tyler." Ali twists the small gold signet ring on her finger. "He's been acting really strange."

"Strange how?"

She pulls her hair to the side; it falls across her face, like a veil between us. "Last weekend at the game, I told him I didn't want to be boyfriend-girlfriend, that I didn't think of him that way. He said something nasty and when I reached out for his arm to tell him I was sorry, he jerked away, popping me in the mouth. It was an accident," she says as she peeks over at me. "But you weren't there."

"What do you mean?"

"I can think back on every terrible thing that's happened to me and you've always been there, making me feel like everything's going to be okay."

I swallow hard, remembering picking her up in my arms in the alleyway that night. "What happened after that?"

"I guess I passed out. Miss Granger took me back to her house, took care of me, but I had the strangest feeling, like you were there. I guess I just wanted you to be there, but I swear, I could even smell you."

"Is my smell that distinct?" I let out a laugh.

"Yeah, it is actually. It's not a bad thing." She gives a slight one-shoulder shrug, tucking her hair behind her ear. "This time of year . . . you smell like dried grains, sweet and kind of powdery. You also smell like diesel and freshly turned soil. And that lotion you use on your hands, the one that smells like rosemary."

"It's not lotion-lotion," I explain. "It's for calluses."

"Fine." She shakes her head. "All I'm saying is, I like it."

I try not to smile like an idiot, but I can't help it. Ali Miller likes the way I smell.

"But Tyler," she says, knotting the string on her sweatpants. "He seems to be getting worse. And that whole thing with the bull . . . it's like he's obsessed with you."

I know I should tread lightly here, but I feel like I can trust her. "This is going to sound insane." I drag my hands through my hair. "But I think Tyler killed that bull. I even dreamt about it. I think he's trying to set me up . . . he's trying to make me look crazy."

"What does Miss Granger think?"

"That's a whole other story." I lean forward, pressing my head into my hands.

"I thought so," she says quietly.

"You thought what?"

"You and Miss Granger."

"No. No . . . it's nothing like that." I turn toward her.

"She's pretty." Ali purses her lips. "And I know she really cares about you."

"Not the way you think."

"Then what is it?" She looks into my eyes. "You can tell me, Clay. Nothing you say will shock me or make me stop talking to you. I did that once before, for the Preservation Society, and it was the worst year of my life."

I look at her and think, what do I have to lose? Maybe she can help me figure this out.

"Miss Granger . . ." I let out a shaky breath. "She thinks I'm some kind of prophet."

"A prophet?" Ali's forehead crinkles up.

"Yeah." I raise my brows. "Like a bona fide spooky religious fortune-telling prophet . . . like from the Bible."

"Okay." She takes a deep breath. "Because of the things you see? The calf . . . the cow ritual thing?" she asks.

"Yeah, but I'm thinking they're probably just nightmares . . . really vivid nightmares."

"Or maybe she's right? You can't deny strange things have been going on around you."

"But that's not all. She also believes we're evil. You, me, Tyler, Tammy, Ben, and Jimmy. That we've been marked for the Devil in some kind of doomsday prophecy."

"Why would she think that? Why us?"

"I think it has to do with the Preservation Society . . . the sixth generation . . . and the mark."

"But you don't even have one . . . do you?" she asks.

"No." I shake my head. "Apparently, I've been able to resist, because I'm a prophet."

She runs her fingers over the back of her neck, like she might actually be buying into this.

"You're not evil, Ali." I take her hand. "I might be completely crazy, but I know that much is true."

"And you're not crazy, Clay. I won't let you be."

Reverend Devers walks past the car, up to the fence. He's got his suit on, the one from Sears, and he kneels down, right in the middle of the sidewalk, and starts praying. A couple of assholes honk as they

drive by, but it doesn't seem to bother him. And it gets me thinking about the priests from All Saints. Miss Granger said something
about a disturbance at the church that made them not trust me anymore. And there was something so odd about the way they were
dressed today . . . almost like they were in disguise.

"Do priests have different outfits?" I ask. "Catholic priests?"

"I'm not sure, but I think they're pretty strict about that. Why?"

"There's somewhere I need to go . . . something I need to check
on, but it's all the way in Murpheyville. If it's too far, I can—"

"I thought you'd never ask," she says with a smile as we pull away.

The farther we get from town, the lighter I feel. Maybe it's Ali,
or the relief of seeing Midland in the rearview mirror, but by the
time we cross the county line, I tell her everything. All about the
dreams. Miss Granger. My Catholic baptism. Sheriff Ely. Lee Wiggins. Tyler and the Preservation Society. The worries I have about my
mom and Jess and Noodle. I tell her everything that's in my heart.
Almost everything.

I don't think I've talked this much in my entire life. And she just
listens and holds my hand and tells me everything's going to be
okay. And by some miracle, I believe her.

42

ALI AND I walk hand in hand up the steps to the church. I open the door and step inside, but Ali doesn't move.

"Don't you have to invite me in?" she teases. "Since I'm possessed by the Devil and all."

It makes me laugh. "Fine. Miss Alison Margaret Miller, won't you please come in?"

"Why thank you, Clay Riley Tate." She takes my hand and we walk down the long grim aisle.

"This is it." I point to the altar with the baptismal font. "They were standing right up there."

"But they never spoke to you?" Ali asks.

"Not directly . . . not in English."

"So they could've been saying anything. They could've been talking about their grocery list."

"Yeah, I guess so." I laugh. "And this is where I had to put on the robe." I point to the screen.

Ali ducks behind it. "Very scandalous," she says as she peeks her head out. "What was it like?"

"Creepy."

"Did the priests give you the pin, or did Miss Granger?"

"She did, but only when we were outside."

"So you stood *here*?" She plants herself directly in front of the altar.

I nod, circling around her, watching the tiniest beam of sunlight filtering in through the stained glass, bending to her face.

"And then what happened?" she asks.

"They asked me to disrobe."

"Miss Granger asked you to disrobe," she clarifies, as she steps up on the altar.

"Yeah." I nod. "I closed my eyes and they splashed holy water on my skin."

"Like this?" She dips her fingers in the baptismal font and flicks me with the water. "Oh no! My hand . . . it's burning," she cries.

I rush over to the edge of the altar, taking her hands in mine.

She starts cracking up. "I'm just kidding, Clay. See, the holy water has no effect on me."

"Very funny." I swing her down from the altar. When I put her down we're standing so close to each other, but neither one of us moves.

And just like that, I'm back to when we were kids again. The first time I thought about kissing her I was ten years old. We'd just seen

Crouching Tiger, Hidden Dragon on TV and we were doing all these karate moves in the woods. She got her foot stuck in a rotted-out log and lost her balance, falling over in the mud. And when I reached in to pull her out, she had mud all over her face, in her hair, but I think that's the first time I ever thought, wow, she's really beautiful.

And when her cat Mittens died, I made him a box. We had a funeral for him and everything. I didn't say much, just how I liked him and how I was going to miss him. Ali leaned into me, and I swear I felt her lips brush my arm. Maybe it was just her chin or her nose, but in my mind, it was her lips, and I kept thinking what if she kissed me and I didn't even know it. Like a secret kiss. So later that year, when we slow danced at the Preservation Society for Cotillion, I kissed her hair. I don't know if she felt it, but when the dance was over, she smiled up at me like maybe she knew and she didn't really mind.

But the one moment that sticks in my mind the most is the pep rally, ninth grade. She ran out of the gym in tears because she fell off the top of the pyramid and flashed the entire school. Even though the guys were razzing me, I took off after her. I pulled her in for a hug, and when she hugged me back, something happened. It wasn't a lightning bolt of lust making me want to rip her clothes off, like something from one of Mrs. Harrison's smutty romance novels—it was the exact opposite. I wanted to cover her up in my arms and protect her from all that. I didn't want to let go. But from that moment on, I couldn't stop thinking about her.

I thought about her when I was doing farmwork, wondering what her chores were like. I thought about her when I was eating dinner, wondering what she was having. I thought about her during class, wondering what college we'd go to, how I'd propose. I even wondered what kind of house I was going to buy her when I went pro. I had it all planned out, and yet, I never said a word. Never made a move.

And then I didn't talk to her for an entire year, so of course she moved on, or at least she tried, which is more than I can say for myself. I was so hung up on the past that I didn't know how to move forward. I had a certain life, a certain version of myself that I wanted to give to her, and when that all went up in smoke, I didn't feel like I was worthy of her anymore. And maybe I'm still not, but it was selfish and cowardly to take that choice away from her. I see that now.

"I'm sorry . . . for everything," I say, placing my hand on her cheek.

"I'm not." She leans into my touch. "It brought you back to me."

The warmth from her skin radiates up my arm, through my body, where it seems to get lodged in my throat.

And in that moment, standing at the altar, it's more than our past, present, and future drawing me in. More than need or attraction. It feels like the hand of God is pushing me toward her.

I take her face in my hands and kiss her. Really kiss her. The kind of kiss you dream about your whole life.

"The chapel is closed," a nun says sternly from the doorway.

Ali and I take a step away from each other and a tiny revolt goes off inside my body. "The door was open," I reply, an embarrassed flush spreading across my cheeks.

"If you're here to look at the church for your wedding, you'll have to go through premarital screening with Father Mercer first."

Ali smiles up at me.

I clear my throat. "I was here the other day. My little sister Noodle . . . er, Natalie Tate, she's enrolled for next year. She came for a tour."

"I know. Did you forget something?"

"No." I shake my head. "I actually came to see about the priests I met that day. An archbishop and a cardinal?"

She purses her lips tight. "We haven't had a visit from the archbishop in ages and certainly never a cardinal."

"But I was here . . . with Miss Granger."

"Poor soul." She makes the sign of the cross. "She's very devout. A good Catholic, but her mind is addled. Those afflicted with maladies of the brain, we must pray for them."

"The priests," I whisper to Ali. "What if it never happened? What if it was all in my head?"

"Come on, Clay." Ali takes my hand, pulling me toward the exit.

I feel the nun's eyes digging into me as I pass. Judging me.

As soon as we get outside, I lean over, bracing my hands against my knees. "If the priests weren't real . . . if I'm seeing things in that much detail, I must be crazy . . . just like Miss Granger."

"We're going to figure this out. I promise," Ali says, rubbing my back. "You have me now. I can tell you what's real."

I try to take a few deep breaths, but it feels like my lungs are already full to capacity. "I feel like I might pass out," I manage to say.

"You're okay. Just breathe." Ali leans me up against a statue. "Just stay here. Let me get the car," she says, as she runs into the parking lot.

I hear the jingling of keys behind me and turn to see the nun locking up the chapel.

I remember there were other people around that day. Witnesses. I know I'm grasping, but there's a lot at stake here. Maybe she doesn't know about the priests' visit because the meeting was a secret.

"The nuns I met the other day . . . a Sister Agnes . . . Sister Grace," I say as I straighten up, trying to act normal. "Is there any way I can talk to them?"

"I'm afraid that's quite impossible," she says, her grim mouth stretching into a pleasant line.

"Why?"

"Because they cut out their own tongues right after you left. And do you know what they said before they put blade to flesh? *Ego causam civitatium sanguine.*"

"I plead the blood," I whisper.

She smiles. "Very good, Clay."

"How . . . how do you know my name?" I murmur as I back away from her.

She watches me and I swear her eyes are pure black. I clench my eyes shut and when I open them again, the nun is gone. Vanished.

I stagger back into the parking lot, into screeching tires as I hit the hood of Ali's car.

"Clay!" Ali jumps out of the car.

"I'm fine . . . I'm fine," I say as I get into the passenger seat. "Let's just get out of here."

As we pull away, I stare at the church. I'm not sure what I'm looking for . . . if what happened was even real. But Miss Granger said there was a disturbance at the church. Something that made the priests not trust me anymore. Could I have made the nuns do it . . . cut out their own tongues?

Maybe I'm the evil one and I just don't know it.

43

I TRY not to look at the wheat as I pull in the drive. I should've finished the harvest days ago, but I haven't made much headway. It doesn't even seem to matter how much time I spend out there, I just keep going over the same patterns, again and again. And ever since that dream about the bull, when I woke up on the combine while it was still moving, I've been afraid of the wheat . . . or the combine . . . or maybe I'm just afraid of myself.

Ali thinks I just need sleep. Maybe she's right. I hope to God she's right, because the alternative is too awful to think about.

I look at myself in the rearview mirror and slap my cheeks before I head in the house. I might be mentally, physically, and emotionally exhausted, but I'm not about to let Noodle see that.

As soon as I open the front door, Noodle comes crashing into me.

I feel her stomach grumble against my leg. "Hungry?"

Noodle nods, but doesn't let go of my leg.

I walk to the kitchen stiff-legged like Frankenstein, dragging her along with me. She starts giggling.

"We've got pancakes," Noodle says, as she takes a seat at the table right in front of a full plate.

"Are these still here from breakfast?" I flick the top one. It's as hard as a rock.

I check the refrigerator. It's practically empty. Pickles, some condiments, and brown lettuce. I told Mom I didn't want her waiting on me for supper, but I didn't mean for her to stop making supper altogether. "This isn't right." I start to head into the living room to confront her, when Noodle puts her hand in mine. "Pancakes are good. Ali made 'em. Don't worry. They'll soften up with syrup."

I look down at her and my heart melts. She doesn't want a fight. And to be honest, neither do I. I'll have to deal with Mom later.

"You're right," I say.

A huge smile takes over her face as she pulls me back to the table.

Noodle thumbs through the stack, picking out the best one and putting it on a separate plate. "For Jess." She grins and licks her lips as she drowns the rest of them in syrup.

I grab two forks. The silverware drawer is practically empty. The mail's piled up. The whole house is depressing, like there's a dark cloud hanging over everything. "Hey, you want to work the fields with me tomorrow after school?" I ask. "I'm having a hard time finishing the front parcel."

"You bet." Her eyes light up.

The sugar seems to go straight to her brain because after a few bites, Noodle starts talking a mile a minute.

With Jess barricaded in her room and Mom in one of her

spells, Noodle's starved for attention, probably been on her own all day.

I feel a little guilty for kicking her one playmate under her bed. Maybe I should help her find it. "I notice you haven't been carrying around that baby doll lately."

Noodle shrugs. "She's busy."

"Oh, yeah?" I try not to laugh. "Busy with what?"

I push the last bite toward Noodle. She crams it into her mouth. "Helping Jess."

"Well, tell her good luck with that."

Hammy comes in the dog door all muddy and gross. Noodle holds down her plate so he can lick up the last bits and then he leaves again.

"Who needs a dishwasher with Hammy around." She hands me the plate.

I take it to the sink, washing it with soap. I spot Hammy out the kitchen window, pacing the wheat again.

"That dog. I swear. What do you think he does out there all day and night?"

"He's busy, too."

"Is he helping Jess as well?" I chuckle.

"No, silly. He's guarding."

"Making sure nothing bad gets in?"

"Making sure nothing bad gets *out*," she says.

I drop the plate in the sink.

I look back at Noodle; she lets out a big yawn, accidentally wiping syrup across her face. Sugar crash.

"Let's get you to bed," I say as I grab the plate for Jess and lead Noodle upstairs to get cleaned up. I run a bath for her and wait outside the door. Ever since Dad died, she wants to bathe herself . . .

dress herself . . . she even cuts her own bangs. Won't let anybody brush out her hair or fix it. That's why she's always got those lopsided pigtails. I guess she's growing up, but not too much, because she's still splashing around, singing her counting song.

She comes out of the bathroom in her nightgown, all pink and shiny. "But I'm not tired," she says as she lets out another giant yawn.

"I know, but I need you to be rested for tomorrow. You've got to be alert on the combine."

"Let's meet in our dreams," she says as she snuggles in. "That way you won't get lonely."

"Always," I whisper.

When I'm done tucking Noodle in, I take the plate to Jess's room. "Jess?" I tap lightly. "I brought you something to eat."

I see a shadow move under her door, hear the shuffling of feet, and then silence.

"Did you have a good talk with Ali today? She said she could come over anytime, or you could go over there . . . whatever you need."

Still nothing.

"I should tell you . . ." I lower my voice. "Mom's not doing so good. It's not like usual. This is something different. She's not talking about Dad . . . she's not talking about anything. All she does is sit and stare at the flies. I'm thinking maybe something died in the wall . . . a mouse . . . I don't know. All I know is that without you around to keep us all in check, things have gotten out of hand. We could use a dose of reality around here."

I listen for a laugh—any kind of reaction—but all I hear is her heavy breath.

"What I said to you the other day, or didn't say . . . that was wrong. It's not too late for you . . . to make something of your life."

I swallow hard and press my palm against her door. "I'm sorry if I made you feel like you're not important. It's been a tough year for all of us. But I'm going to be better. We all need to be better."

I set down the plate in front of her door.

I'm walking toward the stairs when I hear her door creak open. I turn just in time to see the plate slide into her room and the door slam shut again.

She's going to be okay. Jess is a tough girl. I just need to show her that I'm going to step up and lead this family.

It gives me the courage I need to face Mom. Enabling her isn't helping anyone.

I turn on the light in the living room. Mom doesn't even flinch. She's sitting in the same position she was in yesterday. She looks awful, dark bags under her bloodshot eyes, but I've let this go on long enough.

"L.A.W.," I say, watching her spine stiffen. "Why was Dad giving money to Lee Aric Wiggins?"

She clenches her jaw. "Don't say that name in this house."

Normally, that would be enough to shut me down, but I need answers. "It's time," I say as I crouch in front of her, forcing her to look at me.

Her chin begins to quiver, her eyes clouding up with tears. "We're cursed," she whispers. "Your dad was going to take care of it. He was going to fix it. And now, every time I see him, the burns, it reminds me of the shame he brought on this family . . . but something's happening."

"What is it? Tell me."

"Shh . . . ," she whispers, as she peers over my shoulder, so she can get a better view.

246

"This has to stop," I say as I snatch the flyswatter hanging from the nail in the kitchen. "This whole fly business is over."

As I haul back the swatter, Mom jumps up from the couch and grabs on to my arm, but I don't let her stop me this time. I shake her off, hauling back again and again, killing them without mercy. There must be fifty of them now. They don't even move. They don't try to get away. It's almost like they're asking for it.

When I'm finished, I drop the swatter and turn to find her crumpled up on the ground, her shoulders shaking. I feel a stab of guilt when I realize what I've done . . . what this place is doing to all of us.

"Mom, I'm sorry," I say as I go to help her up.

She peers up at me through her disheveled hair. At first I think she's crying, but she's laughing, her face contorted with madness. "I can still hear them," she whispers. "He's coming. He's coming for all of us. We're all going to die."

I'M SO exhausted, I don't even try getting Mom in bed this time.

When I get back to my room, my phone is vibrating. It's a text from Ali.

I've been thinking about the prophecy thing. Miss G has it all wrong, but I think I know the source. It's from an old book in the council archives at PS.

Can you show it to me?

Sure. Anytime. ;)

Now?

Too risky. How about tomorrow? We'll have the whole place to ourselves. After practice. Meet in parking lot?

K.

This is going to sound weird, but I had fun today.

I let out an unexpected laugh. *Definitely weird, but me, too.*

It vibrates again, but it's just Dale calling for the millionth time. One of the things I always liked about him was that he never treated me any different after what happened with my dad, but I don't think I can stand hearing him talk about Ben, or not talking about him. Probably best to avoid him for now with everything that's going on. He's my second cousin and the last thing I want to do is hurt his feelings.

I turn off the phone and pull out the family Bible. I know my dad wasn't in his right mind at the end, but why would he write Lee's initials on such an important family document? And why was he giving him money? I'm sure as hell not going to get any straight answers out of my mom, not in her condition, which leaves me with only one option. I could hang around Merritt's, wait for him to find me, or I could go straight to the source. I know where he deals. I know where he lives. He probably doesn't think I have the balls to go out there, but he's dead wrong.

44

JESS STAYED scarce again this morning—wasn't begging me for a ride. I think about barging in her room to give her a pep talk, tell her to get back on the horse and all that crap, like Dad used to do, but maybe she just needs a few more days to herself before she goes back to school. And if I'm being honest, I'm not ready to deal with it either.

I could use some cheering up, so I take Noodle to school instead.

"Did you see the plane?" Noodle asks.

I look up in the sky.

"Not here, silly. Over the farm."

"What, Mr. Wilson's crop duster?"

"Smaller than that."

"Like one of those drones?"

Noodle shrugs and then tightens her pigtails. "Passed by the crops six times this morning."

"Is that so?" I say as I turn onto Main Street. Sounds like something a Neely would do. Ian or Tyler. Wouldn't put it past either one of them to be spying on me.

"Got lots of rest last night," she says as we pull into the carpool line. "Just like you said, so I'll be ready for the combine."

"See you, squirt." I give her my best "don't worry, Satan's not coming to town" smile and head off to grab some groceries before school.

I don't go to Piggly Wiggly. I figure I can grab some basics out at the store by the junkyard before I pay Lee a visit. Kill two birds with one stone.

I pull up to the store. It's just a cinder block house with a dingy white sign propped up against the side with THE STORE written in brick-red paint.

Some guys are setting up a roadside barbeque in the parking lot. They give me a head nod, but other than that, it's deserted. I'm getting my money together, pulling some change from the ashtray, when I see Lee Wiggins come out with a plastic bag. He's got his hood up, but I'd know that slouch anywhere.

"Wiggins," I holler as I get out of my truck.

He doesn't even turn around, just takes off running at the sound of my voice.

I track him down a narrow path that runs alongside the junkyard. A Rottweiler jumps at the fence, making it bend and spring back, gnashing teeth and pure muscle slamming against the chain link. It scares the shit out of me, but it makes me run that much harder.

I pass the fence and break out of the overgrowth to find Lee standing in front of a burnt-out trailer. I've heard about it, but it's a whole other thing seeing it in person—the warped metal, the charred plastic, right next to his melted-off face. I can't even imagine the force, the sheer amount of heat it took to do this much damage. Enough to kill his two brothers. Enough to maim him for life.

"Come to see Dad's handiwork?" He spreads his hands wide, like he's showing me Disneyland.

"I don't know what the hell you're talking about."

"Sure you do. Think about it, Clay." He takes down his hood, stretching out his neck to show me the full display of his burns. "The explosives. I know you found them in the shed, buried them on the back parcel, but you didn't tell anyone, did you? Sheriff was right there, and you hid it from him. Pretty sure they call that tampering with evidence."

I clench my hands into fists. "How do you know about that?"

"I know all kinds of things." He grins, his mangled flesh stretching tight over crooked teeth. "I know you've been sniffing around Oakmoor, too," Lee says. "Around me and Miss Granger."

"I'm sick of playing games with you," I say, as I get right up in his face. "Whatever it is that you *think* you know? You best spit it out now, while you still have teeth." I shove him and he drops the plastic bag. A package of condoms and some twine sprawls out in the dirt.

I glance down at the condoms. Was it him? Was he the one who was over at Miss Granger's house that night? I kick the box. "Look, I don't give a shit what you do with Miss Granger."

"Is that what you think this is?" He laughs as he picks it up. "You of all people should understand why I need these. I can't be spilling my seed everywhere, now can I? Blessed is the seed."

"I don't know what your deal is, but I need you to stay away from my family, especially Jess. Do you understand?"

"You still haven't figured it out." He grins. "You still don't know who I am."

"Sure I do. You're just some low-life meth dealer. I've seen the bank ledger. Your name's all over it. I get it. Did you feel good taking that money? Getting a decent family man hooked on meth?"

"Meth?" He laughs. "I guess that's an easier pill to swallow."

"Easier than what?"

"The truth!" He opens his eyes as wide as his scarred skin will allow. "You've always wanted to bury your head in the sand. Never understood that about you. Had so much potential. The golden boy with the golden calf."

"What do you know about the calf?" I advance on him. "Was it you?"

"See, there you go again, getting ahead of yourself. Focusing on the wrong things."

"Then tell me." I get right in his face. "What *should* I be focusing on?"

"Your precious daddy wasn't buying meth." Lee stands his ground. "He was paying me off."

"Oh yeah?" I laugh. "For what?"

"For spreading his seed where it didn't belong."

A chill runs down my spine. I think about Neely telling me how my dad had an eye for the ladies. My mom saying he brought shame on the family. Miss Granger asking for Lee's birth certificate.

It feels like the ground's breaking away right under my feet and there's nothing to hang on to.

"Did you know we were born on the same day?" Lee licks his scarred lips. "Just a few minutes apart. I wasn't due for a couple of months, but I still got here *first*. See, I'll always be one step ahead of you, brother."

His initials written in the margin of our family tree . . . the numbers, 11:26, weren't from the Bible, it was the time of his birth. If he was born first, does that make him the sixth?

"How long did my dad know about you?" I ask as I stagger back, trying to keep my footing.

"He knew from day one, but Ma didn't tell me 'til she was on her deathbed last year. I went to him, told him I just wanted to spend time with him, get to know him, but he was too good for the likes of me. Just threw some money at me, and so I took it, and I kept taking it. And when I threatened to go public, he started confiding in me. Telling me things about this town and the Devil. He took a real shine to me. I thought we were finally getting somewhere, forgin' a real relationship, and then he came over that night, telling me how he's sinned, and how it was time to make things right. He gave me a present. Said it was a family heirloom, something a long time coming, generations in the making. Told me I was the chosen one. Special."

"What did he give you? The present . . . what was it?" I manage to ask, but I can hardly breathe. My chest feels tighter than an oil drum.

"Our dear ole dad told me to open it at nine o'clock sharp. Wrapped it himself. I was so excited, thinking he'd finally accepted me. I even started packing up, thinking I'd be moving into your house soon, be a real Tate, and then BOOM!" he screams. "Boom. Boom. Boom," he runs around screaming, as he pounds his fist against the trailer and the side of his head.

"That can't be . . ." I brace my hands against my knees, huffing down air. "He wouldn't do that. He was a good man."

Lee moves toward me, but he's all blurry. "How can you say that when he tried to kill you, too?"

"How do you know about that? How could you possibly know about that?" My eyes are stinging with tears as I sink to the ground.

"It's too late," Lee says, crouching in front of me. "We're just like Cain and Abel, you and me. Why can't you see that? What else do I have to do to make you see the light? One of us has to die for the other to truly live."

I can't stop thinking about Miss Granger . . . how she had Lee's picture tacked under the Tate column, and how she said, "Unless it's not you."

I look up at him, using all my strength to focus in on his face, and I see it now—the pale blue color of his eyes, the broad forehead, the faint cleft in his chin. Like Dad. Like me.

"Do you have it?" I grab his shoulders. "Do you have the mark?" I shake him, but he won't answer. And all I see is red. Everything's spinning around me, the clouds are moving way too fast. There's a high-pitched ringing in my ears, like someone just dropped a yellow jacket nest in my skull. I can't hear . . . I can't feel . . . I can't think . . . the only thing I know is that I need to see the mark. The upside-down U with two dots, above and below. I have to see it.

The next thing I know, he's lying on the scorched earth, his ripped clothes strewn around him, his mangled flesh exposed to the elements. I look down at my trembling hands in disgust . . . and then at his body. There's no mark, but it looks like God chewed him up and spit him back out.

I take off my jacket and cover him up.

"I'm sorry what happened to you. I'm sorry what my dad did. But I am not my father. And neither are you."

"Don't leave," he says as I escape into the trees. "Things were just getting good. I'll be waiting for you, brother," he yells, and I pick up my pace. "We have unfinished business, you and me."

45

I SIT on the edge of the bed of my truck, waiting for Ali to get out of practice, looking up at the sky. I remember when Jess was little, she said she wanted to be an astronaut. I laughed at her, like it was the most ridiculous thing in the world. I wish I hadn't done that. I never see her look up anymore.

As hard as I try, I can't stop going over everything that happened today on an endless loop. Every family has its secrets, I get that, but this is a doozy. It's murder. I think about telling Sheriff, nipping all this in the bud, but I figure it's Lee's secret to tell. And my family's been through enough.

I'm starting to think all of this is nothing more than some fucked-up fantasy world Lee and Miss Granger cooked up together.

That combined with good old-fashioned sleep deprivation. Ali told me to look into it. And it's no joke. Lack of sleep can cause psychosis, memory impairment, and hallucinations. Check, check, and check.

The one thing I'm sure of—Lee Wiggins is crazy. I still don't get what Miss Granger's angle is in all this, but Lee has a legitimate bone to pick with my family. I won't deny him that. And if he wants to try and kill me in some delusional Bible scenario, let him try. But if he makes one false move toward Jess, Noodle, Mom, or Ali, I won't hesitate to finish what my dad started. And if that makes me a monster, too, so be it. I will protect the ones I love until my very last breath.

I spot Ali making her way across the lot. She's wearing her practice uniform with a zip-up red hoodie, her backpack slung over one shoulder. She's like a ray of light in all this. She said she thinks she knows where Miss Granger is getting all of her theories from and if I see it, I might be able to lay this to rest—all the worry, all the uncertainty, all the fear. God, I hope so, because I don't know how much more of this I can take.

"Aren't you a sight for sore eyes," I say as I stand to greet her.

She snatches the cap off my head and puts it on. "I could say the exact same thing about you."

"You even make that ratty thing look good," I say as I close the tailgate.

"Hey, where were you today?" She gives me a lopsided smile. "Everybody was asking about you."

I let out a deep sigh. "Family business."

"Sounds like we might call for a drink." She closes the distance between us.

"Or twelve might be good." I chuckle.

"That can definitely be arranged." She tugs on the hem of my shirt. "So, are you ready to uncover our ancestors' dark history? I'm afraid you're going to be sorely disappointed."

"You have no idea how much I need that to be true."

I lean down to kiss her when horns start blaring.

"Tate!" Someone yells as they drive by. "Good luck tomorrow against the Sooners. Give 'em hell!"

I shake my head. "Let's get out of here."

"It just so happens I know a place where we can be completely alone."

As I lead her to the passenger door, she runs her hand over the side of Old Blue. "This truck is so you."

"What? Worn-out and rusty?" I say as I take her backpack.

"No. Classic. And true."

As I open the door for her, I feel a flutter of excitement. This is the first time she's ridden in my truck in a year—at least conscious.

WE PULL up in front of the Preservation Society and my heart sinks. The main house is all lit up and there's a bunch of cars parked out front. "I thought you said no one would be here."

"It's just us," she says as she takes off my cap, placing it carefully on the dash. "There's a big pregame party over at the Neelys' tonight. Overflow parking."

She starts to open her door.

"Wait," I say as I get out and open it for her. She takes my hand and doesn't let go the whole way up the brick pathway to the front door.

"You have a key, right?" she asks.

"Yeah." I let out a nervous laugh as I find the brass one.

"What? What's so funny?"

"I don't know if you heard," I say as I slide the key in the lock, "but I got caught breaking in here last week."

"Seriously? Clay, you're such a badass," she teases.

"No. It was pretty much the opposite of badass. I didn't realize I had a key the entire time," I say as I try to get the lock to turn, but it's being stubborn.

"Did you have to have one of those awkward talks with Mr. Neely?"

"Oh yeah, and then he sort of blackmailed me into coming to the Harvest Festival."

"And here I thought you came back for me," she says as she slips under my arm, placing herself between me and the door.

I lean into her, brushing my lips against her ear. "I did." And the lock finally gives. "I guess I just needed a nudge in the right direction."

"Well, I'll have to thank him for that someday."

As we step inside the Preservation Society, I notice the door to Mr. Neely's office is closed.

"Come on," Ali says with an excited giggle as she leads me down to the basement, to the end of the long hallway. "I can't wait to show you this."

She slides her hand against the wood-paneled wall and a doorway pops open. I remember looking at this wall the night I broke in. There was a strange rotting smell, but now it smells sweet—too sweet, like it's covering something up.

We step inside and she lights some candles. "There's no electricity in here. They wanted to keep it pure, like it was in the old days."

"Of course."

"But it's kind of nice . . . romantic," she says as she peeks at me over her shoulder.

There's an oversized leather ottoman in the center of the room. Big enough to be a bed. The walls are filled with books and trinkets.

"What is all this stuff?"

"The council archives. This room has been in existence since they built the Preservation Society in 1889. I think maybe they used it as a chapel . . . a sanctuary."

"Sanctuary from what?" I look at her sharply.

"Who knows . . . their parents, maybe?" She gives a cute little shrug. "This is the one place we can be alone. Invisible." She shuts the door. I watch the seams disappear into the grooves of the paneling and instantly, I feel better. Like we just shut out the world.

"Okay." I let out a deep breath. "Let's never leave this room."

"Fine by me," she says as she crosses to a heavy wood sideboard, pouring dark amber liquid from a decanter into two cut crystal glasses.

I take a whiff of the stopper and I guess I make a face.

"My dad's rye." She smiles up at me. "Not the smoothest, but it gets the job done."

"Are you sure it's okay?"

"We do it all the time." She hands me a glass. "Do you have any idea how boring the council meetings are? It's the only perk." She positions herself directly in front of me, clinking her glass to mine. "To us. . . ."

We both take a drink. It burns my eyes, but it feels good going down my throat. Instant warmth radiating throughout my body.

"Now," Ali says as she picks up one of the candles, moving it along the spines of a row of books. "They showed us all this stuff when they turned over the council to us last year, but I never gave it much thought until you started telling me Miss Granger's theory. There's a prophecy, but not like Miss Granger thinks."

She pulls down an old book from the shelves, thumbing through the pages until she finds what she's looking for.

"Here," she says, pointing to the text.

I read over her shoulder, "The sixth generation will inherit the earth, paving the way for a new age."

"That's pretty self-explanatory," Ali says. "When our ancestors founded Midland, formed the council, everything they built was for the sixth generation. For us."

"Okay . . . but there's *six* of us . . . from the *sixth* generation."

"I see where you're going with this, but where's the other six?"

"2016?"

"Grasping." She shakes her head and takes another drink.

I read the next line. "In exchange for our sacrifice and obedience, the lord has placed a protective seal over this covenant." I take another drink. "A seal over this covenant? Like a witch thing?"

"No." She pulls me over to the original land map hanging on the wall. "They're talking about the county."

"Okay. If you squint your eye just right, the dividing lines kind of look like they form a pentagram. How do you explain that?"

"Those were the original plot lines," she says. "Our ancestors certainly didn't get to choose that, or believe me, our plots would all be shaped like potatoes or something."

I study the book with the prophecy in it, holding it up to the light. "It looks like a page might've been torn out."

"Oh my God . . . alert the media, it's a conspiracy." She laughs as she refills our glasses. "Or maybe Jethro just needed a piece of toilet paper. You could go crazy thinking about all this stuff."

"Believe me . . . I know."

"Here, check this out." She pulls an old ledger from the shelf, filled with stats. "These are all the natural disasters to hit Oklahoma in the last hundred or so years. Famine . . . drought . . . tornados . . . floods . . . earthquakes . . . the dust bowl . . ."

"Exactly. And Midland escaped every single one of them. How do you even begin to explain that?"

"You can't. Isn't it amazing? It sounds more like God than the Devil, if you ask me."

"I don't know," I mutter into my glass as I take another drink.

"The way I see it, it's all about perspective. It's like that time we were at the lake, on the floating dock, and we were looking up at the clouds. I saw a dancer. You saw a football player going for the extra point."

"Did I really say that?" I cringe.

"You really did."

"Wow. I was super smooth, wasn't I?"

She studies me, her hazel eyes smoldering in the candlelight. "You were perfect . . . still are."

She clinks my glass again and we drink. It doesn't burn anymore, but there's a weird chalky aftertaste coating the roof of my mouth. The rye moves through my body, coaxing the tension out of my muscles like warm liquid fingers.

"My point is, I can see how somebody like Miss Granger might want to string all this together, connect the dots. I really do, but she's an outsider, she doesn't understand. This town has always been a little off-kilter. I mean, look at our ancestors." She takes my hand, leading me to their photo on the wall. "They came over on a boat from Ireland with no money, no prospects. And when they heard about the land rush, only the craziest of the crazy decided to head west to fight it out for the tiniest chance at free land. We come from a long line of risk takers with nothing to lose. It's in our DNA. But they did it for us. I'm not saying our ancestors were saints, but think of Noodle. She's a Tate through and through. Do you think she's evil?"

"No way." I laugh.

"Well, there you go. We have to hang on to the light. Wherever we can find it."

She laces her fingers through mine, her thumb lingering on my palm, and something vibrates inside me.

"What if we're not cursed . . . but *blessed*."

"What about Jimmy? Or Ben?" I ask, my gaze settling on their family trees. "The last time I saw them, they looked far from blessed."

"Free will. That was their choice. It says right here in the next line, 'Only the strong will prevail.'"

She takes my glass, setting it next to hers on the bookshelf.

"That's how I know that won't happen to you," she says as she steps in close, wrapping her arms around me. Her warmth spreads like embers across my chest. She stands on her tiptoes to whisper in my ear, "You're strong, Clay."

My skin explodes in goose bumps. The feel of her breath on my skin only fans the flames.

She unzips her hoodie, letting it drop to the floor. I try not to look, but I can't help it. She's wearing a white, loose-fitting silk camisole. No bra. "Feel my heart, Clay." She places my hand on her chest. Her heartbeat is like an arrow shooting straight through my palm—strong and steady. The room seems to be spinning around us.

"You must know I've been waiting for you all this time."

Her fingers move down my chest and I swear I can see trails of sunlight and electricity sparking from her fingertips.

She pulls me over to the leather ottoman and lies back, stretching out her long tan legs.

I sit beside her on the edge, willing the room to stop moving. The nail studs securing the leather to the bottom of the bench feel good, like chips of ice against my feverish fingertips.

Ali pulls her rich brown hair over her shoulder. I fixate on the brand on the back of her neck.

When she catches my stare, she says, "In some cultures a woman is marked when she's ready."

"Ready for what?" I ask.

"Ready to become a woman . . . to receive his love."

"Whose love?"

"Yours, Clay." She wets her lips and pulls me down to lay beside her, kissing my ear, my neck. I try to lift my head and get up, but I can't. It feels too good. I gaze up at the chandelier, hundreds of facets sparkling like our own universe.

And in the blink of an eye, she's on top of me. I can't stop staring at the strap of her camisole, teetering on the edge of her shoulder blade. One tiny move and it could slip right off. Or I could make it slip.

She follows my gaze and shrugs, letting the strap fall. "I think you're ready, too."

I try to keep my eyes focused on hers, but the pull of her bare breast is too strong to ignore. It reminds me of the vision I had when I saw her climbing out of the cow. I know I should feel disgusted by it, but I don't. Instead, something primal rises inside of me.

Sitting up, I grasp the back of her neck, kissing her deeply. That overwhelming feeling takes over every part of me. I run my hands down the curve of her waist, and she whispers, "Blessed is the seed."

"What did you say?" A dark ripple of static rushes through me.

"I said, what more do you need."

She starts kissing my neck again and I could so easily close my eyes and disappear into her skin, but that feeling of unease won't leave me. I have the strangest sensation, like we're being watched. My eyes settle on the photograph of our ancestors. I'm drawn to a girl around Jess's age, holding a doll. "I know that doll," I say as I untangle myself from Ali and make my way over to it. It looks like the same doll Noodle's been dragging around since Dad's funeral. I yank it off the wall to get a better look, accidentally dropping it to the hardwood floor.

As I'm leaning over trying to gather the shattered glass, I see a small tear in the photo, exposing something beneath . . . a glimpse of handwriting. I break out the rest of the glass, peeling back the photograph to reveal an old tattered document, with a torn edge, bearing the signatures of the founding families. It's the missing page. The missing piece of the prophecy.

On this day, we form a covenant to protect, serve, and honor our lord. In exchange for these parcels of land we hereby pledge our sixth generation to usher in a new age. Once the seed has been selected, once the blood of the golden calf has been spilled, there will be ten sacrifices. Only the chosen one will be allowed to care for our lord.

"It's true." I inhale sharply. "All of it. They sold our souls for land," I say to Ali, but it's like she's looking right through me. "Did you hear me?"

"We can talk about that later." Ali kneels on the bench, her bare skin glistening in the candlelight. "Come back to me."

Something's off. Something's very wrong . . . with her . . . with this place. "I . . . I need to get out of here." I shove the piece of paper in my pocket and frantically start pressing on the paneled wall until the door pops open.

I can't look back, I can't hesitate, or I know I'll never be able to leave this room. As I careen up the stairs, every cell in my body screams at me to go back, but I keep pressing forward.

As I stagger into the hallway, I hear whispering. I move toward the sound. It's coming from Mr. Neely's office. I place my hand on the doorknob, afraid to open it . . . afraid not to.

The whispering stops, but I hear the unmistakable susurration of breath. Pressing down on the cold brass handle, I nudge the door open.

The room is full of people dressed in long glittery gowns and tuxedos, martinis in hand. They're all staring back at me, but no one moves a muscle. I'm wondering if they're wax figures or mannequins, until one of them speaks.

"Do something, Ian," a woman says through her teeth. It's Mrs. Neely.

My eyes dart around the room. Mr. and Mrs. Miller are here, Mr. and Mrs. Doogan, Mr. and Mrs. Gillman, Dr. and Mrs. Perry . . . all the parents of the sixth generation are present—except for mine.

"What are you doing here? What's going on?" I pant.

I look past them to a television screen set up on Ian's desk. There's a half-naked girl lying on a bench. It takes me a good minute to realize it's Ali on the screen . . . in the secret room. I stare at each and every one of them in disbelief. These sick fucks have been watching us the entire time. A wave of dizziness washes over me. I grasp onto the edge of the desk to keep my balance, when I notice what's in front of the screen. On a swath of black velvet, there's a branding iron. The symbol on the end is plain as day—the upside-down U with two dots above and below. The invitation. Were they planning on using that thing on me? Was Ali in on it? Or did they use her to lure me here? I grasp on to the handle.

"Clay, everything's fine," Mr. Neely says as he steps forward. "But I think you've lost your way. Let me show you back to Ali."

"Stay away from me!" I swipe the metal rod in front of me.

Mr. Neely holds out his arm, motioning for the others to stay back.

I lash the iron through the air, again and again, as I work my way to the door.

Stumbling down the front steps, I drop the branding iron.

I jump to my feet, ready to fight, but they just stand there in the doorway, like I'm some kind of curiosity.

"But, Ian . . ." Mrs. Neely says.

"All in good time." He smiles. "And Clay Tate's time is running out."

46

I RUN as fast as I can down Main Street, but my legs aren't working right. Who am I kidding? My brain's not working right. Cars are honking, people are calling out my number. The lights are too bright, the clouds are moving in way too fast.

"Fuck!" I scream as I stare back at the Preservation Society.

I have to find Miss Granger. I might be crazy, I might be drugged, but I know what I saw. I know what I felt. And that was real. They were going to brand me.

I slap myself as hard as I can, trying to jolt myself out of this haze, but I can still feel Ali on my skin, in my hair, on my mouth. Everything is pulling me back to her, but I can't give in to this— whatever *this* is. I have to hang on until Miss Granger can tell me what the hell's happening . . . so she can fix this.

I wipe my sleeve across my face and cut through some yards to get to Pine Street.

Dogs are barking, televisions blaring, I almost get taken out by a clothesline, but I find my way to her front door.

I start banging. I don't care who sees me. I don't stop until I notice the red streak smeared across the dark wood.

Staring down in fascination at my bloody knuckles, I can hardly feel a thing. God only knows what was in that rye.

Miss Granger cracks the door open. "Clay, what are you doing here?" she asks warily.

"You have to help me," I plead. "I was at the Preservation Society with Ali . . . we were alone, or I thought we were alone, but I think they drugged us and they were watching . . . they were watching us—"

"Watching you what?" she asks as she pulls me inside. "What were you doing with Ali?" She grabs my shoulders.

"Watching us . . ." I break away from her, peeking through the curtains, making sure they didn't follow me here. "I can't believe what just happened . . . what *almost* happened."

Miss Granger sinks to the edge of the coffee table, like she already knows what I'm going to say.

"Ali took me to the secret room . . . the *real* secret room. We had a few drinks . . . we were kissing and stuff, and she whispered, 'blessed be the seed.' She tried to cover it up, but I know what I heard. I went upstairs and I found Ian Neely and all the Preservation Society having some kind of cocktail party while they watched us on a screen. And they had the branding iron out. I saw the mark. And I found this." With trembling hands, I pull out the piece of paper and give it to her.

"Our ancestors . . . they sold our souls to the Devil to get the land. The sixth generation . . . it's all right there. Ten will be sacrificed and only one will be able to lay hands on the lord, to care for him, usher in a new age. And something about the seed . . . what does that even mean?"

I look up at the wall, trying to piece together the information, but it's empty. All of the documents have been removed and there's a fresh coat of paint. I start looking around the room in a panic when I notice a small suitcase by the door.

"You're leaving?" I ask, feeling short of breath. "You can't leave. Not now. I know I said some terrible things. I didn't believe you and I'm so sorry, but please don't leave. I need you to fix this. I need you to save her. I'll do anything you ask."

"I'm sorry I involved you in this," she says, shaking her head. "It was reckless on my part. You don't bear the mark. It's not you."

"But Lee doesn't have it either."

"Not anymore." She gives me a pointed stare and I understand everything. The mark was erased in that explosion, covered up by scar tissue and pain. It was him all along.

"I know you feel bad for your friends, but there's no way you could've stopped this. You must believe me. The Devil is more powerful than you can ever imagine and he's growing more powerful by the second. That's why I'm going to All Saints tonight to prepare for the exorcism."

"But you'll be back, right?"

She reaches out, brushing her hand against my cheek. "There's something I need to show you." She pulls the photo album out, turning to the articles about Mexico City. TWO MISSIONARIES AND FIVE CHILDREN FOUND DEAD AFTER BRUTAL ATTACK AT THE

CHURCH OF GRACE. "Do you remember me telling you about the last case in 1999?"

I nod, wondering where she's going with this.

She turns to the autopsy photos. "The missionaries . . . they were my parents." She brushes her fingers over the photographs. "They were demonologists. They performed exorcisms. This was their last case."

"I'm sorry," I say, remembering the photo from her nightstand. I can't believe I didn't put it together.

"The Church took me in, allowed me to continue their work. My parents gave their lives to save the sixth child," she says as she takes her hair out of the tight knot and pulls it over to the side to reveal some kind of scar.

"The sixth child was me," she says. Taking my hand, she places it against the brand. I'd know that symbol anywhere. "So, I could never leave this behind, even if I wanted to. Avenging my parents' death, defeating the Devil, is my life's work."

It feels strange touching her this way, almost too intimate. I pull my hand away.

"So there's hope for Ali." I clear my throat. "You can save her."

She lets out a gentle sigh, twisting her hair back into the knot. "You're too good, Clay." She smiles, but it doesn't reach her eyes. "I think the Devil underestimated your resolve, but *together*, we can finish this."

"How?"

"The exorcism. I'll return on Saturday to assist the priests that evening at the breeding barn."

"Shouldn't they do it somewhere holy? A place of God?" I ask.

"We need to hit the Devil where he lives."

"I'm sorry I doubted you," I say. "I'm sorry I yelled at you like that. I had no right and I'm—"

"I'm sorry I gave you *reason* to doubt. This has been hard for me, too."

I can't even imagine how this might be affecting her. It's probably like déjà vu with Mexico City. Losing her parents like that.

"What can I do to help?"

"There's still time. You can watch over Ali, protect her."

"But how can I protect her when I can't even be around her without . . ."

"Without what?" she presses.

"When I'm around her . . . I feel like I can't control myself," I say, dragging my fingers through my hair. "And it's only getting worse."

"Then stop trying."

"What?" My muscles tense. "How can you say that after everything I've told you?"

"She's still Ali. The girl that you love. She doesn't understand what's happening to her. Something catastrophic is going on here. I will do my absolute best to save her, but we have no idea how this will end . . . how much time we have left on God's good earth. Or if she'll even make it out of the exorcism. You saw what happened to my parents. It's a natural human instinct to want to be close to the ones we love. God won't judge you for that."

"I can't." I shake my head.

"Then promise me something," she says, her tone determined and serious. "As soon as Ali's free of this . . . *clean* . . . don't waste another moment. If I bring her back to you, tell her you love her, that you can't live without her. Give yourself to her before it's too late."

"I promise," I say, feeling a blush creep up my neck at the thought.

I don't know what to do here . . . give her a hug, a peck on the cheek. Instead, I reach out and squeeze her hand.

"Godspeed," I say.

She looks up at me with a surprised smile. "Yes, exactly. Godspeed."

I'm opening the door to leave when she says, "Oh, and Clay? About the game. *Win*. I don't want to come back to find they've sent a lynch mob after you."

WHEN I go back for my truck, the Preservation Society is dark and the cars are gone. I turn on my phone to find a text from Ali.

Did you get lost? Haha. That rye was strong! I waited, but had to go home. Big game tomorrow. Hope you're in bed having sweet dreams . . . about me. ;) Night

Miss Granger's right. Ali has no idea what's happening to her. In a way, I'm glad. I hope she never has to know the horror of what our ancestors have done to us.

47

THE HOUSE is dark, darker than it should be at nine. Noodle's not at the door waiting for me, which is odd.

As I slip off my boots, I hear whispering coming from the living room.

"Noodle?" I call out.

The whispering stops. There's a long, uneasy pause.

"Hello," I call again.

"She's not here," Mom answers in a low monotone.

"What do you mean she's not here?"

I'm almost afraid to peek my head in the living room, afraid of what I might find. But Mom's just sitting on the sofa, never once taking her eyes off the wall above the mantel . . . off the flies. They're back and they've somehow doubled in number, as if out of spite.

"She said she was helping you."

"Helping me?" I rack my brain, trying to figure out what she means, but Mom's already glossed over.

"Noodle?" I call out as I go in the kitchen. It looks like all the food from the cabinet has been emptied onto the table next to the casserole dish. Potpie night.

Damn it. I forgot the groceries.

And then I remember last night. While we were eating pancakes, I told her she could help me with the harvest after school.

"The wheat," I whisper, acid rising in my throat.

Racing out the door, I push through the crops, the cold air smacking against my lungs.

The combine. What if she tried to do it by herself . . . what if she hurt herself, or couldn't figure out how to stop it and went all the way to Harmon Lake?

"Noodle," I call out in a panic as the untilled wheat lashes against my arms.

There's a momentary break in the cloud cover, the moon revealing the top of the combine about a hundred feet to the west. My legs pump harder.

When I reach the combine, the windows are all fogged up. I jerk the door open to find Noodle, curled up in the seat, clutching her fairy wand.

"I knew you'd come." She rubs her eyes groggily.

"Thank God. Thank God you're okay," I say as I hold her, rocking her back and forth. I can count the number of times I've cried on one hand, but just the sight of her brings everything to the surface. If something happened to her, I'd never be able to forgive myself.

"Sorry," she murmurs. "I fell asleep on the job."

"*I'm* sorry," I manage to choke out. "It won't happen again."

"Is it okay if we call it a night? I'm cold."

"Yeah, it's more than okay." I push her hair back from her face so I can get a good look at her.

She wants to walk, but I insist on carrying her back through the wheat. She feels so small in my arms. She's so smart, such an old soul, that I think I forget how young she is sometimes.

By the time we get to the house, she's almost asleep again; she can hardly keep her eyes open.

I don't even bother getting her washed up. I just tuck her in, clothes and all. "Goodnight, fairy princess Tate," I say as I pry the wand from her hand.

"Jess is tucked in, too," Noodle says as she closes her eyes and nuzzles into her pillow. "In a bed of moss just like a woodland fairy princess . . ." Her voice trails off and she's asleep.

I sit there thinking about all the things that could've happened to her out there and I can barely hold it together. There are two other people in this house and no one noticed she was missing all afternoon . . . all night. I know I said I'd give Jess time, but I can't do this by myself anymore. I need help.

"Jess . . ." I tap on her door, not wanting to wake Noodle. "We need to talk."

No response.

"I know you're in there. I can hear you breathing."

Nothing.

"Look . . . I'm not leaving until you talk to me."

I go to pound on her door, when it swings wide open, a gust of cold air rushing over me. The window's open, her lace curtains blowing in and out . . . *like breath.*

And no Jess.

As I step inside the room to close the window, I bash into plates of untouched food. That wretched doll is lying in the middle of the floor, wearing some kind of schoolgirl outfit. "Damn it, Jess!" I kick the doll across the room.

I think of Lee with that pack of condoms and my blood turns to venom. Is that how he's getting back at me? She doesn't even know he's her half brother. I feel sick to my stomach. I want to go out to the trailer park and drag her ass back here, but I know if I see Lee, I'll kill him. That's a fact.

I tear downstairs to the phone in the kitchen and start dialing Miss Granger, but she's on her way to All Saints right now and I don't want anything interfering with that. The only other person I can think of is Sheriff Ely. Despite our differences, he's a friend of the family. He cares about Jess. He's the only person in this town who had the decency to tell me what's going on right under my nose. He can probably track her down quicker than anyone.

I dial his number.

"Sheriff? It's Clay Tate."

"Are you ready to talk now?" he replies.

"No. It's not that." I keep my voice low, even though I know Mom's gone to the world right now. "It's Jess." I swallow hard. "You were right. She's not here. I think she might've run off with the Wiggins kid."

There's a long pause. I hear Greg Tilford running his mouth in the background.

"Tell you what?" Sheriff comes back on the line. "Why don't I come on over and get the details."

I crane my neck to peek in the living room. "It's really not a good time."

"This is Jess we're talking about."

"You're right." I grit my teeth. "Just make it quick."

I DO some dishes. Straighten up the best I can. I try to get Mom to move upstairs, but she refuses to leave the couch.

I sit down next to her and take her hand, but it's completely limp. I wonder if she even knows I'm here. "Jess ran off, but we're going to find her, bring her back."

She doesn't even blink. She just peers over my shoulder, her eyes fixed on the wall . . . on the flies.

"Jesus." I exhale as I follow her gaze. The wall's more black than white now. There must be a hundred of them. I know they're just flies, but it gives me the creeps. I don't have time to deal with this right now.

"Just don't talk about the flies . . . or God. Just keep it together for a couple more days . . . that's all I'm asking."

She blinks once and I take it as a yes.

Turning off the lights, I leave her to the dark.

WHEN I hear a car coming down the drive, I start going over everything I need to say, but when I hear more than one set of boots on the drive, all of that goes out the window. I swing open the front door, watching Sheriff and Tilford walk up the steps.

"Evening, Clay." Ely tips his hat. "You know Greg Tilford."

"Deputy Tilford," Greg adds.

Sheriff shoots him a withering look.

"We just need to ask you a few questions."

My heart picks up speed. Why would they both come out here for this? "Is something wrong? Is Jess in some kind of trouble?"

"No. Nothing like that." Sheriff shakes his head and then stares out over the crops. "Looks like you've got a ways to go on the wheat. You're cutting it a little close, wouldn't you say? First frost's gotta be right around the corner."

"Yeah." I rub the back of my neck. "I've been a little distracted lately."

"Why don't you tell us about that?" Tilford pulls out a notebook.

And that's when I realize, they're not here about Jess . . . they're here about *me*. They still think I had something to do with all this.

"It sure is cold out here." Ely blows into his hands and rubs them together. "Would it be all right if we talk inside?"

Tilford stares me down, as if saying no isn't an option here.

"Just for a few minutes," I say as I open the door. "But we have to keep it down. Noodle's asleep and Mom's not feeling well."

As I lead them inside, I'm looking around at everything in a whole new light. The dried mud on the wainscoting could be blood. The worn pine planks in the entry, like someone's paced them raw with worry. The seams of the wallpaper curling in on itself revealing the black mold underneath, like the whole place is rotting from within. The home of a killer . . . "Mooder in Midland" . . . and then I think about the flies. Mom sitting there staring at them like it's the second coming. That's all I need.

I can tell they want to look around, but I steer them straight into the kitchen. Tilford walks right into Hammy's bowl; the sharp sound of metal clanking against the cabinets makes me flinch. I motion toward the table. Tilford goes to sit in my dad's chair at the head of the table and Sheriff shakes him off.

Tilford stands back, leaning against the hutch.

"So, about Jess," Sheriff starts off. "When was the last time you saw her?"

"I've been taking food up to her the past couple of nights."

"She hasn't been feeling good?" Greg asks. "Like your mom? I didn't realize there was a flu going around." His flat eyes probe into me. He knows damn well it's no flu.

"Is this because of what happened at the Preservation Society with Jimmy Doogan?" Sheriff asks.

I feel the hair on my arms bristle. "This has nothing to do with Jimmy," I say a little too forcefully. "She's just been having a hard time, hanging around with the wrong crowd."

"You're talking about the Wiggins kid?" Tilford smirks. "That's the understatement of the year."

"I don't know what you heard, but Jess is a good girl."

"I know that . . . I know Jess," Sheriff says soothingly. "Deputy Tilford needs to learn when to shut his mouth." Ely glares at him. "So the last time you really laid eyes on her was the night of the Harvest Festival?"

"Yeah, I guess so." I focus my attention back on Sheriff. "Miss Granger took her home." I lean forward. "But I saw Lee today," I say quietly. "Out by the trailer park . . . and he had a box full of condoms."

"If I were you, I'd be thankful for small favors." Tilford says under his breath.

Sheriff lets out a long sigh. "At least you know they're being safe."

"No, you don't under—" I swallow the rest of my sentence. That's the last thing this family needs right now.

"And where were you that night? The night of the Harvest Festival."

I lean back in my chair. "Haven't we already been over this?"

Tilford starts scribbling down notes; the sound of pen scraping against paper sets my teeth on edge.

"Look, are you going to do anything about this or not?"

Sheriff gives me a sympathetic nod. "I'll get out to the trailer park, put out some feelers. Like you said, Jess is a good girl. She's probably on a lark. She'll come home when she's ready. I see it all the time. Promise me you won't be going out there. Leave it to the law. You hear me, son?"

I nod and stand up, signaling that it's time for them to do the same.

"Oh and Clay, I've been meaning to ask. Do you have any tattoos or marks on your body?"

"Plenty of scars from playing ball. You know that."

"Anything unusual? Something that looks like this." He pulls out a folded-up piece of paper from his breast pocket and hands it to me.

The upside-down U with two dots above and below. I try to keep my face as expressionless as possible, but I can feel a bead of sweat running down my temple.

"Nope." I hand it back to him.

"Never seen it before?" he asks. "Huh. How about that."

"Why?"

"No reason." The right side of his mouth twitches. "You wouldn't be hiding it, would you? Somewhere in plain sight."

"I think I'd know if I had a brand."

"See, that's funny." He scratches his jaw. "I never said a word about a brand."

I feel my insides crumble. "I think it's best you get on your way," I say as I lead them out of the kitchen.

"Do you hear it?" my mom calls out as we pass the living room.

"Ruth, is that you?" Sheriff doubles back, flicking on the light.

She's standing in front of the couch, her body a tight wire, pointing at the wall above the mantel.

"I'll be . . ." Ely stares at the wall. "Strange time of year for flies . . . wouldn't you say so, Clay?"

Tilford swats the air in front of him. "Looks like you need an exterminator."

"He's coming . . . he's coming for all of us," Mom whispers.

"Who's coming?" Ely asks.

"Just ignore her—"

"The seed will inherit the earth," she says. "And the sinners will rejoice as the blood of the golden calf rains down on the innocent . . ."

"Okay . . . I told you this wasn't a good time. She's not feeling well," I say as I take Sheriff's arm, leading him to the front door.

". . . and animals will fornicate with humans," Mom yells from the living room. "And the stars will fall down from the sky. The gateway to the underworld will open up, swallowing all that is good and holy and right . . ."

I get them out the door and we all seem to take a deep breath at the same time.

"Looks like you've got a real problem in there, Clay," Sheriff says.

"The mom, or the flies?" Tilford chuckles.

"Look, I know, okay?" I drag my hand through my hair. "She'll be fine in a few days. It'll pass. I promise."

They start to walk back to their car when Sheriff says, "Oh and Clay . . . one last thing."

I turn, my shoulders collapsing a little.

"How long has it been since you got a haircut?"

"About a year, I guess."

"So, you started growing it out after your dad died? Any particular reason?"

"I always kept it buzzed for football, but when I stopped playing, I just didn't feel the need."

"But now you're playing again . . . and on the council. Interesting." He presses his lips together and bobs his head. "I'll make a note of that."

As I pass the living room, I flick off the light again.

I can't even look at her. It hurts too much.

I take a shower. The water's scalding hot and never wanes. I try not to think about the reasons why—Mom stopped bathing weeks ago and Jess is gone. It makes me shudder in the warmth.

Wiping the steam from the mirror, I drag my hands through my hair, pulling it back from my face. It's weird how Sheriff was asking me about my hair . . . and all that talk about the mark . . . asking me if I was hiding it in plain sight.

And that's when it hits me.

My hair.

The priests checked my body, but what if it's on my scalp. . . . like Miss Granger's?

48

I GRASP the sides of the sink to steady myself and take in a few deep huffs of air before I start rummaging through the cabinet, looking for my clippers. They're in the back, wedged between an empty box of Tampax and some Elmo bubble bath. With shaking hands, I turn it on. The blades are rusted, the batteries old, but it still works. My eyes are blurry, stinging with tears, as I rake the clippers along my scalp, shearing off clumps of heavy dark-blond hair.

"Please don't let me have the mark. Don't let it be true."

The dull grinding sound, the fine strands hovering in the air like bits of spiderweb caught in a breeze, my raw scalp, the hair clogging the pipes, the desperate sucking sound of the drain . . . it reminds me of that night I found Dad in the breeding barn—the drain in the floor clogged with intestines and viscera.

With every pull of the razor, horrible images flash through my mind. The bull, blood gushing from his throat. Lee's scarred skin stretched tight over jagged teeth. Jess looking back at me on that cot with dead eyes. Jimmy kneeling at the altar offering his gift to God. Ben strung up on the goalpost like Christ. The nuns cutting out their tongues. Noodle suckling from the dead calf. Ali crawling out of the cow. "I plead the blood" echoing in my mind.

"Stop!" I scream. I shut my eyes, trying to get away from the memories, but they're always there, scratching at the surface, begging for release.

I force myself to look at my reflection, inspecting every inch of my scalp. I let out a huge burst of pent-up air when all I find are the familiar bumps and planes of my skull.

"Thank God," is all I can manage to say. "Thank God."

AFTER I pull myself together and get everything cleaned up, I wrap the towel around my waist and go into Jess's room, sinking to the edge of her bed. She can't have been gone long, because she's been taking the food. I saw a shadow pass under her door. Heard her footsteps. I'm sure of it. But I've been seeing all kinds of things lately. I look toward the window. Maybe she's been climbing the drainpipe, coming in and out as she pleases. I just can't believe she'd leave Noodle here with Mom, knowing the state she's in. I want to wring Jess's neck.

I get up and open her window, hoping by some miracle that when the sun comes up, she'll be in her bed, or better yet, waiting for me in my truck with those awful boots pressed up against my dash.

I search her room, looking for any kind of clues, but she's taken down every photo, every personal item. I think about how opposite we are. All I do is cling to the past and here she is trying to erase it. I can't imagine how hard it's been for her . . . living in this house . . . living under this cloud of death and depression. She's the only one who had it right and I brushed her off like she was nothing. Like she didn't matter. I think about her out there with Lee Wiggins and my blood boils. I think about him touching her and I want to kill something.

"I'm going to make this right, Jess."

I lie back on her bed, staring up at the handful of glow-in-the-dark stars I put up for her ninth birthday. She wanted to be able to wish on a star whenever she felt like it.

"Star light, star bright, first star I see tonight,

I wish I may, I wish I might, have the wish I wish tonight."

I close my eyes.

Just for a minute, I tell myself.

A low sizzling sound accompanied by a warm glow is coming from the window. I walk toward it, staring out over the burning wheat. A repulsive charred stench lingers in the air. The flames form a perfect circle. Inside, there's a girl with reddish hair, her lithe, naked body bathed in eerie green light.

Noodle slips her hand in mine. "Isn't it beautiful?" she says as the flames engulf the girl's body. "This is all for the chosen one."

We stand there, watching her burn.

And I feel nothing.

———

I WAKE in Jess's bed, covered in a cold sweat, to find the decrepit baby doll lying next to me, her dead eyes glinting in the early-morning light.

A disgusted rage fills me; I grab the doll by its neck, flinging it out the window.

I'm leaning against the frame, taking in huge gulps of fresh air when I see Hammy pick up the doll in his teeth.

"Leave it, Hammy," I holler at him.

He stares up at me, like he's looking at a ghost, and then buries it at the edge of the wheat.

49

IT's FRIDAY. Game day.

I get Noodle on the bus and make arrangements with Mrs. Gifford to sit with her after school until I get home.

On my way to Midland High, I stop at Merritt's to fill up the tank, but it's really just an excuse to look for Jess. I know I promised Sheriff I wouldn't go out to the trailer park, but he didn't say anything about the old campgrounds. The thing is I'm not even mad anymore. Just worried. I don't want Jess getting hurt. If Lee decides to share that little story with her, it could scar her for life.

I hike out into the pines, calling her name. Every insect scrabbling over the pine straw puts me on edge. Lee could be anywhere out here and this is his turf. For all I know, this place could be booby-trapped.

I come up on the old campgrounds, just a handful of busted-up cabins. I peek inside. They reek of mold and animal droppings and other things I don't even want to think about.

I come to a big twelve-foot-diameter circle of fresh upturned soil. It reminds me of the circle in my dream last night, only there's twine dividing it up, like a geometric puzzle. Maybe sectioned off for a garden.

I step over the twine to get a closer look at the pile of trash in the center of the circle, but the more I look at it, the more deliberate it seems, as if the items have been placed here with great care. I rub my arms, but it's not the chill in the air giving me goose bumps. There's a pair of gloves on the handlebars of a little kid's bike, an elaborate men's belt buckle with a bull on it, clumps of dirty hair stuck in the ground, a jar of deerflies, and a Bible open to Genesis 4:12. I know that verse. That's the story of Cain and Abel.

"Lee," I whisper. This is all his doing. A sick feeling twists inside me. I stagger back out of the circle, nearly tripping over the twine. This isn't trash at all, but some kind of fucked-up shrine to my family. The gloves are covered in dried blood—they're the same gloves that went missing when I discovered the calf. The bike is Noodle's. I've been looking for that thing for over a year. The jar of flies—he must be the one who's putting them in the house. And the belt buckle belongs to Dad. That's his 1982 rodeo championship prize. One of a kind. The same one we buried him in.

I make it to the edge of the woods before I get sick, and when I look up again, I can see the twine isn't some random puzzle. The circle's been roped off to form a five-pointed star. A pentagram.

Lee's the one who's been orchestrating all this. Not Tyler. It's beyond blackmail at this point; it's personal. He wants my family to suffer for what Dad did to him. But I'm not putting Jess at risk to protect Dad's secret. To protect our legacy. Dad ruined that when he stepped out on Mom. Then again, we were ruined a long time before that. When our ancestors sold us out for land. For this. I grab a handful of soil and throw it as hard as I can.

I hear a rustle, something snap in the pines. I whip around but there's no one there. Could be an owl, or an old branch, or it could be something a hell of a lot worse than that.

As I'm hauling ass back to my truck, I dig my phone out of my pocket and call Sheriff Ely.

He doesn't pick up; I leave a message.

"I went out to the campground looking for Jess. I know, I know, but there's something you need to see out there. And I think you may need to check Dad's grave, too. By the way, Lee is my half-brother. Just found out yesterday and I guess now you know why he and Jess shouldn't be together. Find her for me and I'll do something for you. Put all your money on Midland tonight."

50

As I pull into my spot at the back of the lot, it looks like a scene right out of some cheesy high school movie, not the center of some doomsday prophecy.

Everyone's decked out in red and black, the pep girls are out in full force—their soft bodies, easy smiles, ripe for the taking. Not that I ever would, but most of them make it clear they'd do anything for the team. Sometimes I think it would've been better that way, just to get it over with, but even now, with everything that's going on, I look at Ali waiting for me by Tyler's car, and I know why I haven't done it. I feel it all the way to my bones. I want Ali to be my first . . . and my last. That much I'm sure of. And I'm going to do everything in my power to make sure we get that opportunity.

People are flitting around like it's Christmas morning; there's an undeniable electricity in the air, but the longer I look at the scene, the clearer it gets.

All of the students seem to dance around the Preservation Society kids, what's left of them, circling, hovering, but never making direct contact, like they've been choreographed on an endless loop, and I can't help thinking of the flies.

The flies.

"Hey!" Dale opens my door, nearly giving me a heart attack.

"Jesus, Dale." I sigh as I get out of the truck.

"Why haven't you called me back and what the hell happened to your hair?"

"Not today, Dale," I mutter as I grab my bag.

He sits on my hood. He knows how much I hate that.

"What? You're too good for me now that you're back on the team? With Ali?" He's flicking a lighter over and over again and all I can think about is my nightmare last night—that girl being burned alive.

I knock the lighter out of his hand and grab his shirt, pulling him off my truck. "You don't know what the hell you're talking about."

He blinks hard. "What's gotten into you, cuz?"

"Just back off." I let go of him and walk toward Tyler's car. I feel bad, but I don't want him anywhere near me right now. There's too much death and uncertainty.

Ali slips her arms around me, running her hand over the back of my head, over the quarter-inch stubble. "There you are," she says, and just like that I could melt into her, forget last night ever happened. But I can't do that anymore, because tomorrow, Miss Granger will be back with the priests and all of this will end. One way or the other.

"Save it for after the game," Tyler says without looking at us as he heads into school. "Give him some incentive to win."

"We're all going out to Harmon Lake tonight," Tammy says with all the excitement of a sloth. "Bonfire."

Ali smiles up at me, fresh as a newly tilled field. I trail my fingers down the red and black ribbons dangling from her braids and I have to believe all of this is going to work out.

If the Devil is real, then so is God.

And I have to believe he's watching out for us.

51

THE STADIUM is packed. I don't have to see it. I can feel it. The thunderous roar of boots stomping the bleachers in time with the marching band. The hum of the Jumbotron leaking through the thick concrete walls.

Some of the guys are praying. Some are taking it out on their lockers. I like to sit real quiet, study the playbook—clear my mind of any distractions. Before, it was simple worries like passing my trig exam or wondering if Ali liked me, not worrying if the Devil is coming to town for world domination. But worrying's not going to help anybody. Miss Granger is doing her part. I have to do mine. She told me to win this game and that's exactly what I intend to do. And the truth is, I want to win. I want to feel something other than pain and confusion and loss and madness. This is something I know how to do. I can run a play. I can throw a ball. I have no idea what's going to happen tomorrow, if there'll even be a tomorrow, but this moment is mine and mine alone.

Eddie Landers comes by, giving me a thumbs-up. I know there was a lot of talk after my dad died, people saying I'd lost my arm. Lost my nerve. Sure, I've got something to prove, but it's more than that. Football was always the one place I could let it all go. All I had to do was put that ball over the goal line. How I got it there was up to me. My call. My domain. My team. Some people might say quarterbacks have a God complex, but I don't want to be God. I just want to feel connected to something bigger than myself. For one night, I don't want to think about my dad or my family or Lee or Ali or the wheat or the Devil. All I want to do is play ball.

"You ready, Tate?" Coach's hand comes down hard on my shoulder. "It's showtime."

He gathers us around to bend a knee.

"We've had a hell of a week—hell of a week!" he yells. "Lost one of our own. Tonight, you don't play for your mama or your daddy or your girlfriends. You play for Big Ben. Ben Gillman. He loved this team more than anything in the world. He loved football. His funeral's on Sunday at Newcomers. I expect all of you to be there and I expect to be burying him with the winning ball from tonight's game. The *winning* ball! And we've got this. We got our captain back—the Tate-en-Nator. You listen to every goddamn word that comes out of his mouth out there. He knows how to bring home the W. And you know what happens if we win this?"

"Women!" one of the guys calls out. A low chuckle rumbles through the locker room.

"Well, yeah, I'm sure there'll be plenty of that. Despite our checkered season"—everyone stares at Tyler—"you'll have a chance at redemption. You'll be heroes. Tonight's not just any game. We're playing our rivals, the Sooners. Whether they win or lose, they're going to State, but we have the opportunity to show 'em what we're made of. This is the real championship right here. There won't be a trophy, there won't be any rings . . ." I feel eyes on me from every direction. I know they all blame me for taking it away from them last year, when I lost it out on that field and nearly killed that kid. "But you'll be able to hold your head high in this town for the rest of your lives. The Sooners want to take that away from you. But this is our turf. We need to show them how real men take land . . . by force, like our ancestors did before us."

I almost burst out laughing. If they only knew.

"We're faster, tougher, smarter . . . and we will take this field. We will take what's ours! On three."

"One, two, three."

"Pioneers!"

We storm through the doors and onto the field.

The band strikes up our fight song, the rush of pom-poms, the roar of the crowd, the lights, the cameras. This is Oklahoma football. No fucking joke.

On instinct, I glance up at the stands to where my parents used to sit. Mr. and Mrs. Neely are there now, clapping and screaming with a crazed look in their eyes. I shake it off. Not now. I can't let anything get in my way, get in my head.

The Sooners fans are booing us as we take the field.

As much as they want to see me fail, they're looking for magic. They want to believe. They're looking for salvation. Redemption. And if throwing a pigskin ball at fifty miles per hour like a spinning Scud missile precisely into the hands of your receiver isn't magic . . . I don't know what is.

We huddle up. First play of the night.

I know what they're expecting, I've always played it smart, but I don't want to take this slow and steady. We need to show them what it's gonna be like—set the pace. "We're not going for a first down," I say to the team. "We're going for the touchdown. Miracle Whip, for Ben. Are you guys with me?"

They answer in unison without the slightest hesitation. They trust me out here.

"Who's my runner?" I ask.

"I got this." Tyler nods.

"You sure? Because I'm going to deliver that ball right into your hands. If you drop it, that's on you."

"I'm sure."

Tyler's putting up a good front, but he looks nervous.

"Okay. After the first pushback, I want all eyes on Neely. Protect him out there."

We break and get into position.

"Walleye 24. Trent 43. Pine 22. Hut."

The offensive line is gunning for me—coming at me from every angle. After the initial hit, I send my guys down the field. Fake to the left, fake to the right. I spin out of a tackle, giving them as much time as possible to get into position. A guy's coming at me—280 pounds of pure pain—but I stand my ground, waiting as long as I can before I let go of the ball. I take the hit; it knocks me clean off my feet, crushing the wind right out of my lungs. I lift my head, but all I see are blurs of light moving in the inky darkness. I hear the crowd going crazy. I look up into the stands, but they're empty now. I clench my eyes shut and when I open them again, hundreds of people are walking onto the field. They're smiling, but their eyes are pure black orbs—inhuman and hungry.

"He's coming," they chant as they crowd around me. "He's com-ing," they say as they reach out to touch me.

Not now. Not here.

"Tate!" A hand reaches through the wall of bodies, pulling me to my feet and away from the darkness.

"We did it!" Tyler grabs onto my helmet, forcing me to look him in the eyes. The other guys ram into us, whooping it up. I stagger back and look around the stadium—everything's back to normal. I must've blacked out for a minute . . . that's all.

I glance over at Ali cheering on the sidelines, beaming with excite-ment, the end of her red and black ribbons grazing her shoulder blade. She has no idea what's coming for her. For all of us.

Tyler jerks my face mask. "Are you with us, Tate?"

"Yeah." I pull away from him and get my head back in the game. I shut it down, all of it, until it's just me and the ball again.

Play after play, touchdown after touchdown, I let go of every-thing I've been holding inside of me. The anger, the hurt, the fear, the violence, the lust, the confusion, the rage, until there's nothing left of me, until we've annihilated the Sooners, brought them to their knees. I've sent them off this field in humiliation and I'm not sorry for it. I did what I came out here to do and now it's time to move on.

I sign the ball. R.I.P. And that's the last time I'll touch a foot-ball.

And I can finally live with that.

52

THE RIDE to Harmon Lake is like something out of a dream: the ache in my muscles from a hard-won battle out on the field, the feel of Ali's warm body nestled against me, her hand on my thigh— dangerously close to everything I wanted before all this happened.

It's probably a mistake giving her a ride like this, being this close to her before the exorcism, but I want to protect her. I know Miss Granger says it doesn't matter, that it's still Ali, but when I'm with her, in that way, I want it to be for real. For keeps. Mind, body, and soul. Nothing clouding our judgment. It's probably corny and maybe I'm kind of corny, but I think we both deserve that much.

But she's certainly not making it easy.

Ali's kissing my neck, running her hand over my chest. "We don't have to go to the lake, you know. We could just get lost," she says, gently biting down on my ear.

"Lost, huh?" I laugh. "In this two-stoplight town?"

She slides her hand down to unbutton my jeans. I almost hit the mile marker sign for Harmon Lake.

I barrel into the makeshift lot and slam on the brakes. There's a ton of cars already here. I can see the glow of the bonfire in the distance.

"Ali . . ." I put my hand on top of hers to stop her, but she's not listening to me.

"I can tell you want to," she whispers.

I let out a shuddering breath as she frees me from the rest of the buttons. I start to say something when she lowers her head.

I want to stop her, I know I should, I *will*. "Ali," I say as I pry my hand off the steering wheel and pull back her hair so I can see her face, but that only makes it worse.

"Pioneers!" A guy screams as he passes the truck, raising two twelve-packs above his head.

Ali giggles, but she doesn't stop.

As much as I want to forget everything and disappear into her, into this moment, I grasp onto the back of her neck, feeling the brand beneath my thumb, the raised mark . . . the invitation, and pull her off me. "This isn't right."

"I don't understand." She sits up, pushing her shiny dark hair out of her face. Her eyes are soft brown with flecks of light gold. "Don't you like it?"

"Believe me . . . I do." I look straight ahead at the bonfire in the distance as I button my jeans—anywhere but her soft lips. "Just not like this . . . not yet."

"Then when?"

I tighten my grip on the steering wheel. "If you can just give me a little more time."

"Is this about Miss Granger?" Her eyes well up with tears. "Were you with her last night? Is that why you left me at the Preservation Society?"

"There's a lot more to it than that."

"I'm not going to wait forever, Clay. Time's running out," she says as she gets out of the car.

"Ali, wait!"

She turns back. "I've tried everything. I want to be with you. I thought this was settled. But I can't make you choose me."

"Ali, it's not that. It's always been you—"

"Then show me." She takes off into the woods.

I will my body to calm the hell down and go looking for her.

I've been to some ragers out here, but never anything like this. Lynyrd Skynyrd's blasting, people are wasted, a few couples are practically doing it right out in the open. The bonfire's huge and putting out a ton of smoke. And there's a weird herb smell, same thing I smelled in the secret room at the Preservation Society. You can probably see the smoke all the way to Gerard County. Dumbasses. This party's going to get busted before they even shoot off the fireworks.

I fan away the smoke, looking for Ali, when I spot Tyler dancing on the bed of a truck with some girl. His hands are all over her ass and she's grinding up on him. The girl turns to face me, and I do a double take. It's Tammy. She sees me watching her. She smiles as she leans back, kissing Tyler. It's not a peck on the cheek, it's a full-on kiss with tongue, but Tammy never takes her eyes off me.

A bunch of guys from the team start howling and whistling at them. And I want to rip their heads off.

"She's staring right at you, man. She wants you." Pete Adams elbows me in the ribs with his beer bottle. "The quiet ones are always the kinkiest," he adds dreamily.

"Grow the fuck up," I say to Pete as I push through the crowd to get to her.

This isn't Tammy—the Tammy I know would never act like this. I've got to get her out of here before she does something she regrets.

"Think you've had enough." I grab on to her and lift her off the truck bed.

"I knew you'd choose me," she says, wrapping her legs around me.

Prying her off me, I set her down. "I'm getting you out of here."

"I'm not leaving until you kiss me right here . . . right now. Like you mean it."

"Oooh . . ." A crowd gathers round.

She doesn't realize what's happening. What's inside of her. What's driving her.

I take a deep breath to tell her that's not going to happen, when the smoke hits me. I stagger back a little, the ground tilts, the fire's spinning in front of me.

I squeeze my eyes shut. I'm trying so hard to focus. I feel like I've seen this all before but I can't figure out from where.

I open my eyes to see Tyler whispering to Tammy. Is the Devil speaking through him? I saw him whispering to Jimmy down in that cell at the Preservation Society. I saw him whispering to Ben on the field after he turned on me at practice, and now this . . .

"Relax, Clay." Tammy steps forward, and suddenly she's taking off her clothes. "Come skinny-dipping with me."

"This is the Devil, Tammy. This isn't you." I take off my coat so I can wrap it around her, but a bunch of guys grab on to me, holding me back.

"Let her do it, man."

She just smiles as she strips down naked right there on the muddy bank. "Come with me, Clay, please." She takes off her glasses and pulls the elastic out of her hair, wading into the dark water.

I jerk out of the hold to find everyone raging around me, egging her on. They don't understand what's really happening here.

Tammy swims out to the floating dock where they've set up the fireworks and climbs up, lighting a flare.

"He's coming, Clay," she calls out. "He's coming for all of us."

The green glow of the flare . . . her pale naked body . . . the reddish sheen to her hair . . . I've seen this before, but in my dream the girl was encircled by flames.

The fireworks.

"No . . . no!" I slip off my shoes, diving into the frigid water.

"Yeah, Tate. Thatta boy." People are yelling after me.

"Tammy, stop!" I scream as I come up for air again. The smell of sulfite and gunpowder hits my nostrils. It's so dark; the water's so murky. In the fading glow of the flare I can just make out her silhouette as she's pulling the caps off a bunch of M-80s, emptying the contents around the dock.

"Blessed be the seed. This is all for the chosen one," she says as she drops the flare, setting off a circle of flames on the dock, which swiftly engulf her body. She screams in agony as the fire burns her hair, her skin, but she doesn't move an inch.

"Jump in the water!" I call out to her, but she doesn't listen. I try to grasp on to the ladder and pull myself up, but the metal's scalding hot.

As I sink back into the water, all I can do is watch the flesh melt off her bones, until she's nothing more than a charred mass.

I look back at the pandemonium on the shore. People are screaming, taking off, running into the woods. Sirens are blaring in the distance. But that's not what makes me freeze in place. Stepping out of the woods toward the shore is Noodle. She's in her nightgown, dragging the dead calf beside her.

53

"CLAY TATE?" A voice booms over a megaphone, harsh lights blinding me, making my vision of Noodle disappear. "Step out of the water with your hands up."

For a second, I can't even process what they're saying. I turn away from the floodlights, looking back at the floating dock, at Tammy's charred remains, and I know how it looks. I'm treading water in front of her goddamn corpse.

I think about taking off, swimming as far as I can. If I reach the creek it could carry me all the way to Love County. But then I think about Noodle, Jess, and Mom. All I have to do is hang on until tomorrow. Miss Granger will be back. She can fix this. They've got nothing on me except being in the wrong place at the wrong time.

When I get close enough to the shore to stand up, Deputy Tilford storms in and grabs me, throwing me down onto the muddy bank, drilling his knee into my kidney, as he cuffs me.

"Sheriff!" I scream into the blur of flashing red lights. "I need to talk to Sheriff Ely."

"I'm the deputy in charge," Tilford says as he hauls me to my feet. "Sheriff's out there looking for your sister. Lost cause if you ask me, but I'm more than happy to get some alone time with you."

"Tell him to go to the campground," I plead as he drags me to his police car and crams me in the back. "Find Lee. Find Jess!" I manage to get out before he shuts the door.

The volunteer fire department finally arrives; they're rushing out with the hose and gurney. They don't know it, but Tammy's been dead since I had that vision about her last night. Just like all the rest of them.

As we pull out of the lot, I see Ali in tears, standing next to Tyler's car. Tyler smirks at me and puts his arm around her as we drive by. He still thinks this is some kind of competition for her.

But I'm beyond that. This is about her soul.

54

AT THE courthouse, they have me in a windowless room with mint-green painted concrete walls. The clock on the wall is broken, but I've been here for hours, maybe all night. There's a large particleboard table and two metal folding chairs. I see a camera in the corner, its tiny red light blinking at me like a warning. *Don't say anything. Keep your mouth shut, Clay.*

When the door finally opens again, I sit up straight, the cuffs rattling around my wrists.

I'm disappointed to see it's just Greg Tilford.

Begrudgingly, he sets a cup of coffee in front of me. I take a drink, letting it scald my mouth. Anything to warm me up.

He tosses a puke-colored scratchy wool blanket at me. I manage to get it over my shoulders. "Thanks," I whisper as I sink into it.

"You ready to talk now?" Tilford drops a thick folder on the table with a thud.

"I already told you. I was only trying to help. I saw what Tammy was doing and I tried to stop her."

"That's where I'm having trouble." Greg leans in. "Eyewitnesses are saying that Tammy wanted you to go skinny-dipping and you pushed her off. They said you were acting crazy, talking about the Devil."

"Don't I get a phone call? I want to make a phone call."

"Which reminds me," he says as he opens the folder, scanning through the papers. "Looks like you've been calling Miss Granger quite a bit."

"So? She's my counselor," I say, trying to get a glimpse at what's in that file.

"You have things on your mind, Clay? Things you need to confess?"

I gulp down the rest of the coffee. "I want to talk to Sheriff."

"We haven't been able to reach Emma Granger yet, but we've seen your school records." Tilford flips through some of the pages, scratching a dark patch of stubble he missed on the side of his neck. "I'm thinking you learned all this from your daddy. Graduated from pregnant cows to people."

"Where's Sheriff Ely?" I rub my wrists. " 'Cause he'll tell you. I had nothing to do with any of this. It's just a huge misunderstanding."

"Oh, yeah?" Greg smirks as he pulls out a piece of paper and slides it over to me. "How about this list of library books you've checked out in the past year? Schizophrenia. Mind control. Hypnotism. The occult. Prophets?"

"Th-that was before," I sputter. "That's when I was trying to figure out what was happening."

Greg leans forward, alert and tense. "Happening to what? To *you*? You think you're some kind of God . . . some kind of prophet? You hearing voices, Clay?"

I stare down at the fake wood grain on the table. *Just keep your mouth shut.*

Greg lets out a deep sigh. "I'm just trying to understand. You've got to help me out. Your dad goes nuts . . . breaks into the breeding barn, kills all the pregnant cows with a metal crucifix, and tries to get to the bull. The remaining cows stampede him to death. You accuse the Preservation Society of being involved in his death . . . you say all these families are in on it . . . some kind of conspiracy theory." He lays out school photos of Tyler, Tammy, Ben, Jimmy, and Ali in front of me. "Now, fast-forward a year, you join the council, that same bull from the breeding barn gets its throat slit, and three of your fellow Preservation Society pals turn up dead under very suspicious circumstances. And it just so happens that you're the one who discovered their bodies."

He then lays two crime scene photos down. "Here's Jimmy bleeding out at the altar. Ben strung up on the goalpost like Jesus Freaking Christ. You had some kind of altercation with each one of them before they died. You've got all these books on mind control and Devil worship and prophets and you're telling me that's a coincidence?"

"Yes. That's exactly what I'm telling you."

He lets out an explosive laugh. "Then you must have the worst luck in the world!" I pull the blanket tighter around me.

"And then there's the brand." He slides close-ups of autopsy photos across the table. "Jimmy's brand was on his lower back. And Ben's was on his calf. Of course we don't have any evidence of

Tammy's mark, because this is what she looks like now." He places a photo in front of me and I cringe. Looks like something from the bottom of Mr. Miller's smoker.

"But I think it's safe to say she had the same mark. Wouldn't you say so, Clay?"

The dregs of the burnt coffee brings the stench of death right back to me. My stomach's churning, but I refuse to give in, I refuse to let him know he's getting to me. I swallow the bile burning the back of my throat and force myself to look him straight in the eyes. "I didn't do this."

"We did a little digging. You know what that symbol means?"

"No." I try to act disinterested but I can feel the heat spread up my neck.

"That's funny. 'Cause I think you do. It's a Devil worship thing. You drew the same symbol on your math folder." He slides over a copy of the front of my folder.

"I probably just saw it on one of them and drew it. There are lots of drawings on that folder."

"I'll give you that one, but that sure as hell doesn't explain *this*." He pulls a photo from the back of the file and leans back in his chair with his hands laced behind his head.

I steel myself and look down at the photo. It's an aerial shot. It takes me a minute for my eyes to adjust, to wrap my mind around what I'm seeing. It's our farm. And then I remember the other day when Noodle saw the plane . . . the drone. That must've been how they took these. I can see the roof of the house, the equipment shed, my truck in the drive, the combine in the middle of the field, and the breeding barn—but that's not what has my heart in a vice grip.

There's something in the crops.

A symbol.

The upside-down U with two dots above and below, clear as day, carved into the wheat.

"This can't be." I shake my head. "This must be some kind of hoax. Neely must've doctored this or someone must've done this to the field while I was sleeping," I sputter as I take a closer look.

"It says here Sheriff paid you a visit after Jimmy died. Said you were acting strange and that you weren't using the same pattern your dad used to clear the wheat." He flips through some pages in his notebook. "You told him, and I quote, 'I'm using the force.'"

"Look." I pull against the shackles, the sharp noise rattling me. "I can explain all of this . . . there's got to be some kind of logical explan—"

"Here's what *I'm* thinking," Tilford interrupts. "You got them all drugged up, and then you branded them. Is that part of your sick little ritual? You mark them for death, just like cattle, and now you're picking them off one by one."

"Really?" I laugh as I jut my head back. "So I'm a druggie now, too?"

Greg grins. "You know that cute little blonde who came in earlier to take blood and hair samples?" He pulls out a pink slip of paper. "Toxicology came back with high amounts of salvia in your system."

"*Salvia?* I don't understand . . . how the—oh my God, the bonfire . . . the smoke . . . that must've been what they were burning at the bonfire. Why everyone was acting so crazy."

"We have dozens of eye witnesses all saying the same thing. The only person acting crazy was *you*."

"Someone's setting me up." I try to stand, but the cuffs won't allow it. "Lee Wiggins!" I blurt. "He has something to do with this. He's got a grudge against my family . . . against my dad."

"Is this about your sister? Jess? She was last seen running away from you after the Harvest Festival. What happened between the two of you? 'Cause I heard you walked in on her and Jimmy Doogan in the basement of the Preservation Society? Did he humiliate you, Clay?"

"No, it wasn't like that." I jerk against the cuffs.

"Did she soil your family name?" He keeps firing at me. "And now she's missing. People saw her around town with a known meth-head and you don't even go looking for her?"

"I didn't know she was missing until I called Sheriff last night."

"I don't know what's worse!" He gets in my face.

I'm trying to hold it together, but he's riding me so hard. I don't know how much more of this I can take.

"I went out to the house last night to notify your family of your arrest. That's no condition for a little girl."

"What are you talking about?" I sit up ramrod straight.

"Your mom was in a catatonic state, wasn't keeping house, bathing. All she could talk about was those flies."

"She's fine. She'll be fine." I strain against the cuffs.

"She's far from fine, Clay. She's at Oakmoor now."

"What?" My throat goes bone dry. "What about Noodle . . . where is she?"

"She's with her guardian. Ian Neely."

"No." I take in a sharp inhalation of breath. "Listen to me . . ." I lean forward as far as the shackles will allow. "She's not safe there. I know he's your cousin, but I'm telling you, he's one of them . . . he's not what you think he is."

"So the whole town's in on this, huh? Setting up poor Clay Tate. I'm done listening to this bull crap." He starts gathering the papers.

"I'll tell you anything you want, just get Noodle away from Ian Neely. Put her in foster care. Maybe she can stay at All Saints. She's enrolled next semester as a day student, but I'll pay for her to board. She'll be safe there."

"The only thing she needs protection from right now is *you*. She even said you threw her doll out the window. What kind of sick fuck takes a doll away from a little girl?"

"Have you *seen* that doll?" I yell.

As he gets up to leave, I can't help thinking, what if he's right? What if none of this is an accident or a coincidence? Maybe I didn't need the symbol on my skin because I'd already carved it into the wheat. An invitation all over my land. Maybe I'm the one who brought the Devil here and I don't even know it. Could I be that screwed up? Is this what happened to my dad? Am I the chosen one? Is that why he tried to kill me in the end?

Just as I'm on the verge of spilling my guts, telling him everything, the door slams open. Sheriff Ely's standing there.

Greg walks out into the hall. They exchange words and I swear I can see the blood drain from Tilford's face. After a few tense minutes, Tilford comes back in the room. "Clay, it appears I've made a mistake," he says as he unlocks my cuffs. "You're free to go. I'm sorry for the inconvenience," he adds, but he can't meet my eyes.

Inconvenience? I want to punch his lights out, but I'm so fucking relieved. I rub my sore wrists, looking up at him in shock, thinking this must be a joke . . . some kind of test. A minute ago it seemed like he was ready to lock me up for life.

"I don't understand. What's happening?"

Tilford won't meet my eyes. "Sheriff Ely will fill you in."

I turn to see Sheriff standing in the hall; I start to ask him what the hell's going on, when he takes off his cowboy hat. The only other time I've seen him without his hat on was at my dad's funeral, so I'm pretty sure whatever he has to tell me, I don't want to hear.

55

SHERIFF'S TREMBLING as he reaches forward to shake my hand. His eyes are bloodshot; there's dirt caked under his nails. He looks like he's been through hell and back.

"Is it Ali?" I force the words out of my mouth.

"Ali?" He seems taken aback. "No, son. No, it's Jess."

"You found her?" I let out a sigh of relief.

"We found her." He looks down at the ground. "You were right. She was with the Wiggins kid." He presses his lips together so tight they turn white. "Lee confessed to everything. He's the one who forced Jimmy, Ben, and Tammy to kill themselves. Threatened to kill their families if they didn't. He slit that bull's throat, put that calf in your field . . . carved the mark in the wheat . . . put salvia in the bonfire. Said he did it for the Devil."

"I knew it." I let out a huge gust of pent-up air. "Well, can I see her? Can I see Jess?"

"That's why I'm here." He swallows hard. "We need you to identify the body."

"The body? What body?"

"Jessica's body." His voice quivers as he struggles to meet my eyes.

"No," I whisper, feeling the floor drop out from under me. "How? Why?" I brace myself against the wall.

"I'm guessing she died about two days ago. We found her out in the woods behind Merritt's at that campsite. The Wiggins kid suffocated her, buried her alive." He nearly swallows the word.

I grit my jaw, choking back any emotion. "I need to see her."

"Are you sure you're up for it? 'Cause we can wait a bit . . . you can talk to someone . . . get something to eat."

"I don't want to talk and I don't want a fucking sandwich. My sister's dead for Christ's sake."

He grips the brim of his hat so hard I think he might crush it. "This way," he says as he places it back on his head.

We take the elevator down to the bottom floor. It's where they keep the bodies until they can be released to the funeral home or shipped off to Gerard County for autopsies. It's the longest elevator ride of my life.

I remember having to do this last year when Dad died. Every town official was gathered round, watching me, rubbernecking for the best view, but this feels different. The hall's empty; the fluorescent lights flicker. It's so quiet. All I hear are Sheriff's boots clacking against the worn-out linoleum.

"Where is everyone?"

"There's a storm coming. Everyone's hunkered down at the school. Emergency personnel only."

"A storm?" I whisper. The lights flicker.

We enter an examining room. There's no sheet to peel back. She's just lying there on a metal table, naked as the day she came into this world. The sight of her takes my breath away.

"Goddamn it, I'm sorry," Sheriff says as he grabs a sheet from the rack and quickly drapes it over her.

Tears sting the corners of my eyes as I force myself to look at her. The first thing I notice are the bruises around her throat—and all I can think about is fastening that locket around her neck the other night at the Harvest Festival. I took her there. I put her in that position. I was so wrapped up in Ali, and Mr. Neely, and all this Devil shit that I didn't even see what was happening. I did this to her. She was my sister . . . my own flesh and blood. She's been dead for two days and I didn't even know she was gone. I should've checked on her. I should've gone in her room. While I was playing ball, getting close to Ali, she was out there rotting in the woods. Left there like a piece of trash.

Trash.

"Wait . . . was she . . ." I choke on the thought. "Was she buried in that circle?" I manage to ask.

Ely looks down at the ground and I know it's true.

"I was there . . . I was right there. The dirty clumps of hair sticking up from the ground. I must've stepped right over her body." I grit my jaw so hard my teeth creak. "I failed you," I whisper as I try to brush her hair back, but it's matted with dirt and bits of moss.

Moss. Just like Noodle said the other night . . . that Jess was tucked in a bed of moss like a woodland fairy.

I wipe my sleeve across my face, but the tears won't stop flowing.

Sheriff Ely places his hand on my shoulder. "I'm sorry for your loss. What's happened to you and your family in the past year is enough pain for ten lifetimes."

I tighten my grip on the edge of the metal table. My shoulders are shaking so hard, the moss in her hair trembles with each heaving breath. I let out a sob and then clasp my hand over my mouth. I wonder how long it took for her to die. What she thought of before she took her last breath. It kills me that she couldn't see the stars.

I'm not sure how long I stand there. Minutes . . . maybe hours. When I'm done crying, I take the edge of the sheet and pull it up over Jess's face. I've seen enough death to know this isn't her. It's just an empty shell. Jess must be in heaven. I have to believe that. The thought of anything else is too much to bear.

"Sheriff." Greg clears his throat from the doorway. "A twister was spotted over the county line. Near Gillmans'."

"I'll be . . ." Ely replies in a daze. "First tornado to cross the county line in a hundred and twenty-seven years." He straightens his badge. "I guess I need to man the alarm."

"I'll get Clay checked out," Tilford says. "Make sure he gets his belongings, take him wherever he needs to go."

"Is that all right with you, son?"

I nod. It's the best I can do. I still want to deck Tilford for riding me so hard back there. I know he was only doing his job. But still.

As Sheriff heads off to deal with the alarm, Greg escorts me to the elevator.

"What floor?" I let out a jittery sigh, uncomfortable being in yet another confined space with him.

"That's up to you."

I glance back at him. "Look, I don't know what you're getting at, but—"

"If it were me, I'd want to kill the guy who did that to her." He pauses, an obnoxious smirk tugging at the corner of his mouth. "Want a shot at him?"

"Wiggins?" My heart races. "Is he here?"

"Private holding cell on the fifth floor . . . no one here but us chickens. I figure I owe you one. They ordered him up a nice steak dinner from Garrison's, too. First-class treatment."

I unclench my fist long enough to push number five.

56

GREG UNLOCKS the cell, pushes the door open, and steps back.

Lee's standing there in his jumpsuit, grinning at me, like he's been waiting for me.

I don't waste a single breath. I charge after him, pounding him into the ground. He doesn't even try to fight me; goes down like a sack of grain. I haul back and punch him in the jaw so hard I hear it pop out of place. But still, he's got that grin.

"Do it, Clay. I've been waiting for you," he grunts. "Thought you'd come for Jess a lot sooner."

In a burst of rage I head butt him. He falls back, stunned at first, and then starts laughing. "She was practically *begging* for it in the end."

Picking him up off the ground by his jumpsuit, I slam him

against the wall. I start wailing on him with everything I have, a rage so hot and full of acid, I want to put my fist straight through his chest.

"Blessed be the seed," he says as he takes the blows.

I punch him in the gut and he doubles over.

He starts to sing. It sounds like a nursery rhyme. "The first to fall will pray, the second to fall has come to play, the third to fall will shiver and burn, the fourth to fall, a lesson to learn, the fifth to fall will eat his words, but six and seven will go to heaven, eight will be a grave mistake, the ninth will be for goodness' sake, the final one to fall, the tenth will be the one to bind them all."

"How do you know that song?" I shake him. "That's Noodle's counting song. Have you done something to Noodle?"

"I'm ready to eat my words." He straightens up to face me. "Let me serve our lord."

I haul back to punch him again, my fist trembling, aching for contact. His face is raw and bloodied, but still, he manages a smile. His eyes—the irises have all but disappeared. They're pure black now. And what I see in their reflection scares the shit out of me. Who's the animal now?

"Aren't you going to stop me?" I pant as I look over my shoulder at Tilford.

"You deserve this," he says with a dark glint in his eyes. "Courtesy of Ian Neely."

"Neely?" I exhale as I let go of Lee. He collapses to the ground, a puddle of mangled flesh and broken bones.

"Do it, Clay," Lee whispers, blood streaming down the corner of his mouth.

Lee wants me to kill him. Neely wants this, too.

But why? If I do this, if I take his life, will I be one of them? Is that how they'll finally pull me in?

"Fuck you." I spit on Lee. "I'll let the good state of Oklahoma take care of you."

On my way out, I smear my bloody thumb across Tilford's star badge, which is pinned upside down. The sign of the Devil. "I know you're one of them. Tell Neely thanks, but no thanks. Better yet . . . I'll tell him myself."

"Don't leave me like this," Wiggins screams. "You're Cain and I'm Abel. Let me be the fifth. You have to finish it. Let me serve our lord." His wail echoes down the hall.

57

I RACE down the stairs, a high ringing in my ears, the sound of my fist pounding Lee's flesh, bones snapping, fluorescent lights pinging.

As soon as I leave the building, the cold air hits my split knuckles, making me wince, but there's still acid and hate coursing through my muscles.

I start running. It's like my body knows where I'm headed long before my brain can process it, but I'm heading straight for the Neelys' house.

I can't let him take Noodle from me.

"Noodle!" I scream as I barge into their house, tearing through rooms. There's a grilled cheese on the kitchen table, cut into little triangles, just the way Noodle likes it. It's still slightly warm in the center. They can't be far.

I start to head upstairs to check the bedrooms when the sirens begin to wail. I freeze in my tracks. This is the first time I've heard the tornado alarm in my entire life. It sounds alien going into my eardrums, making my heart beat double time. Could Midland be getting its first tornado since the land rush? And what does that mean?

I know they set up a town shelter at the school, but some of the original houses have storm shelters. I go out back to look for a cellar hatch, and that's when I notice how quiet everything is. Other than the mournful wail of the siren, there's no cars, no kids playing or dogs barking. The air is completely still and humid, and there's a sweetness. The wind chimes just hang there like broken bones. The dying leaves cling to the branches, unstirred. Everything feels suspended. The sky is the strangest color, green with swirls of peach. But the clouds circling Midland are the color of gunmetal . . . death.

"Noodle!" I scream into the void, but the stillness seems to swallow it whole. It's like every living thing has vanished from the earth. Maybe they know something I don't. Maybe this is the end.

I run back inside and grab a set of car keys dangling from a hook in the kitchen. I realize this is grand theft auto, but it's an emergency. I have to find Noodle. I have to find anyone at this point so I can be sure all of this isn't a dream.

As I open the garage door, I let out a burst of nervous laughter when I see Mr. Neely's bright-yellow Hummer. Dickmobile. Like father like son.

I turn the engine, and Ted Nugent comes blasting through the stereo. I start stabbing at it with my finger to make it stop, but I only end up jamming the buttons. I roll down the windows to try and get away from it, but it's no use. At least they'll hear me coming.

The shops on Main Street are deserted. I get out to peer in the window of Gus's Shoe Shop. The door's open, but there's no one there. It's like everyone just walked out of their homes . . . their stores . . . their lives . . . but where did they go?

I see a black sedan racing down Main Street, turning on Route 17. I jump back in Neely's car and take off after it. I'm going seventy and I still can't catch up. I wonder if it's state police.

The farther I get out of town, the duller the tornado sirens become. I'm grateful for it. Now, if I can just figure out how to silence Ted Nugent, I might be able to think. As I'm fiddling with the stereo, I hear screeching tires, followed by a cloud of dust in the road up ahead.

I slow down, hoping they didn't get in an accident. As I approach, I'm trying to remember how to do CPR, but when the dust settles, I only find an abandoned car. I get out and track the skid marks in the road—must be twenty-five feet of burned rubber, but what made them slam on their brakes? And where the hell are they now? There's a little peach on the license plate. Georgia. The inside of the car looks pristine, like it just came off the lot. I check the glove box. Registered to a Thomas Dixon from Atlanta. Why would he be way out here? We're not anywhere near a major highway. Maybe he's looking for shelter from the storm. A few wrong turns, maybe he panicked.

I scan the surrounding fields. It's just a bunch of overgrown grazing pastures, part of the Neely farm. Nothing around for miles.

Getting back in Neely's car, I drive ahead to see if I can spot anyone. Then I notice the other cars. It's sporadic at first, until they're lined up one after another on either side of Route 17. Some still have their doors wide open. Engines running. Some of the cars I recognize from town, but others are from as far away as New York City.

I weave in and out of the vehicles as far as I can go, until a semi's blocking the road. Abandoning Neely's car, I cut through overgrown pastures, yelling out to anyone who might need help, but there's nothing, not even a bug scrabbling over the dirt. The wind's picked up now. It doesn't come in fits and gales—it's like Mother Nature's expelling one long endless steady breath. It makes the tall grass sway and shiver, like that mental patient sitting under the tree at Oakmoor.

It sends an icy chill over my skin.

The sky lets out an ominous groan. I look up. All the clouds seem to be amassing over the dividing line between our farm and the Neely ranch. *The breeding barn.*

And it dawns on me. This is no ordinary storm. This is God and the Devil . . . a battle between good and evil . . . this is everything coming to a head.

I pick up my pace. As the breeding barn comes into view, I see Miss Granger's car out front. Two figures in long black dresses are dragging someone from the car.

I wave my hands in the air. "Hey . . . hey there!"

As I get closer, I see they're not dresses, but robes. Of course . . . it's the priests from All Saints, and they're dragging Tyler Neely into the barn, his body contorted like a piece of plastic melting in the sun.

Miss Granger emerges from the car, pulling a girl out with her.

Ali's shaking and crying. "Please don't do this. Why are you doing this to me?"

"Wait," I scream as I close the distance.

"Clay . . . help me!" Ali says.

The priests come out of the barn. Ali's bucking and wailing like a pinned animal, but as soon as the priest with the reddish goatee lays his hand on her forehead, her body goes rigid, her eyes roll back in her head. The sound that escapes her twisted mouth is something straight out of a nightmare. A screeching wail of agony.

It takes me aback.

I watch as the priests drag Ali into the barn, but this isn't Ali. I know that now.

"Please don't hurt her." I try to go after them, but Miss Granger steps in front of me, blocking my path.

"This is for the best," she says.

"What's going on? There's cars everywhere . . . from all over the place . . . just abandoned in the road."

"Probably storm chasers," she says as she glances up at the menacing sky. "After all, this is a historic event. One hundred and twenty-seven years in the making."

"But where is everyone? Oh my God, Noodle!" I suddenly remember, looking back toward town.

"She's fine. She's with the rest of the community at the school. She'll be safe there." Miss Granger takes my hands. "I heard what happened to Jess . . . about Lee." She looks down at my swollen, bloody knuckles. "I'm so sorry, but soon this will all be over."

"It's time," one of the priests calls from the barn.

"Let's do this," I say.

"No, Clay." She shakes her head. "You can't stay for the exorcism."

"What are you talking about?" I stare at the barn door. "I can't leave her."

"I don't want you to remember her like this. Ali wouldn't want you to remember her like this."

"What do you expect me to do?" I swallow hard. "Just wait out here . . . and do what?"

"Pray." She squeezes my shoulder before disappearing inside the barn and latching the door behind her.

58

I PACE the red earth in front of the barn, listening to the horror that must be happening inside—the bellowing of the priests, the holy water sizzling against skin, the screams of agony coming out of Tyler and Ali.

I run around the barn, like I did on that night when I saw Ali emerge from the cow. I get glimpses, but the priests hover over them, their black robes engulfing the scene. I press my face against the splintery wood. Ali screams out in pain. I can't stand this . . . not being able to do anything to help her.

The sky groans and I wonder if Miss Granger's right. I haven't prayed since Dad died, but I'm willing to try if it will help Ali. I'll do anything to make this stop.

I tear myself away from the barn and go to the only place that makes sense.

The wheat.

The place where it all began. Where it will end.

I keep walking until I can pretend their screams are just the wind whipping through the plains. A low grumbling thunders above me. As I look up at the sky, at the dark clouds amassing, I'm suddenly afraid for Ali's soul.

"Is this what you want?" I scream up at the heavens. "You want me on my knees?"

I drop to the ground, my hands digging into the fertile soil, the very land my ancestors traded our souls for . . . their own flesh and blood. "For this?" I scream, hot tears streaming down my face. "You can't let the Devil take her for *this*!"

A bolt of lightning strikes over the breeding barn, making the hair on my entire body stand on end.

"I hear you. I feel you," I call up to God, my chin trembling, my body weak. "I'm sorry I turned my back on you after Dad died. I'm sorry I didn't see. You've kept me strong, kept me safe. I'm asking for a second chance. I won't waste it. I'll make you proud . . . you'll see. But I need your help right now. There's a girl back there"—I glance toward the breeding barn shrouded in inky darkness—"a girl I can't live without. Ali. I know you've been watching out for her, too. But I need you to take the Devil from her. I need her to walk out of that barn. I need her to come back to me. I can't do this without her. She's everything I've ever wanted. Give me this one thing and I'll never doubt you again. I'll marry her. Just please bring her back to me the way she was before. It might be my last chance. *Our* last chance."

I clench my eyes shut and whisper, "I plead the blood. I plead the blood." I feel the bitter wind whipping across my face. I hear the groan of the breeding barn. The sky screaming in my ears. "I plead the blood. I plead the blood." I say it over and over again until the screaming subsides. And when I open my eyes there's a sliver of golden light trying to break through the clouds.

And just like that, I know it's God. He heard me. If that tiny speck of light can break through the darkness, it might be enough to save her. All of us.

I run my palms over my head, lacing my hands around the back of my neck, and stare up at the sky, at the golden light overpowering the darkness.

I let out a joyous burst of laughter.

That glorious Oklahoma sky—it'll make a believer out of anybody. Even *me*.

The light spills over the wheat, making it look like fields of gold.

I start running back toward the breeding barn, my heart pounding with anticipation.

The barn door creaks open and I stop. I don't even dare take a breath.

Ali walks out. She looks different. Like a thousand pounds have been lifted from her shoulders.

I know that dress—cream colored with tiny pink rosebuds on it. It's the same dress she wore on the night she came to my room . . . the night I kissed her and she ran out of my house crying.

"Clay." Ali runs toward me, flinging her arms around my neck. "Where have you been? I'm so happy to see you."

I tense up at first, but the feel of her in my arms, the sound of her voice . . . this is Ali. The *real* Ali. "I've been waiting for you," I say as I hold her tight. "Thank you," I mouth to Miss Granger, who's standing in the doorway of the breeding barn, tears streaming down her face. Whatever happened in there, it clearly took a toll on her.

I pry Ali's arms loose. "I'll be right back."

I walk over to Miss Granger. "Is Tyler—"

"He didn't make it." She wipes her sleeve across her face.

"What happened?"

"He couldn't be saved," she says as she closes the door to the barn behind her. "But Ali's clean. She's free of this darkness."

"Thanks to you."

"No." She gently takes my hand. "Thanks to *you*. I think it's your love for Ali that saved her. That pulled her through."

"What happens now?" I ask, trying not to imagine the horror of what's inside that barn.

"Take Ali to your house. Give me a few hours to clean up here. We'll come for you at sundown. Everything will be clear."

I start to turn, when she reaches for my arm.

"And, Clay. Remember your promise. Love is a beautiful thing. You've seen how precious life is. How precious time is. Don't let it pass you by. You don't have to be alone anymore. She's going to need you, like you were before. God is giving you a second chance. Don't waste it."

I look back at Ali, the halo of light caressing her skin as she twirls a stem of wheat. Her hazel eyes are so warm and bright. She's wearing the peaceful smile I've always known. A ripple of wind rushes over her, making her skirt flutter against the top of her knees. She's more beautiful than ever.

"I promise," I whisper.

I take a deep breath and walk toward Ali. She reaches out for my hand, lacing her fingers through mine. I feel a rush of euphoria, a calmness pass over my soul. We walk hand in hand away from the breeding barn and into the wheat.

Into our future.

59

I TAKE Ali upstairs to my room; it's the one place that doesn't remind me of death. Noticing the trash bags covering the windows, and how wrong it looks, I hurry to take them down, which floods the room in hazy light.

Ali sits on the edge of my bed, brushing her hair back from her shoulder. The freckles have faded so much over the past year that you can hardly see them anymore.

I sit next to her. Being with her like this—in my room, the same dress, the scent of her hair—it's like déjà vu, but there's a hint of sadness in her eyes, a depth that hadn't been there before, which tells me, on some level, she remembers everything. I can hardly stand being this close to her and not touching her. The agony, the waiting, everything we've been through.

"There's something I need to tell you." I swallow hard. "Something I've wanted to tell you for so long."

"Clay—"

"I love you, Ali," I blurt. "And I want to marry you."

She takes in a short inhalation of breath. "Yes." She smiles, her warm hazel eyes filling with tears. "Do you know how long I've waited to hear you say that? Yes. Of course I'll marry you."

When I reach over to wipe the tears from her cheeks, she leans in and kisses me. Her lips are soft, warm and wet. I keep waiting for her to pull away, but she seems to crave the closeness, the intimacy as much as I do. She runs her fingers over the back of my head, my back, before moving on to the buttons of my shirt.

I hold on to her hands, pressing my forehead against hers. We stare at each other, breathing in time.

"Are you sure this is what you want?" I ask.

"We've waited long enough."

She kisses me again, deeper this time, and it feels like I'm diving off a cliff at the quarry—life or death can be waiting for me below, but it doesn't matter.

As she takes off my shirt, I unzip the back of her dress, nice and slow, giving her plenty of time to stop me. She doesn't. I've dreamed about this moment for so long, and now that it's here, I'm scared.

I let out a shuddering breath as she smooths her hands over my stomach, my muscles tensing under her touch. She shrugs out of the straps of her dress, letting it pool around her waist. I kiss her shoulder, her neck, her collarbone; her skin seems to warm beneath my breath like sunlit honey.

She starts to unbutton my fly. It's so tight. But as soon as she gets the top button undone, the rest of the silver buttons pop open. We both laugh a little.

Swallowing my nerves, I run my hands up her thighs, under the skirt of her dress, when she stands abruptly and I think this is it—I've gone too far, but she only pushes the rest of her clothes to the floor, stepping out of the fabric.

I stare up at her in awe. Her tousled hair, her flushed cheeks. It's like I'm seeing her for the first time.

She pulls me to my feet, kissing me, helping me out of the rest of my clothes. I feel so vulnerable under her gaze, but it feels right, like everything in my life has been leading me to this moment.

She eases down on the bed, her dark hair spilling over my pillow, her beautiful skin touching my sheets. I can't believe she's here, that this is really happening, but I can feel it in every part of my body, every bit of my soul, pulling me toward her, like this is home.

I lower myself on top of her. She takes in a deep gasp of air, and I freeze. Everything inside me wants to keep going. But I don't want to hurt her. My body trembles with restraint.

"Do you want me to st—"

She leans forward, kissing me. Her tongue is no longer timid, it's strong and insistent, full of need. She pulls me into her. I groan with how good it feels. I was worried I wouldn't know what to do, but it's like my body knows. I try to be gentle, but the way she's grabbing onto me, the way our bodies seem to fit together in perfect symmetry is more than I can bear. Together, we're striving for something higher than ourselves. We're all tangled up in each other to the point where I'm not sure where I end and she begins. It's like we're one person. One entity, moving in time.

Every care, every worry vanishing—I feel myself disappearing into her. Everything's building . . . mounting . . . yearning. And in one moment, an explosion of images race through my mind—her black eyes, her body slick with blood when she climbed out of the cow, the dead cat clutched to her lips—but I can't stop. I keep going, moving inside of her, until there's nothing left of me. A flurry of blood and darkness and desire and need. Life and death in a single impulse.

I rest on top of her, afraid to move . . . afraid to look at her. I'm embarrassed by the thoughts that ran through my head, but when she strokes the back of my head and whispers, "I love you," I know it's okay . . . that this is real. It's Ali. It's me.

I'm taking her in, every bit of her smell, her sweat, her breath when I feel her stomach grumble. I laugh into her shoulder as I collapse next to her. She lets out a gentle sigh as she turns onto her side. She's asleep.

I slip out of bed and pull on my jeans. I didn't think I lasted all that long, but the sky's getting dark now.

Ali's stomach growls again. She stirs, but still doesn't wake.

I kiss her on the forehead. "I'll find you something to eat."

I go downstairs to the kitchen, and flip on the light switch, but there's no power. I pick up the phone—the line's dead, too. That's weird.

I look at the bills fixed to the refrigerator. It seems like we're caught up, but who knows how long Mom's been slipping.

It doesn't even matter. As soon as I deal with Jess's funeral arrangements, get Mom the help she needs, I'm selling this place. Lock, stock, and barrel. I don't owe my ancestors shit. I know Noodle won't understand, but she'll get over it. Maybe Ali and I will take her all the way out to California. Jess always talked about wanting to go there. I can just see Ali and Noodle playing in the surf, making sand castles.

I catch my reflection in the glass door of the cabinet—my goofy-ass smile. Despite everything, all this tragedy, I'm happy. We're finally clear of this. There's nothing but blue skies ahead.

I open the cabinets to find they're barren. Just some stale saltines and a little bit of peanut butter left. This'll have to do. I place the items on a plate and grab a knife.

As I head back toward the banister, I hear the buzzing. I want to ignore it, but it's so loud now. How did I not hear it before? As soon as I step into the living room, my knees buckle.

The wall above the mantle is a quivering black mass, but it's not random anymore. The flies are in a perfect formation of the cross that once hung there. The cross my father used to kill the cattle.

I drop the plate of food and clasp my hands over my ears, but I can still hear them. It's not just buzzing . . . it sounds like they're saying something, whispering. I listen closer.

"He's coming, he's coming, he's coming, he's coming," over and over and over again, like a drone. This is what my mother was hearing . . . it was *real*.

"This can't be happening. We did the exorcism. The Devil's been banished from this place." I stagger out of the room, searching for the flyswatter, when I hear Ali scream.

Running upstairs, my heart stutters as I enter my room. Ali's huddled in the corner, a blood-smeared sheet wrapped around her, sweat covering her sallow face.

"What happened?" I ask as I edge toward her. "Did I do this to you?"

"I don't know." She's panting. "But something's wrong."

What is it?" I crouch in front of her.

Slowly, she pulls back the sheet to expose her swollen and stretched stomach.

"What the hell?" I collapse back on my heels.

"Clay," she says in terror as she reaches out for my hand. "There's something inside me . . . something *alive*. Feel it."

Tentatively, I let her place my palm against her stomach. The moment I make contact with her skin, I feel something pound against my hand.

Ali screams out in pain.

"I . . . I don't understand." I scoot back.

She lets out a guttural moan as her stomach rolls and heaves.

I dig my fingers into my skull, trying to pull myself together, trying to think. "We have to get Miss Granger . . . and the priests . . . they'll know what to do."

A loud insistent bark pulls my attention. I look out the window to see Hammy standing at the edge of the wheat, hackles raised, growling at the dirt. A small hand emerges from the ground and all I can think of is Ali climbing out of that cow. I watch in horror as that fucking baby doll crawls out of the hole and stands on its own two feet. The doll looks up, fixing her big, shiny black eyes on me, and grins.

"It's alive," I whisper.

It was the doll that was moving around in Jess's room all that time. The doll from the photo of our ancestors.

The baby doll takes off running into the wheat with Hammy chasing after it.

I press myself against the glass to get a better view.

And that's when I see them.

The others.

60

HUNDREDS OF people are walking through the wheat, straight for our farm.

I blink hard, hoping this is just another vision, but there's something about this that feels all too real . . . inevitable. This is supposed to be over. Maybe they made a mistake. Maybe I needed to be exorcized, too.

"We have to get out of here. We have to get back to the breeding barn," I say as I gather up Ali's clothes. "We're going to have to run."

"Run? I . . . I can't. You're going to have to leave me here and get help."

I scoop her up in my arms. "I'm not leaving you. No matter what happens . . . no matter what you see . . . I'm with you. Do you understand?"

I force her to look at me, relieved to find it's still Ali . . . the girl I love with the soft hazel eyes. "Just hang on to me," I say as I carry her down the stairs, past the flies and their sickening whispers. I open the front door to find the perimeter of the wheat filled with people, with hundreds more pushing through behind them. Some are complete strangers . . . some I recognize from town.

"Dale," I yell. He smiles, but it's not his smile. His eyes are pure black—dead and inhuman.

This is just like my dream . . . the vision I had during the game.

Dale's one of them now, along with Greg Tilford, Reverend Devers, Mrs. Gifford, Mr. Cox . . . they're all a part of this now.

"Clay . . . what's wrong with them?" Ali asks. "Why are they smiling like that? What's wrong with their eyes? Why won't they help us?"

I take off running with Ali in my arms toward the Neely ranch. "Don't fucking come near us," I scream as I cut through the wheat, but they're everywhere. They don't try to grab us, but they're following. Watching. It's so dark now that I can hardly see more than a few feet in front of me, but I can hear them breathing all around me.

I'm never going to make it all the way back to the barn carrying her like this. I see the silhouette of the combine in the distance and I pick up my pace.

I'm hurrying to stay one step ahead of these freaks, but I can't afford a misstep. Ali's in bad enough shape as it is. She muffles an occasional scream into my shoulder as her stomach roils and heaves. It only seems to be getting worse. My muscles are burning, but I keep going. Whatever's happening to her, Miss Granger will know what to do. She has to. I can't lose Ali again.

As I'm hoisting Ali into the cab of the combine, I hear the keys drop out of my pocket. "Damn it."

I get down on my hands and knees, feeling my way around the discarded wheat stems, and I hear one of the stalks snap. I look up, afraid to see anything, afraid not to, but it's pitch-black now.

"Clay, hurry," Ali pleads.

I grope around in the dark. "Come on . . . please," I whisper. As soon as my fingertips brush the cold metal, I let out a huge gust of pent-up air. "Got 'em," I call out.

Gripping the keys in my hand, I climb into the combine.

"You ready?" I ask.

Ali's still in a lot of pain, but she nods as she settles on my lap.

I turn the key; the engine roars to life, the headlights illuminating hundreds of bodies crowded in all around us. Ali screams, nuzzling her face into my neck. They're just standing there in the wheat, staring at us, with rictus grins and those black eyes.

"Go . . . go!" Ali yells.

I shake off the terror building inside me and grind the tractor into gear.

Sheriff Ely staggers in front of the headlights.

"Wait," he yells, waving his hands around.

His eyes are normal. He's not one of them. I try to slam on the brake, put it in reverse, turn the wheel, but nothing's working. I even pull the key out of the ignition, but it still won't stop.

"Get out . . . get out of the way . . . move!" I yell, but Ely just looks up at me in shock as the combine lurches forward. There's a horrific scream, followed by a huge bump as fresh blood splatters the windshield.

"Oh my God . . . my God . . . I killed him!"

I think about opening the door and jumping out, but Ali's doubled over in pain. We'll never be able to make it on foot in her condition.

The people are barely moving out of the way as the combine moves forward, like they don't care if we run them over or not. Not that I could stop it, even if I wanted to. The combine has taken on a life of its own.

Through the blood-smeared windshield, I keep my eyes trained on the breeding barn. It's lit up from within, like a beacon in the dark.

Just when I'm trying to figure out how I'm going to get Ali out of the moving combine, it stalls out about twenty feet from the barn. I jump out and help Ali down. Miss Granger's standing outside, waiting, as if she's been expecting us.

"I knew you could do it," she says with a pleasant smile.

"No . . . you don't understand . . . I hit Sheriff with the combine . . . he's dead." Ali groans in pain. "She needs help . . . there's something wrong."

"In here," Miss Granger replies, as she motions inside to a bed of fresh-cut wheat covering the breeding platform.

I set Ali down. "There's people coming," I say as I hunch over, struggling to catch my breath. "Hundreds of them . . . they've come for us . . . just like my vision at the game. I thought this was over."

"Don't worry, they'll be here in time."

"In time?" I ask as I check on Ali. "In time for what?"

A drop of blood lands next to Ali in the wheat. I'm looking at her body trying to figure out where it came from when Ali clamps her hand over her mouth and points toward the ceiling. I look up to see Tyler rigged into the breeding apparatus—the artificial insemination gun shoved down his throat. The priests are suspended from hooks on either side of him, their black robes swaying gently.

"Oh Jesus!" I shield Ali's eyes. "You didn't tell me about the priests. Why didn't you tell me they died, too?"

"Would it have made a difference?" Miss Granger says nonchalantly.

I try to pick Ali up, get her away from the stench of death, but she screams out in agony. "Stop. I can't move."

I set her back down again. "Help her! Can't you see she's in pain?" I turn to see Miss Granger opening the barn doors to the hordes of people.

"Don't!" I stand in front of Ali as if I can protect her from the mob gathering around the breeding platform. They're smiling at us, like we're some kind of entertainment.

"You still don't understand, do you?" Miss Granger says. "Jimmy, Ben, Tammy, Jess, Tyler, Sheriff Ely, the priests . . . that was all for this to come to pass. It was right in front of you all along."

"What are you saying?"

"I was with Reverend Devers and Jimmy that night at the church. I thought you almost caught me when you got close to the garage. Ben was in my bed the night you woke from a nightmare and came over to my house. You ran your hand right over his jean jacket hanging on the back of my chair. It's a shame, really, because I'm certain I could've had you that night. Lee was supposed to be one of the sacrifices, but you weren't man enough to finish the job. That's okay. I'm devout. I can still be of service, for goodness sake."

"Why are you saying this? It can't be—"

"I was beginning to wonder if you could even pull this off, the dirty deed." Her gaze shifts to Ali. "You were stubborn with your virgin whore complex. But when she offered herself to you and you refused, I knew what I had to do. I had to make you believe I took the Devil from her, made her pure again, so you could pour your demon seed into her. The priests had to pay the price, but it was well worth it. Was it worth the wait, Clay? Everything you hoped it would be?"

I feel a blistering heat take over my face. "How long have you been one of them?" I ask as I scan the barn, trying to come up with an escape plan.

"I should've died that day in Mexico. But I offered my parents instead."

"You killed your parents?"

"I set them free." She smiles up at me and I feel sick to my stomach. "You were so easy to manipulate, Clay. Drinking my tea. Telling me your deepest darkest secrets."

"The salvia. That was you?" I look around for anything I might be able to use as a weapon.

"I needed you off balance. Especially when you saw what happened at the rebirth ceremony, Ali emerging from the cow. I needed you to believe it was all a bad dream. I think deep down you knew, didn't you? You kept seeing it over and over again. Did you see it when you were bedding Ali? I bet you did." She smiles coyly.

"What do you want from me? What do you want from Ali?" I yell as I stand guard.

"We're here for the birth of our lord," she says, her gaze shifting to Ali's stomach.

"That's impossible . . . we just . . . I mean . . . Ali was a virgin before tonight."

"Is that your highest concern? That she was a virgin for you?" Miss Granger rolls her eyes. "So provincial, Clay. But yes, Ali saved herself for you, poor wretched cow. Our lord works in mysterious ways." Her smile deepens. "Blessed be the seed," she exclaims. "Satan chose *you* to deliver his seed. And you chose Ali. It's the highest honor."

I don't want to believe it, any of it, but when I look at Ali writhing on the breeding platform, the witnesses gathered around, I know it's true. I have to get Ali out of here, to the hospital, so they can abort this monstrosity growing inside of her. I look back at her and my heart is breaking. How could I have been so blind . . . so stupid? The seed . . . I was the seed all along. That's why my dad tried to kill me that night. He knew. He saw something in me . . . something evil. I remember the bull kneeling before me. All this time, I thought someone else killed the golden calf, but it must've been me. I started it all. I brought him here.

Ali holds out her hand to me, beckoning me closer.

I sink next to her on the breeding platform. "I'm so sorry . . . I didn't know . . . I didn't und—"

"The prophecy," she grunts through the pain. "Only the chosen one will be able to care for the lord. As the chosen one, you're the only one who can touch him . . . maybe the only one who can hurt him, too." She looks up at the ceiling pointedly.

I follow her gaze to the flash of silver glinting in the candlelight—an upside-down crucifix hanging from the neck of one of the priests.

"I can't." I shake my head rapidly, thinking about what she's asking me to do.

She grips my arm. "If you don't stop this . . . we're all going to die. Think of Noodle."

I push her damp hair back from her face. Acid floods my throat, my shoulders start to convulse, but I choke it back. I choke back everything. Grabbing a bail of hay, I climb up and jump, snatching the crucifix from the priest's neck.

As I stand over her belly, the crucifix at the ready, I glance nervously at the horde behind me, but no one moves to stop me. They just keep smiling.

"Do it," Ali pleads.

"God help me," I whisper, my entire body trembling.

As I raise the crucifix over my head, ready to impale the child, something reaches inside of me, grabbing hold of my heart. My mind wants to, but my body won't let me. "I can't," I cry out. "I can't do it."

"There, there, now," Miss Granger says as she places her hand on my shoulder. "Do you think the Devil would let *you* stand in his way? You were nothing more than the seed."

Burning with rage, I whip around, plunging the crucifix into Miss Granger's neck, her warm blood splattering across my face.

"The ninth will be for goodness' sake," she sings in a childlike voice as she sinks to her knees.

"W-wait." I grab on to her. "How do you know that song? That's Noodle's song."

"Thanks to you, he's coming, Clay. He's coming for all of us. There's only one more sacrifice to make." Her gaze settles on Ali.

I look at Ali and all I can see is her climbing out of the cow, split right down the middle. The rebirth ceremony, that was real. All of it was real.

"If they need another sacrifice, take me," I plead. "Take me instead of her."

"You still don't see." Her final words gurgle from her throat as she slumps over onto the ground.

"Clay . . ." Ali writhes in the bed of wheat. "It's coming," she screams. I run to her side as a ripping wet sound, like something's tearing through bone and muscle, fills the air. I watch in horror as a tiny hand bursts from her stomach. The thing slithers out of her body, to rest on the wheat, covered in blood and viscera.

The crowd takes in a collective sigh as the infant takes its first breath, but no one steps forward to claim it.

"Cut me free, but don't touch it," Ali cries.

I wrench the crucifix out of Emma's neck and use it to sever the umbilical cord. The baby coos. It's a boy. I try not to look at it, but I can feel its power trying to lure me in.

People are kneeling down to pray before him. People I've known my entire life—the reverend, Dale. They don't see what's happening . . . that this is the end.

I crawl back to Ali's side, pulling her farther down the platform, away from the child, her body leaving a wide swath of blood in the wheat.

"I have to get you out of here . . . to the hospital," I say as I try to pick her up, but she stops me.

"It's too late," she says. "Maybe it was always too late for me. Whatever you do, don't touch the baby. I remember from the prophecy. Only the chosen one will be able to care for the lord. If you don't pick him up, no one else will be able to—he'll die." She reaches out to touch my cheek. "You didn't forget me. You're good, Clay," she whispers as her eyes turn to glass.

"No, Ali, no," I cry as I gather her in my arms. "Help me." I look to the heavens only to find the bodies of the priests suspended from hooks, hovering like macabre party decorations.

The child makes a cute gurgling sound. I look at it with such hatred, but it quickly fades. I can feel its power. I can feel him pulling me in, my arms aching to hold him. But I know if I pick up that baby, my life will be over, the world will be over. I've seen the death and destruction left in its wake. I think of my father, lying here, bleeding out as he tried to prevent this from happening, and I know what I have to do. There will be one more sacrifice.

"I plead the blood," I whisper as I tighten my grip on the metal crucifix and open my veins.

I lie down next to Ali, lacing my fingers through hers. My blood warms her hand. If I close my eyes, I can pretend she's still alive, that we're just sleeping in my bed, but I know it's a lie. I thought I could die in peace knowing I made the ultimate sacrifice for mankind . . . that I did something good . . . just like Noodle and Ali said I would, but I've never felt so hollow and alone. I'm angry about everything that's been taken away from me. I'm sad about all the things I'll never see. I glance at the infant one last time, with Ali's dark hair and my stubborn chin, and try to take comfort in the fact that I went up against the Devil and I won . . . but this doesn't feel like winning. It just feels like dying.

The crowd begins to shuffle, followed by hushed whispers. I open my eyes to see a girl with long blond hair.

"Noodle?" I whisper. I haven't seen her with her hair down in years.

She drops the mangy baby doll that's covered in blood at her feet and steps toward me.

It kills me that she has to see this, but I'm grateful I get to say goodbye.

I hold out my hand to her, but she doesn't come to me. Instead, she walks straight for the child.

"This is what I've been practicing for," she says.

As she leans over to pick up the child, I see the unmistakable mark on the side of her scalp, the upside-down U with two dots above and below. It looks like an old scar. Is that why she never wanted anyone to touch her hair?

"No," I shake my head, tears stinging my eyes. "Not Noodle."

As she cradles the child in her tiny arms, she sings to him, a nursery rhyme from long ago.

"The first to fall will pray."

Jimmy.

"The second to fall has come to play."

Ben.

"The third to fall will shiver and burn."

Tammy.

"The fourth to fall, a lesson to learn."

Jess.

"The fifth to fall will eat his words."

Tyler.

"But six and seven will go to heaven."

The priests.

"Eight will be a grave mistake."

Sheriff Ely.

"The ninth will be for goodness' sake."

Miss Granger.

"The final one to fall, the tenth will be the one to bind them all."

Ali. My sweet Ali.

NOODLE'S COUNTING song—it's about the ten sacrifices. She made it up years ago. Is that how long she's been one of them . . . preparing for this moment?

"I think I'll call him Clay," Noodle says as she swings around.

The swoosh of her long blond hair brings me right back to that day in the fields—the day I ran over the golden calf with the combine. It was her . . . crouching low in the wheat. I saw blood on her hand that day, but she said it was a paper cut. She slit the calf's throat and left it there. She whispered to me in my dreams, told me to plow the invitation into the crops . . . she was there before each one of them turned, before they killed themselves . . . at the Harvest Festival, the practice, the bonfire, the lake, the breeding barn. She drove Mom mad . . . pushed Jess into Lee's arms.

Tears sear down my face.

"It's you . . . you're the chosen one," I whisper, barely holding on to consciousness.

She turns and steps toward me, a sweet smile on her face.

"Rest easy, brother. The last harvest is finally over."

ACKNOWLEDGMENTS

First and foremost, I'd like to thank my editor Melissa Frain for going on this gruesome, bloody, and sometimes uncomfortable journey with me. She gave me the artistic freedom to explore every dark corner and brought a lot of tenderness to the story. I couldn't be more grateful.

Seth Lerner is responsible for the gorgeous cover. Thank you.

Standing O for Amy Stapp, and everyone at Tor for embracing my weird, and making this such a joyful experience.

Special thanks to Josh Adams for making this love connection.

To my fearless agent, Jaida Temperly, and everyone at New Leaf, thank you for taking such good care of me.

I owe a huge amount of gratitude to my beta readers/friends, who gave me the encouragement I needed to tackle this story. April Tucholke, Virginia Boecker, Jasmine Warga, Rebecca Behrens, Jenn Marie Thorne, Lee Kelly, Erin Morgenstern, Bess Cozby, Veronica Rossi, Lauren Oberweger, Nova Ren Suma, Libba Bray, Maggie Hall, Jodi Kendall, and last but not least, my muse, Gina Carey, who inspired Noodle.

To my husband Ken, my partner, who listens to all my crazy ideas, props me up when I'm low, and cooks for me when the deadlines are looming.

To my parents John and Joyce, and my beloved sister Cristie, who answered every Oklahoma question with glee, even when she knew what the book was about.

To my daughter Maddie—thank you for all your love and support. The next book is for you.

I wrote *The Last Harvest* for my son Rahm—another strong, silent type. The idea for this book was sparked by one of our late night philosophical conversations. You are wise beyond your years and I'm so grateful that I get to be your mom. Keep seeking.

Finally, I'd like to thank Stephen King, Shirley Jackson, Ira Levin, and V. C. Andrews for warping my brain in the best possible way.